ROBIN TRIGGS

NIGHT SHIFT

This is a **FLAME TREE PRESS** book

Text copyright © 2018 Robin Triggs

FLAME TREE PRESS
6 Melbray Mews, London, SW6 3NS, UK
flametreepress.com

Distribution and warehouse:
Baker & Taylor Publisher Services (BTPS)
30 Amberwood Parkway, Ashland, OH 44805
btpubservices.com

Publisher's Note: This is a work of fiction. Names, characters, places, and
incidents are a product of the author's imagination. Locales and public names
are sometimes used for atmospheric purposes. Any resemblance to actual
people, living or dead, or to businesses, companies, events, institutions, or
locales is completely coincidental.

Thanks to the Flame Tree Press team, including:
Taylor Bentley, Frances Bodiam, Federica Ciaravella, Don D'Auria,
Chris Herbert, Matteo Middlemiss, Josie Mitchell, Mike Spender,
Cat Taylor, Maria Tissot, Nick Wells, Gillian Whitaker.

The cover is created by Flame Tree Studio with
thanks to Nik Keevil and Shutterstock.com.
The font families used are Avenir and Bembo.

Flame Tree Press is an imprint of Flame Tree Publishing Ltd
flametreepublishing.com

A copy of the CIP data for this book is available from the British Library
and the Library of Congress.

HB ISBN: 978-1-78758-038-1
PB ISBN: 978-1-78758-036-7
ebook ISBN: 978-1-78758-039-8
Also available in FLAME TREE AUDIO

Printed in the US at Bookmasters, Ashland, Ohio

ROBIN TRIGGS

NIGHT SHIFT

FLAME TREE PRESS
London & New York

For JK and L

ID: SAB6974/243/21M

Verified: Baurus, RM

Brasilia Province

Received: 051046:0312

Priority: Ultra

Confirmed and verified

Attachment confirmed and verified

Message follows

Private and Confidential

RE: Australis Incident

Madam Director

You will be wondering why an operations executive is contacting you directly rather than going through official channels. You may already be wondering what disciplinary action to take against me. I have thought long and hard about this, and believe me when I say that I would not be risking my career – my entire future – if I did not think that this was necessary. All I ask is that you suspend judgment until you have read this letter.

The staff at Tierra del Fuego became aware of problems at Australis when our regular contacts ceased shortly after the night shift began. As O'Higgins Base, our Antarctic port, was frozen, and because all Antarctic flying is suspended over winter, no action was taken until the following spring. Dr. Gabriel (EUG/4454/555/13M), Technician Istevez (SAB2023/499/24M) and I myself were then dispatched to investigate. Our official report is on the system, should you care to examine it. It is enough to say that the situation at Australis is stable, though I fear we will struggle to keep the lights on this year. The Company will also have lost many millions in profit.

Of immediate concern is the disturbing story we've managed to piece together surrounding the events of the long night. All survivors were given SP-117 by Dr. Gabriel as per standard procedure; all then were interviewed individually and their statements recorded verbatim. The events they describe would be hard to credit had the witnesses not corroborated each other from their differing *viewpoints. These accounts – in addition to the forensic and analytic reports – have been retained on a secure server should you wish to examine them.*

I have deliberately downplayed the significance of these reports so as to discourage curiosity. I have ordered Dr. Gabriel to say nothing; I have checked his record and do not consider him a security risk, but you might wish him reassigned. He and Technician Istevez have remained at Australis for the time being, to help stabilize the situation.

The transcript I am attaching – that of Anders Nordvelt (EUE/6887/274/33M) – is fully representative, and I urge you to read it. I cannot – dare not – enlarge on Nordvelt's narrative in this message, save to say that it suggests that the problems encountered in Antarctica may threaten other Company operations. Indeed, it might not be going too far to say that they may affect the very future of the Company.

I think once you have read the transcript you will understand the reasons for my direct approach. Had I employed the usual chain of communication, my life would now be in serious danger.

I await your instructions.

Ricardo Baurus
Operations Executive
SAB6974/243/21M

CHAPTER ONE

We stood on the pack ice, struggling to keep our feet in a wind that drove the snow right into our faces. I shielded my eyes and watched Fischer and Weng crouching down by the still, suited figure to make certain of what we all knew. The professional part of me sought clues, evidence, footprints. It was hopeless. Our torches illuminated only the smothering blizzard. I tried to find shelter in the lee of the building but the gale seemed to be coming from all around.

Fischer straightened and looked at me, her feet crunching on the freshly fallen snow. Even through her mask I could sense the anguish. Or maybe that was just my imagination, my own terrors reflected back at me.

We had good cause for fear. This assignment was rapidly becoming a nightmare.

Just a few days into the night shift and we had a death on our hands.

*   *   *

Should I go from there, or should I begin with my arrival?

*   *   *

There was no room in the driver's compartment so I rode with the light goods. A small, hard seat and a small, cheap viewscreen were my comforts. I spent hours pacing the small, gray space, watching progress on the screen map. I tried to read, scrolling idly down the lists of titles on my datapad. I flicked from article to article, but nothing could hold my attention. I settled for switching the screen to show the outside world. It was just…gray. All gray and white and brown. Shapeless mounds drawn in nothing colors, and that was all I could see for miles and miles and miles in every direction.

My home. For at least the next six months this forgotten land was to be my home. I was to be the thirteenth man, a late replacement for the old security officer. I didn't know why he had left: the Psych should have anticipated any problems.

Only twelve other people within a thousand miles. Well, I'd always felt alone, even when surrounded by thousands. Maybe that was why I'd been appointed.

The smelting plant was the first I saw of the complex. I watched as the giant factory slowly grew in the crawler viewscreen. I had studied the plans of the base, of course, but it was another thing entirely to watch that monster slowly becoming more solid, more gigantic, as we approached. The buildings clustered around its base were to be my home; just those few small structures and, around them, Antarctica's endless wastes.

"Ten minutes, Mr. Nordvelt," the driver called over the intercom. "Best get suited up."

I was, I think, more practiced than he knew. I had my Antarctic gear on and ready in half that time. My training had been thorough. I stood sweating in the airlock as I waited for the vehicle to come to a halt.

★   ★   ★

I emerged into a rough courtyard and paused to let my eyes adjust. Ahead of me a horseshoe ridge rose to meet a quicksilver crack of sun; gloomy lumps of industry stood within the rough shadow-bowl this formed. The yard itself was floodlit, heavy lamps set on top of adjacent buildings, themselves little more than brutally practical concrete boxes. Beyond them, the great banks of solar panels that topped the greenhouse shone liquid blue. Further structures were just pinpricks of light against the black hillside.

Behind me the crawler was already uncoupling the cargo carriages that made up the land train. Ahead, a fresh row of laden trucks stood ready to be hauled back to O'Higgins Port for shipping to Tierra del Fuego. I had taken the last boat in; this precious cargo of raw materials – coal, oil and iron – would be on the last boat out before the port closed for the winter.

The distances hit me like they'd never done on my long journey here. "Mr. Nordvelt, I presume."

The sudden greeting startled me. I hadn't really been paying much attention to the green-coated figures that had been emerging to greet the crawler as its massive engine growled. They barely looked human in their face masks and body-hugging warmsuits – more like lizards than people. I must have looked the same to them, but I guess they were used to it.

One of these figures had detached himself from the main group and had come to stand at my side. He held out a gloved hand to me when I turned. "I'm Anton," he said as we shook. His voice was clear, the earpieces working their magic in my hood. No chance of lip-reading, though. I could barely see his chin move beneath the mask.

"Commander de Villiers?"

"If you like," he said with a dismissive wave. He started to lead me away from the vehicle, towards the largest of the nearby buildings. Above it loomed the smelting plant and the hill it was dug into. "Don't have much call for rank at Australis. We're far enough from Company eyes. We know why we're here." He broke off to pull open the door – not locked, I couldn't help but notice – and lead me inside. "We all know our jobs – and who we are." He laughed, loud and rough in my ear.

We passed straight into the vestibule; not quite an airlock but similar in practice. It was more like a large cloakroom. I stood to the side, backing against a row of lockers as de Villiers shut the door behind us. He removed his gloves and started to unclip his mask. I followed his example, the air cool – but not cold, not freezing as I'd imagined it would be.

"That's your locker," de Villiers said with a nod. "Still has McCarthy's name on it, but you'll get used to that. His name'll be on most of the things you get here." He laughed again, I'm not sure why. Now his face mask came away and I saw him properly for the first time.

His face came as a relief to me, even with his too-perfect grin and sandy, devilish beard. The journey, the environment – it was like I'd arrived on some foreign planet., The warmsuits and the rest of the winter weather made monsters of us all. He gestured me out of the way to get at one of the lockers behind me, stowed his gear in there as it came off to reveal a relaxed, weathered yellow shirt. It seemed that I couldn't escape the fashion for bright colors, not even here.

I unzipped my suit-front, found McCarthy's locker and pulled at the door. It opened, to my mild surprise: was there no security code, no bioreader? But de Villiers hadn't bothered with one either. I pushed the thought aside, saved it for later, as I set my bag down and began to strip myself of my Antarctic clothing.

"So that's what you look like," said de Villiers, with a little twist of a smile. "Come on, let's get inside and have a chat. Bring your bag."

He led me through the inner door and into the base proper. As soon as I was through I felt the warmth roll over me. It felt almost like the savannahs – a dry heat, and I welcomed it. Maybe it was psychological; the warmsuit had kept the chill from me outside, after all, but still I felt the Antarctic wastes melt away from me.

De Villiers strode casually ahead. "You know the layout of the place?" he asked as we passed doors to the sides of the metal-walled corridor.

"I've studied the plans. There's only the workshop and storage on the ground floor, yes?"

He nodded. We'd reached a door at the end of the hall and de Villiers shouldered it open, turning as he did to raise an eyebrow at me. "You know we're self-sufficient, powered and heated by those solar panels on the greenhouse and by a small oil-lake half a mile away?"

"Yes."

"Good. We can skip all that, then."

I followed him through to a stairwell; it only went downwards. Three floors, I knew – staff quarters. Barracks, headquarters, leisure rooms. Gymnasium. All underground to save heat and power.

"First floor: meeting room, kitchen and refectory, infirmary, recreation room, network room – through which all computer functions are routed, although our relay station, with the actual satellite equipment, is in the comms building half a mile from here," de Villiers said as we descended. "Oh, Greigor – what're you doing here? I thought you were out with Maggie."

A tall, well-built young man had emerged just as we reached the door that led from the stairwell into the first underground level. We all stopped, startled – an uncomfortable meeting.

"Mm? Oh, yes," Greigor said, his eyes wide. He struck me as implausibly, unfairly handsome. He stared at me openly until suddenly snapping back to face the commander. "I just…jus' going now." His voice was a smooth baritone with a little South American lilt, his shirt a deep crimson, patterned with darker patches – flowers, I realized.

De Villiers frowned. "This is Anders. Anders, Greigor Miziara. He works – or he should do – in the greenhouse. The hydroponics."

We muttered greetings and shook hands. His grip was too firm. He kept his deep brown eyes on mine and, though he said the right things, his smile was that of a wild dog eyeing up a rival.

"Right," de Villiers said. "Get on, Greig. We'll see you at dinner." He stared at Greigor's back until he'd disappeared round the bend in the stairs. "Okay. Where were we?"

We descended in silence, footsteps echoing around us.

"Second floor. Crew quarters."

According to the plans, there was nothing but the laundry and the generator below us. Instead de Villiers led me through another door and into another corridor. Still he couldn't help but tell me things I knew already. "My rooms – my office and quarters – are the other way, the corresponding suite." We reached a corner and followed it round to the left. He stopped in front of the first door. The plaque read *McCarthy, G.,* and then below, *Security.* "And here's yours." He favored me with a grin, the encounter with Greigor apparently forgotten. "The rest of the team follow on from yours and mine, and the doctor has her rooms at the far end, by the emergency exit." He tapped a code into the lock – *1-2-3-4* – and ushered me inside. "This is your office. Your bed is through there. Guess you'll want some time to yourself, but don't take too long. I'll meet you in the rec room in an hour."

I turned to see him leaning against the frame of my outer door. I was going to thank him, or agree, or say *something*, but he beat me to it.

"You know you're going to have the most boring six months of your life, huh? Hope you like people, like reading, because God knows you'll have bugger all else to do." He treated me to another of his queer little smiles, but his tone was cold, almost bitter. His eyes froze in the striplights of the office. "Security chief? What a joke. You're thirty-two, right? You look like you're barely out of school. I've read all the Company has on you…"

He paused, and unsaid words rang across the corridor.

"Damn, I want to know who you slept with to get placed here." De Villiers grinned again, teeth white. "I mean, you're— no offence, kid, but you hardly compare with the rest of us on experience. Come through the Company system, right? Never seen how the real world works. Guess we'll all be like you someday." He stared at me, scrutinizing me closely. "Still, maybe that doesn't matter. I don't know what they told you back in Tierra, but you're only here because we have to have *someone*, you know that? You'll walk out of here, your wallet three times as thick and your pick of jobs to walk into. And what'll you have to do for that? Nothing. There's no crime here, none at all. No crime, no drugs, no alcohol, only thirteen people, including you. But because it says in some Company rulebook that we must have a commander, a doctor and a chief of security, here you are." He paused. "Welcome to Australis, Mr. Nordvelt. Good to have you aboard." He shut the door on me, and I was alone.

★　　★　　★

My office was small and spartan, not a single spot of humanity. To call it functional would be an understatement. It felt like a cell. I stood with my back to the door and looked. A bare metal chair for visitors, a desk with compscreen, a chair for me and, in the corner, a filing cabinet. God knew what I'd need that for; nothing gets written down anymore, or at least nothing that needs to be kept. On the right-hand wall was another door, marked *Private*.

I dropped my bag to the floor and went to the other side of the desk. On the compscreen the Company logo floated silently. I was tempted to scan my biometrics and get straight to work, but – well, why rush? Instead, I went to the internal door and stared at the key panel. The commander hadn't given me the code. I tried the handle, but it wouldn't shift. I shrugged, tried *1-2-3-4* and it opened. De Villiers had obviously meant it when he said they hadn't much use for security here.

The room beyond was almost as colorless as the office. Fractionally smaller than I was used to in my old home, in the blocks – except now I wasn't sharing with three other men. To my left was a wardrobe. I looked inside and saw one of McCarthy's blue-gray uniforms still hanging. There was a gray armchair facing a viewscreen, a metal table with another compscreen and two chairs, and a metal-framed bed. I ran an idle hand over smooth beige blankets, took in the white pillowcases. There were two metal shelves on one of the walls, and a cupboard for clothes. I wandered into the small kitchen area – just a workspace, a combi-maker and a cupboard – and opened the cupboard to find two cups. Almost as if they'd allow one guest, but no more. As if they expected every member of crew to make a friend – but only one.

There was another door in the far corner: the washroom. Toilet, shower and sink.

This was my home.

I dragged my bag inside, shut the door. First thing I had to do was change the code – just for my peace of mind, to give myself some sense of privacy. But even then I couldn't quite accept that this space was mine; not since I was five had I had a room of my own. I kept looking for a second bedroom, feeling for the air currents, for signs that someone had been here. Of course I'd known it'd be like this, but the emptiness still sent the hairs on the back of my neck quivering. I'd no idea how I was going to stay sane with only twelve other people for a thousand miles.

But the Psych said I would. So I would.

I sat in the armchair and I became aware of a low vibration. It was everywhere; it had always been there, I'd just not noticed it until now. I looked up. It was the smelting plant, I knew – or maybe it was the refinery, or the recycling plant, or the mineworks. It was *industry*. And it would be here as long as – longer than – I'd be.

Best get used to it.

I pulled my bag towards me and opened it up. Everything I owned was in there, in that small holdall. I felt inside, lifted out the neatly folded plain gray shirts and put them on the floor. Below were my few personal items: The letter from my first love; the picture she'd drawn for me, so long ago now; the rosewood-inlaid puzzle box I'd had for…for as long as I could remember. And the memcard: outdated technology with outdated memories. My fingers brushed across the silk-smooth face of a photograph. I didn't need to draw it out to know what it was: the only picture of my parents I had. I don't know why I kept it. The memories were always…complicated. Love, hate and anger. Mostly anger.

Textbook case…. Has trouble forming relationships…. Low self esteem…. I bit back memories of old Psychs. That wasn't me anymore.

At the bottom of my holdall was my book. The one truly precious object I owned. A real, paper-and-ink hardback in its tatty, torn dust-jacket. I pulled it out, ran my fingers over the sleeve. *The Adventures of Sherlock Holmes.* Second edition. 1893. I knew all the words intimately, knew every stain, every faded comma.

Why would the Company send me here? There must be a reason. Maybe it was to balance of the rest of the crew with a loner, an invisible one.

I withdrew my hand from the holdall, realized I'd taken the memcard with it. I turned it through my fingers and welcomed the cold, the isolation − I *swam* in it. After all, I'd chosen this; I'd applied for the job, wanted the promotion, wanted to see another side to the world. And then it'd been too late for second thoughts.

I surged to my feet, a flash of impatient anger (…*subject to mood swings, but capable of keeping control…*) burning away my insecurity. I strode to the compscreen and slid the memcard into its slot before scanning my fingerprints on the reader. The Company logo flared on the screen and faded, and I had access to the base files.

I clenched my teeth. Sod de Villiers. Sod him and his condescension. I was here to do a job, and I was going to do it properly. I set myself to reading about evacuation procedures once more.

★   ★   ★

I stood in the doorway of the rec room and waited awkwardly as the occupants looked me over. There were four people in there, four people who had been working together for nearly six months, who knew each other, and to all of them I was a stranger.

The room was at least twice as big as my quarters and felt almost comfortable; two large settees seemed to demarcate one area, and beyond them a large wooden table filled another. On the wall, a large viewscreen hung next to a map of the continent. The screen pulsed with random patterns that vaguely kept time with some orchestral work, the volume quiet enough for conversation.

"It's Anders, right?" A woman stood, crow's feet deepening as she smiled. "Don't just stand there," she said. "Come and sit down." She had auburn hair that was running to gray. It clashed with her shapeless burgundy jacket.

"I—" I started to move towards her but, off-balance, brushed some papers from the pinboard that was stuck on the wall by the door. A handful of loose sheets fell, and I stumbled in my haste to gather them together.

"Here, let me give you a hand," the woman said, and I heard her advancing across the carpet.

My face burning, I caught a glimpse of poker and chess league information before she was with me, and the damage, such as it was, was quickly repaired.

"Sorry," I mumbled.

"Stupid, old-fashioned thing," she said with a wave of a hand. "Anton likes it, but really it just gets in the way. Here, come on. I'm Julia Fischer. And you're Anders." She eased me into the seating area. "This is Mikhail, and Fergie. That's Weng over there."

I tried my best to recover my poise, to make myself smile and look attentive. The blond one, Mikhail, wore a T-shirt bearing the logo of the West Coast Warriors, whoever they were. At least he was smiling like he meant it. The other, Fergie, just scowled at me.

The fourth person, an Asian girl with fierce eyes, was seated at the table, chessboard in front of her. She'd given me the briefest of glances as I entered, and was now staring back at her game. I had hoped to try and work out who was who from the personnel files I'd been reading, but now I found I'd forgotten every single word.

"So good to see new blood here," Fischer went on. "McCarthy was such a bore. Tell us about yourself, Anders." She leaned towards me, just on the edge of my personal space. She had sat herself beside me, and from the corner of my eye she seemed somehow angular, predatory.

I shrugged away the feeling and groped for the words I could never stop practicing in my head. "Well, I'm from Sweden originally, from a small town you've probably never heard of," I said with false brightness. "But I've lived most of my life in England—"

Fischer cut me off. "Not that. We know all that."

"*You* might," the man she'd called Fergie grumbled from his seat. He had a distinct Scottish accent, low and rumbling. "Not all of us have access to the medical files, you know."

Fischer ignored his input. "Tell us about *you*, Anders. What makes you tick?"

"Give the man a break, Julia," the other man, Mikhail, said. He had sharp, high cheekbones, blue eyes. His accent was American. He gave me a quick smile before turning back to Fischer. "The man's only just met us. Let him catch his breath." And then to me: "You're lookin' at my shirt? Are you a Warriors man? Best team in the world, no doubt." He grinned.

This was not going as I'd planned. I glanced around for help, then shrugged awkwardly. "I'm not really up on sports, I'm sorry."

His smile flickered. "I play for my local team," he mumbled. "Or I will do, when the shift's done."

"Your name – I thought you'd be—"

"Russian? Yeah, I get that all the time. My parents are Finnish, but I was born and brought up in California."

"Doesn't stop us from calling him a commie, though," Fergie said.

"Hey, I'm not the one dissing the Company all the time—"

"So what are you into, Anders?" Fischer cut into what was, to judge by Fergie's rolling eyes, an old argument. "What's your *passion*? Music? Poetry? Sex?" She smiled lasciviously, showing me her teeth.

She was too close; I could feel her breath on my neck. I edged away along the seat. "I don't know what to say," I faltered. "Books – old books, I mean…. Old films, too." I shook my head.

"If you like old things, the doctor's gonna love you," Mikhail said.

"Do please shut up, Mikhail," Fischer said without looking away from me.

I shifted, uncomfortable in this conversation. "Really, I'm just here to do my job."

Fergie laughed. "Yeah, and what a job you've got. Got to keep us from attacking each other, from sabotaging the plant, from, from – I don't know, from eatin' the yellow snow. What made you want to come here anyway? Middle o' bloody nothing."

"Well, you know," I said with an apologetic shrug, "it was a promotion, right? I mean, they're offering good money to come here…" I trailed off as I didn't get the understanding nods I'd expected.

"Do you have a partner? Are you gay?" Fischer asked from nothing. I blinked. "No. No."

Then her smile really did reach her eyes, but before she could say anything else, de Villiers burst into the room.

The man was beaming, his presence as large as a Norse god. It seemed as if I saw him for the first time; he was big, yes, but no bigger than Mikhail, no broader than Fergie. But he radiated energy and dominated the space.

"Well met, my friends," he boomed. "Making yourself at home, Anders? You have no drink. Micky, get him a – what will it be, Anders? Coffee, tea, water? – get him a coffee, and one for me whilst you're at it."

Mikhail got up in silence. His face was a mask. Just a few moments ago he had been open, fully engaged. Now he was sealed, no emotions showing. Fergie was the same. The Scotsman may not have been particularly friendly before, but better that than this blankness. And Fischer—

The doctor had stiffened too, making no attempt to conceal her distaste for the commander. She glared at him, hatred in her eyes. The look was gone in a second, but it had been there.

It was as if everyone had thrown on their masks. A game I'd become very good at playing over the years.

Fischer was already on her feet and made a point of looking at the clock. "I must get on," she said. "Nice to meet you, Anders, we'll catch up later."

"As will we, my little chickadee," de Villiers said with a grin as she swept past him towards the exit. "What shall we say? After dinner, in my room?"

Fischer paused momentarily in her stride, her face frozen. For a moment I thought she was going to slap him, or maybe just ignore his fake flirtation, but then she gave an almost infinitesimal nod, and left.

I frowned. I had no idea what I had just witnessed. I just had a sense of – of *wrongness* about the situation. I opened my mouth, then closed it again. What could I say?

The smell of coffee had been slowly percolating around me, and I looked at Mikhail. He was standing in front of a combi-maker, waiting. In the silence, disturbed only by the background noises of water heating and the music from the viewscreen, he glanced at me, saw my expression. He shook his head briefly. *Say nothing. Make nothing of it.* Then he turned back to the maker and started to pour the drinks.

The commander couldn't have been unaware of the response to his arrival. But he gave no sign, no indication that he saw any problem. He kept smiling as he sauntered further into the room. "Hey, Weng," he said to the Asian woman. "Is this today's chess challenge? Let's have a look." De Villiers stepped up to the table, first to her shoulder and then to the other side of the board. "God, do we have to listen to this rubbish?"

It took me a moment to realize that he was referring to the music. To me it had become an inaudible part of the background.

"Put something decent on, Fergie, there's a good chap," he said.

"Anders?" Mikhail said softly, and I turned so he could pass me a cup of hot coffee. I smiled my thanks, and he nodded back, bending to my ear. "Don't worry about…about the doctor and the commander," he said. "They're always like this – they have a… fractious relationship." He straightened before I could reply and took another mug over to the commander.

I turned back to watch Weng and de Villiers as Mikhail returned to his seat, and angry guitars kicked from the speakers. I hated this new sound instantly, but I didn't let that show on my face.

De Villiers sipped at his drink and sighed theatrically. "Okay, Weng, I can force mate in three. You do any better?"

The girl looked up at him, but her hair covered her face and I couldn't see her expression.

"This is a toughie. Want a hint?" De Villiers idly moved a piece – then another, and a third. "There you go. Easy when you know how, ain't it? You should give Anders a game. Maybe you'll have a chance against him." The commander took another sip of coffee and turned back to us on the settees. Weng stared at his back, and this time I did see the anger, the rage, in her face.

"We'll have to get you in the leagues, Anders," de Villiers said. "You play, I take it?"

"I'm not very good."

"Now that's exactly what I wanted to hear."

"I think I should go back to my room." I stood. I no longer wanted to be here, in this atmosphere.

"Don't go, Anders!" the commander cried heartily, as if all this were a joke to him. "Stay here, get to know us – let us get to know you."

"Later, maybe. It's been a long day."

"Well, dinner'll be in an hour or so, when the rest of the crew get back. Join us then and meet everyone."

I nodded and left.

CHAPTER TWO

De Villiers, A. Commander of Operations, Australis mineral exploitation base
  Married, three children
  In Company employ 34 years
  ...

I scanned the data carefully, but without access to his personal logs I had no explanation for the way the other members of the crew had reacted to him. There were no personal reports, no hints of how former crewmates had found him to work with.

Seven years' command of mining operations in Ghana
Four years' command of mining operations in Turkey
One year deputy command of mining operations in South Africa
...

His work history was impressive; his suitability for Australis command undeniable. But these were all professional records. I had no access to his Psych reports, and the only mention of his life beyond work was that he was married with children. I could have dug deeper – as chief of security, I had some access to personal files. But de Villiers outranked me and it would have been a gross intrusion. Besides, what was I looking for? All I had was the barest of first impressions, and the responses of people I didn't know. Not nearly enough.

Company Overseer, Debringas Mine, South Africa
Assistant Overseer, Debringas Mine, South Africa
...

Maybe that was just how he was – infuriating, condescending, far too large for his surroundings. Maybe he was putting it on for my benefit to make sure I knew he was the boss. Maybe. I drummed my fingers on the table, frowning both at the screen and at myself.

I logged out of the base computer system and switched off the machine. It was time to go and show myself to the rest of the crew.

★   ★   ★

I got to the refectory early. The table was set for the forthcoming meal so I knew I was in the right place, but there was no one else present. I hesitated at the doorway, unsure whether to sit or stand or leave. Then I heard singing from the kitchen – a man's soft tenor. The door between the two rooms looked at me invitingly, and after a moment's hesitation I went through.

The kitchen was larger than any I'd been in before, though that wasn't saying much. I guess that for a group catering situation it was tiny: a bank of hobs and an oven and a grill, with work surfaces and cupboards all around the walls. A double door at the rear was swinging, allowing that voice to reach me in waves.

Something was roasting in the oven, and two huge pans were simmering on the hob. The smells were rich and earthy, with hints of garlic and spices. It immediately put me in mind of the Middle East, of hot open places far away from the frozen poles.

The singing suddenly grew louder as the doors at the far end of the room swung open and a man stepped through. He was tall, with neatly cropped black hair and a tidy beard, his skin a deep tan. Dressed in chef's whites, he started as he saw me, the melody caught in his throat. He was carrying a packet in his right hand – more spices, I thought. Or salt, or sugar.

A smile acted as an apology. "Hi," I said. "Am I allowed to be here?" I cursed myself for the stupidity of the question as soon as the words were out.

"Y-yes," the man stuttered. "Yes, of course." He recovered himself a little and crossed to the hob, setting the packet down before giving the pans a stir. As he lifted the lids, smells erupted: a mix of vegetables steaming together in one of the vats, and something I couldn't place in the other. Some sort of cereal, perhaps: rice, or pasta. I began to feel hungry. Real, properly cooked food was a luxury. I'd had my share, for sure, but I was not a rich man. It was all insects and soy protein, save for the occasional holiday treat.

"You must be Mr. Nordvelt," he said, glancing over his shoulder at me. "Excuse me for not shaking hands. I'm a little busy here." His voice had an Arabic lilt and his smile contained an apology.

I nodded to his back. "And you're Mr. Ben Ali?" Surely he must be the man listed as the chef.

"Abidene. Or Abi. I'll be another ten minutes, I think. Would you prefer to wait in the other room? We can talk better there – when I'm not so distracted."

I returned to the dining room and walked straight into a conversation that stopped as soon as I was seen. It was Fergie, talking to a Chinese woman – not Weng, as I'd thought momentarily, but an older lady. She was tiny, the top of her head barely reaching the Scotsman's chin.

"Anders," Fergie said a little louder than necessary. "What were you doin' in the kitchen? This is Maggie, by the way, from hydroponics. Maggie, this is Anders—"

"—McCarthy's replacement, of course. Good to meet you."

She'd recovered quicker than Fergie. I wasn't supposed to see the look that passed from him to her, but I did. *Secrets. Secrets and lies*, I thought as I shook Maggie's hand. Her skin was dry and smooth in the way that fine sandpaper feels smooth.

"Don't let me interrupt," I said, and couldn't resist asking what they'd been talking about.

"Oh, nothin', nothin', just the state of our work," Fergie said, again blinking first. "That sort of thing…."

"I do a lot of experimental work, you see," Maggie said smoothly. "As well as trying to keep us fed, I'm playing with modified crop strains to see what grows out here. Not outside, obviously – although that's always the dream – but under glass."

Beside me I felt Fergie relax. I must have been successfully distracted.

"Maggie's our gardener," he said. "We're not self-sufficient here yet – not by some way – but that's the aim."

I decided not to fight it. I let myself be diverted as Maggie told me more of her work. And despite my reserve, I found myself being charmed. She showed me McCarthy's old seat – my seat – and, head propped on my hand, I listened as she told me of her ambition to make the Antarctic green. To feed the world by erecting glasshouses across the continent, with soil replaced by water and powered by the long summer sun.

"So will you be dormant in winter? No winter harvest?" I asked.

She hesitated. "Well, that's where being sited near all that oil comes in handy. That fuels us for the winter," she said with a grin.

The door to the corridor opened and Fischer walked in, accompanied by a beautiful black woman. She couldn't hide her looks, although it seemed as if she'd tried. She was wearing oil-smeared overalls, black hair cropped close. She wore no makeup, no jewelry, solid boots on her feet. But she was perfect nonetheless.

Her name was Max, and she was the maintenance engineer.

I didn't get to talk to her that night – merely the briefest introduction. Her seat was somewhere in the middle, next to Greigor, and I was concentrating too hard on being polite and diplomatic. The table must've been organized by rank, and I was at one end sitting across from Fischer. De Villiers was at the head, of course – I was on his left side. And to *my* left was Keegan, a fair-haired Englishman introduced to me as the base's meteorologist. Abidene sat at the far end of the table, nearest the kitchen.

The food was good, a mix of Mediterranean pulses and vegetables and synthetic meat direct from Company vats. It was served with a rough wine, acidic and overflavored. I was surprised: I'd thought they'd have something better than that. Maybe the batch hadn't been kept properly. Must've been alcohol-free. Real wine was too expensive for most people these days, and the Company would never have paid to have a batch of the good stuff shipped out to a working base like this. Besides, de Villiers had said that there was no alcohol to be found on Australis.

As soon as he swept into the room and assumed his position to my right, de Villiers had started to monopolize the conversation. He'd started with a few overloud questions about how I was fitting in, whether everything was to my satisfaction – not caring whether I had an answer or not – before gliding straight into a dirty joke shared with Keegan. He addressed a few remarks to Weng, who was seated next to Fischer. She ignored him, attention focused on her food. Greigor too kept trying to talk to her; the young man seemed almost obsessive in making sure she had water to drink, had salt and pepper and whatever else she might need. Weng did not so much as glance at him. Eventually he gave up and turned his attention to Max on his other side. At least he got conversation there. I just tried not to stare at her.

Fischer ate in silence, a faraway look in her eyes as she methodically worked through her plate. She seemed completely different from the self-possessed woman I'd met earlier – she kept slumping in her seat, then shaking herself together for a moment. I was about to ask her if she was all right when de Villiers cleared his throat and got to his feet.

"Ladies and gentlemen, a moment please."

I looked at the faces around the table. Polite impatience. Disdain. And Fischer was ignoring him completely, just mopping up the remnants of her meal.

"I'd just like to say a word to welcome Anders to the team here at Australis. I'm sure he'll fit in very well here – the Psych wouldn't make the same mistake twice." He laughed and a few of my fellows smiled.

Abidene was scowling at the end of the table. He got to his feet and started clearing the plates away. If de Villiers thought that rude, he gave no indication.

"I know you'll all do your best to help the lad settle in, that you'll bend over backwards to accommodate him." He grinned and flashed me a quick wink, although I couldn't see any real warmth behind the gesture.

I hated this. I was never one for attention, just wanted to do my job in as quiet a manner as possible, to learn quickly, to fit in. I took a deep breath. Time. That was all I needed, just a little time to get to know people and all would be well. I mean, how hard could it be? There were only twelve other people here; it wasn't like the thousands I'd been surrounded by in the blocks.

I made myself smile and mumbled my thanks to Abidene as he silently removed my plate.

"We all know," the commander went on, "how important this base – this project – is to the world. We provide the resources to keep the wheels of civilization turning after the collapse of nation states—"

He shot a quick look at Maggie, mischief in his eye. I looked to her in time to see an expression of disgust being carefully wiped from her face.

"We look for new ways to feed the hungry," de Villiers continued. "We're the pioneers. You should be proud to be a part of this, Anders. We don't want any disruptions."

His sudden focus took me by surprise, but he swept on before I could work out what he meant.

"Now, as you all know, tomorrow brings the equinox. The end of summer and the start of the long night. The year's only sunset! When is it forecast for, Keegan?"

"Tomorrow, Cap'n? Sixteen forty-seven."

"I'm expecting us all to drive up to the ridge to toast the sun – a little bit of old-fashioned pagan fun. Show Anders what sort of people we are, right? So make sure everything goes smoothly in the morning, okay?" he said with a laugh. "I don't want any problems holding us up. Now – Abi! Another bottle of wine."

★   ★   ★

I lay in my bed, hands behind my head. The taste of wine lingered in my mouth; it really must have been a bad bottle. I felt okay though, just tired.

What was wrong with Fischer? She'd been so strange. In the afternoon she'd been sharp, even abrasive – never to be ignored. But during the meal she'd seemed...absent. And then, when the food was finished, a tuck of the head from de Villiers and she'd followed him meekly from the room.

No one else had seemed to notice, or at least they hadn't considered it worthy of comment. Most of them had gone straight to the rec room, or to their own quarters, as soon as they'd finished their food. I'd been delayed by introductions to a miner called Dmitri and Theo, an oilman. Handshakes and hellos, the awkwardness endless. I'd found myself mesmerized by a small crucifix that kept bouncing on a leather cord round Theo's neck. Everyone seemed nice enough, though; they seemed to understand my shyness. The woman, Max, she'd disappeared before I'd got more than a smile, and Greigor after her. Fergie and Maggie had slipped out too.

I wondered what they might have been talking about, that they'd shut up as soon as they saw me. Nothing work-related, surely. I couldn't help but imagine they were talking about me.

And then de Villiers: he just had to seize the spotlight. His little speech... The way he'd looked at me, that little glare when he'd said he didn't want any disruptions. Almost as if he had reason to distrust me.

Or was I just being paranoid?

I turned over and tried not to think about it.

CHAPTER THREE

My whole body ached next morning. My mind was awake, but my body didn't want to comply. I showered, glad not to have the water rationed, and worked some of the kinks out of me. It was late – later than I was used to – and I felt the need to work, to justify my existence here.

So I dressed in my basic gray fatigues – the gaudy colors that marked austerity fashion just sat wrong on me – and went into my office. I turned on the computer. At home in the blocks, my inbox would have been full of alerts: problems for me to investigate, to allay, to dismiss. When you get hundreds of people squeezed into a small area, crime is almost inevitable.

There was nothing. In Australis, people solved their own problems.

It seemed that de Villiers was right: I was going to have a very quiet time here.

And maybe that was why I was looking for things to be wrong, why I was so puzzled by Fischer, by Maggie and Fergie. Because I wanted a mystery to solve, and because I couldn't bear the thought of being superfluous, of being useless.

For want of anything better to do, I tried to access McCarthy's old reports. Reading them would make me feel that I was at least *trying* to work.

Except I had no access. Something was wrong. It was asking for a password, but my bioscan should've granted me immediate clearance. I shook my head. I'd already seen how little the crew cared for security; a backup system would surely be redundant.

I tried my Company ID: nothing. Frustrated, I stared at the screen.

At least I could use the basic, common programs: examine the layout of the base, check the mail servers and the CCTV records. I just couldn't get any deeper. I glanced at my book, my puzzle box, on the desk beside the screen. I considered accessing the music from my memcard, but that would have calmed me, and right then I wanted to be angry. Damn the incompetence.

I contemplated the screen in front of me for as long as I could bear before I went in search of de Villiers.

★   ★   ★

The corridors were quiet, the artificial light making a mockery of time. I glanced at my watch: half past ten. I'd spent a week at the southern tip of Chile to try and get accustomed to new circadian rhythms, but I had precious little knowledge of how Australis itself operated, or of how the crew considered time when all was darkness outside.

I took deep breaths as I walked. There was no point going in all gung-ho. It was probably just a mistake, just needed a word and it'd be sorted. It never occurred to me that de Villiers might not actually be in his quarters.

I frowned at the blank door. All I wanted to do was work, to find my purpose – and I couldn't do a thing, not one useful thing. I slammed my fist into the cool metal, echoes spilling down the corridor.

"You know, I'm impressed. It usually takes longer than this to get riled by the commander."

I spun round; I hadn't heard Fischer approaching. She eyed me strangely as I mumbled an apology. She stood straight and proud and, though she was a good two inches shorter, gave me the impression of looking down on me. There was a faint scent of something sweet about her.

She smiled, her eyes becoming sharp. "Anton will be up at the mine. What did you want him for? Anything I can do for you?"

"…No. No, nothing, just – I just had some problems with my compscreen."

"If you want technical help, you'd be best to talk to the janitor."

"The janitor?"

"Max. That's what she calls herself." Fischer half-smiled. "But she'll be up at the mine as well. Sorry. She and Anton are usually up there, tinkering, tinkering."

"Tinkering with what?"

"Trying to make things run better. Anton cares about digging more than he does for any human."

"But – he seems personable, though."

Fischer raised an eyebrow, smiling with something more like genuine humor. "Trying to gauge my reaction, Anders?"

I shrugged and brought a smile to my own lips.

She laughed at my tacit acknowledgement. "Anton and I have an understanding," she said. "I don't particularly care for the man, but he has his uses. Mostly in that he keeps out of my business."

"You seem very relaxed about it." I was, I realised, actually enjoying this conversation. I could keep up with this aspect of Fischer's personality. My earlier frustration had dissipated.

"About what, in particular? Talking about my colleagues? You're going to be here for at least six months. We all are. If you haven't got a handle on the politics of twelve people by the end of the shift, then you really aren't worth… Well, let's just say that I wish you well. I don't know you, Anders, but I'll tell you this. We're all one big family here on Australis. Not necessarily a happy family, but working this close with the same people, day in, day out, builds a certain…loyalty. If you're here to break that up, then you're not going to be popular."

And, just like that, the fun was over. "Why would I be here to break you up?"

She gave me a long, contemplative look but said nothing.

"So – look, all I want is to do my job—"

"Job?" She laughed. "Job? You've not got any *job*, Anders. Not if—" She broke off. "Look, you're just here to sit back and enjoy yourself. Read. Flirt. Fuck. Just find a way to pass the night shift without going insane, or driving anyone else insane. If you can do that, then maybe the Psych's got the right person after all. And for God's sake, call me Julia. We're going to be spending a lot of time together. Best get…familiar."

★   ★   ★

It seemed that everyone else had work to do, for no one was in the rec room. I made myself a strong coffee and drank it in silence. I accessed the viewscreen and flicked through the menus for a while without putting anything on. I was restless; back home I'd have gone out for a walk. But in Antarctica? I just couldn't face the prospect of getting suited up and fighting with the conditions.

I thought of Weng, and why she might hate de Villiers. I thought of Greigor, with all his Latin elegance and those eloquent looks that put me in mind of some classic Hollywood heartbreaker. I thought of Max.

I went to the refectory. There was no one there either – I wondered what Abidene might be doing, if he had any other duties or if he was already working on the next meal. Maybe he was talking crops with Maggie.

The room was spotless; if it had been used for breakfast, there was no sign. I hadn't eaten yet, so, just as I'd done the night before, I pushed my way into the kitchen. It too was pristine. I found a half loaf of bread, carefully wrapped, in a cupboard. I located a knife and cut myself a piece, feeling like a naughty child. I had no idea if this was allowed or not, but I made a good effort to leave everything as I found it: I rinsed the knife in the sink, swept the crumbs I'd made into my hand – and then to the sink. The loaf went back in the cupboard.

The bread was coarse and dry – almost like the wine had been – and I wondered if it had been produced here on the base. I swallowed it down and took another bite.

And then I heard Abi's voice from the storeroom. I froze on my heels, the sudden urge to flee strong within me. I strained my ears, trying to make out the words.

"De Villiers," I caught. "De Villiers and his parties… Can he not just carry on with his work? He is insufferable—"

"Well, what do you expect—" A woman's voice, not one I could immediately place. Words I couldn't catch.

"I don't know what the Company was thinking, putting him in charge. He turns everything into a competition, into a game."

"It's who he is. Too late to do anything now."

Abi muttered something in response.

"You think I don't know that? I have to watch Greigor—"

Maggie? Could be.

"—have to limit de Villiers's influence before—"

"Oh, damn the commander. Damn the Company!"

"You don't have to shout. You—"

But she quietened and I lost the conversation.

I stayed there, not moving, for a little longer, but I didn't get anything else. I put the last of the bread into my mouth and slipped away.

I was going to have to keep an eye on the chef and the scientist.

★　★　★

It was the woman, Max, who came to take me out to witness the equinox.

I hadn't seen anyone for hours – not since I'd run into Fischer. I'd been in my rooms, where, as I didn't seem to have any formal duties, I'd done my best to pass the time by adding to my journal and trying to make my room my home. I'd failed; there was no way, with my pathetic bag of possessions, that I could make the place seem like anything other than a drab box. In the end I fell asleep across my bed, a wave of tiredness sweeping over me unexpectedly.

The knocking on my door woke me instantly. I jerked up, thinking I must have dreamed the disruption, but then it came again: a firm rapping, and someone calling. "Mr. Nordvelt? Are you there?"

I took the few paces to the door and opened it. There stood the beautiful woman from last night – Max, the one who called herself the janitor, still wearing dirty old overalls. They struck me as much more attractive than the loud shirts of the doctor or Greigor.

"Mr. Nordvelt. Anton – the commander – he asked me to fetch you for the party."

I blinked. "The party. The equinox?"

She nodded. She seemed a little nervous. It was natural, I suppose – I was a stranger to her. But it didn't help me to relax.

I tried to smile but it didn't feel right on my face. "Call me Anders. So we're going out, then? Do we need anything?"

"We have to suit up, obviously. But Abi should have the food sorted, and the commander has the drink—" She paused and shrugged. "Are you coming?"

So I followed her out of my office, down the corridor and to the foot of the stairs. It was funny how she seemed a lot more confident when she was moving, graceful in her work boots, comfortable in her skin.

"So, how are you settling in?" she asked as we ascended.

"Not too bad. It's only been a day. I've not met everyone properly yet."

"You'll get used to it. I really like it here. Once you're used to the quiet, you'll see how beautiful it is."

"Antarctica?"

"Well, I'm not talking about this stairwell."

"Why do you call yourself the janitor?"

She laughed; she had a good laugh. Not the decorous twinkle of the debutante, but something deeper, earthier – more *real*, somehow. It was impossible not to smile back at her.

"'Cause I get to clean up everyone else's mess. Why else?"

"Isn't it a bit beneath you?"

"I started it myself. When the others use it it's a nickname, that's all. You must know the staff structure here on Australis – de Villiers in overall command, you as security, and Fischer as doctor? Then there's the support staff – Keegan, Weng, Abidene, Maggie and Greigor. They're the scientists, the researchers. Even Abi – he's developing new nutritional supplements with Maggie. They're the clever ones, not like us grease-monkeys." She grinned. "But we're all researchers in a way. Pioneers." She paused to shoulder open a door. "Where was I? Oh, yeah – Fergie and Dmitri are the miners, Mikhail and Theo the oilmen. I don't have a set role like the others. I fix things when they break – and when other people break them. Hence I'm the janitor."

"Do they keep you busy?"

She laughed again, her voice echoing down the corridor. "Yeah, busy enough. Anton's full of ideas, and it's usually me who has to either implement them or explain why he's being ridiculous."

"It sounds as if you like the commander."

She stopped, one hand on the door that led to the vestibule, and thus to the exit. She wasn't smiling now. She held my eyes and paused for a long time before answering. "Who have you been talking to?"

"No one's said anything, I just..." I trailed off, gesturing vaguely.

"All I'll say is that he's good at his job, and we work well together. I'm not in the habit of spreading gossip about my colleagues." Then she smiled again, defusing the tension. "C'mon. Let's get suited up."

★   ★   ★

The warmsuits were clever, and essential if you wanted to survive in the wastes of Antarctica. The green scales on the outside were simply flexible solar batteries that powered the circuits beneath and provided constant warmth – and in the long winter they could be charged from any electrical outlet. But the real magic was in the face masks we wore to protect us from the cold and the wind. The masks not only kept us from frostbite, but also managed to mimic normal human speech – even in the most hostile of conditions.

There was a microphone fitted into the mouthpiece and a transmitter over the ear; that was simple. The genius was that the mask measured how loudly you were speaking, and in what direction. The sound that was received by your companions was therefore what they'd have heard had you not been wearing it: very useful in a blizzard, or a gale. So you could lean close to whisper, or shout so all could hear. It was meant to feel natural, intuitive, and after a while it was. If only it were as easy to tell people apart by sight: everyone looked the same in their suits and masks.

The heavy red sun was bisected by the horizon. I shivered at the sight of winter's first stars, but I wasn't at all cold. Must have been a psychosomatic reaction.

Max closed the base door behind me, and it sealed automatically. She loped across the icy tarmac towards a building as anonymous as the rest of the base. Only Maggie's greenhouses were instantly recognizable to a newcomer like myself. I followed Max, boots gripping easily on the smooth surface.

"So what's the plan?" I asked as she reached the door of the new structure.

She hauled it open, bracing herself against a wind I barely felt. "We're riding out about three miles to a ridge nearer the pole. It's a nice spot, with shelter from the wind. The rest of the crew should already be out there."

She let me slip past her, then followed me in. The door slammed shut behind us, but I noticed it wasn't sealed like the barracks were. There was no vestibule; it was obvious that no attempt had been made to heat the building.

The lights came on automatically as we moved inside. The room was full of three things: vehicles, parts, and space. It was clearly a repair shop as well as a place to park. The walls were cold and bare and there were few touches of humanity. Much of the floor was empty. There was a 4x4 in one corner, huge spiked tires designed for crossing the ice. There was also what looked like a crawler that had been cut in half. It was, I realized, a sort of shunting engine designed to line up carriages for the crawler to take back to O'Higgins. There were a pair of vehicles with one wheel at the front and twin tracks to the rear, like a cross between a motorbike and a snowmobile. One looked ready to go but the other was half-dismantled, apparently raided for parts. From my training, I knew they were half-tracks.

"You ready?" Max asked, and without waiting for an answer strode to the working vehicle and swung her leg across. In her mask and suit, she looked like an alien queen about to ride into battle.

"You want me…?"

"Pillion. I take it you don't have a problem riding behind me?"

I could hear the amusement in her voice. I smiled behind my mask and mounted – a little clumsily – at her back. Ahead of us a chain-link metal door took up most of one wall. Max started the engine and, at some unknown signal, the door rattled up into the ceiling.

"Any chance of the mechanism freezing?" I asked above the low growl of the motor.

"Ha. Everything has a chance of freezing – that's one of the things that keeps me so very busy. I just thank the gods of global warming that it's not like it was twenty years ago." The engine growled as she eased the throttle open, and steadily we accelerated into the wasteland.

★　　★　　★

At first it was hard to make anything out. The sun was too low and too bright, and anyway I was trying to peer out from behind Max's back.

But gradually – as first we swung north to ease around the minehead, then east and finally south – I began to adjust to the glare, and to relax.

And I had my first real experience of Antarctica.

I couldn't feel anything, not really. That was the problem with all the protective gear – it dulled the senses. The wind was just a gentle pressure on my body; there was no sense of the biting gale that whipped ice flakes across the plateau. The only physical sensations were those of the seat beneath me and the prewarmed air that was allowed to filter through the mask. But I saw things that took my breath away.

Every color. I'd not expected all the colors…

"Pretty, isn't it?" Max called back to me.

I could only nod, murmur vague agreement. It was the sun, reflecting on the ice. Refracting like a spill of oil. Every dip, every rise, every hole and every angle – each met the light in a different way. It was a kaleidoscope, a prism that shone without any sort of unity or plan. And further from us, where the land stretched away and the angles merged, the ice became a blue-brown collage until it met the sky.

In the distance, great rock formations stretched fingers upwards as if in a gesture of defiance, black against a dying sun.

And, aside from the complaints of the half-track and whispers of the wind, it was silent and still. No birds, no mammals, just me and Max crossing an empty plateau. Terrifying. Magnificent.

After a little time I became aware that we were traveling parallel to an ice ridge. We'd been out for something like twenty minutes; I guessed we'd covered just a few miles. When the ridge started to sink back into the plain, Max gracefully arced the track across it and swung us slowly along its far side. Half a minute later and I saw figures in the distance.

★　　★　　★

It was an oddly incongruous gathering: eleven people, specialists all, sitting on the side of an ice ridge in Antarctica and having a barbecue. Several of them had removed their masks, had them hanging over their chests from the attachments at the neck. An old barrel served as the firepit, and there was plenty of coal for fuel.

Unmasked, Abidene was doing the cooking, which seemed to consist mostly of rebutting de Villiers's attempts to interfere. I noted the looks the chef gave the commander whenever his back was turned, and Abi's studied blankness whenever de Villiers spoke. The food was mostly various soy- and mushroom-based products of the sort that anyone could buy anywhere in the world.

"Anders! Max!" de Villiers boomed as Max parked the half-track near another four that had evidently brought the others. There was also a 4x4, which must have been used to bring out the supplies. "Welcome! Here, grab a beer, the food'll be a few minutes yet."

Max unfastened her mask as she swung herself off the vehicle. Holding it in one hand, she took a deep breath and gave a yell of joy as she exhaled. When she turned back to me, her eyes were watering from the cold. She grinned. "C'mon, Anders, take yours off." She blinked, and wiped away the tears before they could freeze on her face.

"Yeah, come on, kid, show us what you're made of," de Villiers added. He picked up a bottle from a collection on the ice and lobbed it to me.

I caught it easily. I too had dismounted and was stretching my legs. I hesitated for a moment. De Villiers and Max were waiting for me to unmask. Behind them Abidene was focused on the food, and on the other side of the fire were the rest of the crew. One or two mask-wearers were facing in my direction, but I couldn't tell if they were paying attention to us.

I reached up and unfastened the clips that held my mask in place. I hesitated for a moment, then pulled it off.

The cold hit me like a hammer.

I gasped as the blood shrank from my face; my glove was rough against my cheek as I brushed away tears. But the air was clean and fresh in my lungs. The experience was like my first step on a foreign planet. Never had I taken in such an unpolluted breath. I gasped again as a smile spread across my face.

Max was smiling at me. De Villiers was nodding. I felt like I'd passed some initiation ceremony.

"Don't keep it off too long," Max cautioned. "When you start to go numb, put it back on for a few minutes. Keep your skin alive."

"Come on," de Villiers added. "Let's join the others." He strode back to the barbecue and immediately started to tell Abidene how he should be doing it. I saw the flash of irritation in the chef's face, quickly hidden, as the commander tried once again to take over.

★   ★   ★

Despite de Villiers's assertions that he could have done it better, the food was good and, out there in the wilderness, I felt more alive than I'd done in years. I made small talk with the rest of the crew and drank – in my unmasked moments – what proved to be a pretty acceptable beer. I spoke with Theo, even spent a little while throwing a ball around with him and Mikhail. I was clumsy, unfamiliar with the game, and every time I dropped a pass or missed my aim they'd laugh and I'd turn away in embarrassment. But I persisted, and when Mikhail finally erred and had to chase the ball down a steep slope, I grinned as Theo gave a sarcastic cheer.

I spoke with Maggie, with Abi – with everyone except Weng, who didn't appear to want to talk to anyone. Apart from her, the mood amongst the crew seemed good. The only strange thing was that people kept appearing and disappearing as they took off, then replaced, their masks as the cold got too much. You'd be talking to someone, then you'd glance away, and when you looked back, you'd be talking to alien blankness. It made it even more surreal that their voices weren't muffled. But I got the hang of it quickly enough, and soon was getting plenty of practice at removing and replacing mine. As a system it worked well, and I began to notice differences in stature and the way individuals held themselves. It helped that people tended to call their colleagues by their names more than they normally would.

After a while I noticed something odd.

I'd gone a little way apart from the rest, and was sitting with my back to a rock. I wasn't feeling antisocial – I'd have welcomed company – but for a moment I just wanted to take the weight off my feet and to stare at the sunset with another beer. When I looked back at the group, it took me a few seconds to realize that people were missing.

I frowned behind my mask and tried to work out who had wandered off. Three people: I could hear de Villiers laughing, so not him. And the smallest, slightest figure must have been Weng, and next to her Greigor, only a little taller but much broader. And there was Theo, and Dmitri—

The puzzle resolved itself when Maggie, Fischer and Keegan ambled back from behind a fold in the land. They were all unmasked and laughing, and I put it out of my mind until I saw Max.

She was chatting, mask off, with a man I couldn't immediately identify. The conversation seemed quite natural and friendly. There was someone else there too, possibly Fergie. She was holding something. Gesticulating with it. A small, thin tube, paper-white, almost hidden, invisible within her fingers. It was only when she put it in her mouth – then immediately took it out again to say something – that it clicked with me.

Cigarettes. You barely see them nowadays; they're a rich man's affectation. I'd met a few smokers in the blocks – usually with the cheap bootleg stuff – and of course part of my job was to keep dealers in check. I'd been questioned at length about my experience of nicotine and cannabis and all other intoxicants as part of my interview for this job. I'd submitted to a blood test and given a urine sample, and I presumed that everyone else here had too. To have smokers here was just strange.

De Villiers was watching, mask off, in the background. His expression showed distaste as he scowled at Max. But he said nothing until she raised a lighter in her other hand. I could've sworn he looked straight at me before snapping a couple of words at the janitor. She immediately took the cigarette from her mouth and hid it at her side. I pretended not to notice as she looked at me too. Then she walked off, accompanied by Fergie, and was soon swallowed by the barren landscape.

★　　★　　★

We stood together to watch the sun finally disappear below the horizon, the year's only sunset. It was hard to believe that this was the last we'd see of it for six months – it just didn't seem real, especially as there was still plenty of light. The moon shone down on us, and around it stars began to break cover. We had no need of our torches when de Villiers drew everyone together for a few words. First he made us all take off our masks, the better to mark the moment. I glanced around, seeing faces pinched with the cold. There were a lot of smiles; I saw Mikhail whisper something to Maggie, whose lined face crumpled into barely contained laughter.

"Well now," de Villiers began. "It's about time for us to head back, I think. But before we go, I just want us all to raise a glass – or a can, at least."

I was nearing the end of my third drink, almost wishing it were real alcohol. I almost felt like I belonged out there, that I was entitled to smile, even to laugh.

Childhood trauma enhances fear of basic human interactions... The words of the Psych seemed to be melting away in the cold.

"Ladies and gentlemen, you don't need me to tell you how important the work we do here is. Our research may one day feed the world. The resources we're pulling out of the ground – each day we're providing a good chunk of what we laughingly call civilization with light and heat—"

"Get on with it, Anton," Fischer interrupted. Even she was less acid than usual; she sounded more impatient than really annoyed. "It's cold out here, you know."

"And it's going to get a lot colder. Ladies and gentlemen, a toast. To the crew of Australis base, to the year's only sunset – and to the start of the long night. Here's to the work ahead – to the night shift!"

CHAPTER FOUR

We chased our moon-shadows across the ice and back to the base. Max was quiet; I was quiet. Five half-tracks raced across the wastes, leaving the 4x4 in their wake; the engines were all I could hear. The wind was beginning to pick up as we arrived back and pulled up in the workshop-cum-garage. Clouds were building in the dark distance, and as we dismounted I heard Keegan mention that we were in for a blizzard.

De Villiers, Max and Dmitri waited to help unload the 4x4. The rest of us hurried past the floodlit buildings and into the barracks. I was tired and a little heavy-headed, and as soon as my suit was off, I slipped away and into my room. The clock on my computer told me it was just after five. Soon it would be pitch-black outside.

It was far too early to settle down, so I took the luxury of another hot shower. I felt a spark of guilt over the waste of water – had I still been in the blocks, I'd have far exceeded my daily ration – but I must have spent a good half hour in the steaming cascade, rejoicing in the experience and feeling truly alive.

I was drying myself, naked in the main room of my apartment, when the doorbell chimed. Hurriedly, I threw my clothes back on and went barefooted into my office and opened the outer door. Weng stood before me in the corridor. She stared up at me defiantly.

"Weng?"

She said nothing, just looked at me with those piercing brown eyes.

"Do you want to come in?"

She nodded and I stepped back, my feet cold on the floor. I could see her taking in my crumpled clothes and my wet hair. I realized that I'd never actually heard her speak – surely she wasn't mute?

I backed away and stepped around my desk. Weng turned and carefully shut the door after her before standing behind the visitor's chair.

"Take a seat," I said, still unsure if this was an official or a personal visit.

She shook her head.

"What's on your mind?"

For a moment I thought that she would say nothing; I had a vision of her simply turning and walking out. But she didn't move – stayed utterly still. She just stared into my eyes as if she were trying to read my mind.

When she finally spoke she had a strong accent but her words came slow and clear, as if she was challenging me to misunderstand.

"Are you here because of me?"

"What?"

"Are you here because of me?"

"W-why would I be here because of you?" I stammered, unable to think of anything more coherent to say.

She stared at me for a long time, then turned on her heel and left without another word.

★　　★　　★

"Anders, take a seat. What can I do you for?"

The commander leaned back in his chair, the undoubted ruler of his kingdom. I felt small beneath his intense blue eyes.

"I felt we should have a talk," I said awkwardly.

"Personal?" He gave a little grin and crossed his legs. "Or is it business?"

"Business."

"Ah. Right. Well, what's on your mind, mate?"

"There are a few... Look, I'm having trouble accessing some computer files—"

"Trying to look me up again?"

"What?"

"Gotta say, I thought you might've come see me earlier. You accessed my work record, didn't you?"

"How did you—"

"You think I don't keep an eye on what people are up to? If anyone's looking into me, I want to know about it, right?" He spoke mildly but the look he was giving me was warning enough. "I put a trace on. So what's your business looking into my past? You think I'm not doing a good job here? Or are you planning to hunt through the whole crew's past?"

"I just—"

"Just what?"

God, this conversation had got out of hand so quickly. I was totally wrong-footed, could see no way but awkward honesty. "I wanted to know why the crew reacted the way they did – when you—"

"That's none of your damn business."

"You – wait, you think it's not the business of the chief of security to know what's happening on his territory?"

"*Your* territory?"

"I didn't mean—"

"I've met people like you. People who've spent their whole lives – what was it, since you were six? – their whole lives in the Company system. No understanding of the real world. Think the sun shines out the Company's arse."

"I don't—"

"You're the new man, Nordvelt. I get the best out of this crew. If you're here to get in my way—"

"Why would I do that?"

"Listen," he said. "I know these people and you don't. I don't mind giving them a little leeway…let them get away with a few things to keep the machine running smoothly."

Of course he did. "The wine we had with the meal last night: that was real, wasn't it? Anything that rough must have been produced here. And the beers this afternoon. They were alcoholic too."

He looked away. "I didn't see you complaining when you were drinking them."

"I didn't know they were alcoholic. I might have got drunk—"

"Got drunk?" He laughed, a bear's roar of laughter. "God, you can't handle a few glasses of wine, a few cans of weak beer? What are you—"

"That's not the point," I snapped.

"Listen, Nordvelt, I run this base so it works as efficiently as possible. That means keeping my staff as happy as possible. You've only been here for a couple of days; imagine what it's like after six months. With another six to come. The tedium is…difficult. I recognize that. So I make allowances. As long as it doesn't affect their work, I allow the personnel here a little latitude. You'd better respect that, or the next six months are going to be…unpleasant. For us all."

"Is that a threat?" The voice didn't sound like mine. Maybe it was the beer. De Villiers was right: I wasn't used to drinking, didn't know what I could be like.

"Not a threat. A warning. We need to work together, Anders—"

"I should report this."

"Yeah, ruin everything I've worked for here? You really want to do that, kid? It might be hard for you to see, but I operate in the real world. I know what it takes to get things done out here—"

"I can see just fine."

"Fine. See this. I want this place to thrive. I want to work with you. We're on the same side, right? You want to prove you're no Company shill—"

"You want me to turn a blind eye to this."

He didn't answer straight away. He just looked at me. "Did you want anything else?"

That was it? That was all he had to say? "Where does it come from?"

"What?"

"The alcohol. And those damn cigarettes I saw."

He turned away slightly. "I have no idea."

"How can you—"

"I have no idea," de Villiers said again.

I leaned back in my chair and stared at him across the desk. "Why did McCarthy leave?" I asked at length.

De Villiers grunted. "Health issues. He had headaches and trouble sleeping. And he had terrible nightmares when he did get off – God, did he go on about it—"

"You're saying that it was nothing to do with your decisions?"

He paused. "I think it's fair to say that McCarthy and I never saw eye to eye."

"He disagreed with you over this."

"Not strongly enough to report me. But he was a military man –

a United Nations peacekeeper, back in the days when the UN had teeth. He could never let go of that."

"What do you mean?"

"I mean he was arrogant and inflexible."

"Like you, then?" I regretted it immediately, but too late. The words were out there.

But De Villiers just burst out laughing, the anger gone in an instant. "Yeah, I suppose you're right. I guess the idea was for him to straighten my shoulders and me to round his. We got on all right most of the time, you know – found a way of working."

"Which was?"

"He didn't see our drinking. I made damn sure no one was drunk at work. Like I'd ever do that anyway. Lost enough friends at…at other jobs." He glanced at a photograph on his desk. "Anyway, McCarthy, we'd have sorted out our issues, but he got these headaches, sometimes laid up in bed for days." He shrugged. "Look, Anders," he said, leaning forward, "I don't have a problem with you, kid, I really don't. But I don't trust you. Don't trust any Company lapdog."

I flushed but he went on before I could speak.

"I want us to work well together. Maybe I should have told you the truth initially, but I wanted a chance to gauge you first, see what kind of person you are. I knew that computer block would bring you here, give us a chance to…talk. But Max and whoever else spoiled that plan by being so obvious."

"You're asking me to condone actions that clearly violate Company policy."

"What I'm asking you to do is pretend you've not been indoctrinated in that damn orphanage and step into reality. We're on the same side, Anders. We both want this place to succeed. The world needs these resources, needs the coal, the oil – and if Maggie can make hydroponics really work, then we can—"

"Yes, I've read the mission statement." I was dry, conflicted.

"You really want to put an end to that? To put these people out of work?"

I hesitated. I had no wish to cause trouble: I was going to have to work with these people for another six months. I hardly wanted to be the man who took away all their pleasures.

And what if everyone just lied? Would my bosses even care?

"I'll think about it," I said.

"Good man." The commander seemed to assume that he'd gotten my silence. "Now, was there anything else?"

"You'll remove the block on my computer?"

He waved an arm vaguely. "I'll sort it when I have a moment."

I stood to leave.

"Anders," de Villiers called after me. "Don't worry. Don't stress, kid. You'll have a good time here, maybe even make some friends – reckon you could do with a few, right? Think about what I've said."

★   ★   ★

I wanted to go for a walk. I wanted to consider – or to not consider – on my own, to throw off any lingering effects of the beer and work out what I was going to do. It was what I'd always done before, when I'd prowl the late-night concrete cliffs that used to be home.

No chance of that here. Too dangerous outside, especially with a blizzard coming.

So I stomped round in circles and replayed the conversation I'd had with de Villiers. It was clear now why he'd been suspicious of me; it made sense. He'd been encouraging rule-breaking and was scared I'd report him, maybe even get him removed. He saw me as an automaton, a Company drone. Question was: was he right?

Yeah, I'd been through the system. Yeah, I thought the Company was our best hope as a species – they'd basically bought the world, and the world was a better place for it.

Nice of de Villiers to point out my need for friends. I didn't know if he'd inferred it from my personnel file or from my Psych reports, or if he'd just worked it out over the course of a few meetings, but I'd never really been close to anyone in my old life. My friends lived in film and in fiction, so far removed from this age of decay that we could have been on different planets.

When my feet took me to the rec room, and when I saw that the crew were watching an old movie, I felt such a desire to sneak in and watch from the back of the hall. I wanted to be carried away. I wanted to be somewhere else, someone else.

Instead I went back to my room, accessed my memcard and let my mother sing me to sleep.

★　　★　　★

I was awakened by an alarm from my computer. It took me an effort to rise; my limbs felt heavy, my mind unrested. I'd been dreaming. I remembered the emotions – fear, anger, determination. I'd had a mission, something that would have given me peace. But that accursed alarm – the memory fled, leaving only a vague sense of anxiety, of *unrightness*.

There'd been something of my last interview in there too: something of having a problem to solve, one that I couldn't quite grasp, couldn't shift…like the puzzle box that sat next to my compscreen…something I had to do…

I shoved the sensation from my mind and forced my body to move. I was stiff and had to roll onto the floor before I could get to my feet.

The alarm was in response to a Priority One message – the type only to be used in critical situations. I wondered if it was one of the crew messing me around, a practical joke for the new boy. But I couldn't ignore it. I silenced the noise and accessed the message.

It was de Villiers. "Nordvelt, get the hell out of bed," he said. It was a visual recording, dated just half a minute earlier. On the screen, his face looked lined and worried. Not a joke, then. "We have a situation at the comms building. Get here at once."

I dressed hurriedly, grabbed a caffeine tab from the kitchen and strode out.

★　　★　　★

The comms building was half a mile to the southeast, on the track up to the minehead. Why they'd built it out of the main complex I wasn't sure; maybe the builders had thought the extra height gave a clearer signal. I looked up, the slope rising sharply before me, but I couldn't see beyond the courtyard. Keegan had been right; heavy snow had fallen overnight. It was still falling steadily.

Three sets of half-covered footprints led away from the barracks in the direction of the garage but I ignored them and went straight for the hill. A half-track would have been quicker but I was yet to drive solo and this wasn't the time to try.

The climb took around twenty minutes – it wasn't too far but it was steep – and I was once again glad of my warmsuit and mask. My boots gripped easily on the snow-dusted ice. I was anxious.

After just a few minutes, I intersected a rough road created by the tracks of successive vehicles. I walked in them for easier footing, and after only a quarter of an hour more, I could see figures up on the hillside: two of them, and a parked half-track. A few yards to my right, a conveyor wound around a massive outcrop. Silently the wide belt carried coal to the courtyard from the minehead above.

What I couldn't see was the comms building.

At first I thought it must have been obscured by the snow. Then I thought I just wasn't close enough.

One of the figures saw me, and beckoned for me to hurry up. In their suits it was impossible to tell who they were, but one of them must have been de Villiers. I started to walk faster, using the treadmarks I was following as a sort of stairway. I stumbled; I'd tripped over a piece of metal half-buried in the snow. It was too big to belong there, and, curious, I scraped away at it with my foot as I regained my breath.

A horrible realization crept over me. I looked back up the hill.

What I had tripped on was bent, buckled and broken. It had been a radio mast. It lay on and under a field of snow-covered bricks.

I couldn't see the comms building because it wasn't there anymore.

I couldn't see the comms building because it was beneath my feet.

★   ★   ★

De Villiers, Max and I sat in the commander's office, each of us cradling a coffee, each of us ashen-faced.

"Okay. So we've got emergency lighting up there. We've got everyone we can spare clearing the rubble, and you've had a look, Max. So what's the prognosis?" de Villiers asked.

She shrugged. "We're completely cut off. We've no way of getting in touch with Tierra del Fuego. The only sat-phone we had was mangled in the wreckage. Comms still work for each of the buildings individually, but we can't get word from the minehead, or the oil well, to the barracks without someone making the journey. I could probably link hydroponics into an internal system, given a bit of time." She smiled humorlessly. "At least then Abi could call Maggie and Greigor in for dinner."

"So we're isolated," de Villiers concluded.

"And we're not expecting another transport until the spring."

"Can someone not drive back to the port at O'Higgins and send for help?" I asked.

"Even if it wasn't insanely dangerous," de Villiers snapped, "none of the vehicles we have here have the range. Even if we loaded them with petrol, strapped barrels to the back and roof, they'd barely make it a third of the way. If you can't say anything helpful, Anders, shut the hell up. If you had any other duties, I'd tell you to get out and get on with them."

"But there must be an automatic contact signal. Surely a plane will be sent when it ceases?"

De Villiers ran a rough hand across his brow. "Sure, they'll know – Tierra'll know, but no planes will be able to land here in winter. And no boats can dock at O'Higgins; the port freezes up. There's no help coming from outside, kid."

"So we're stuck."

"Well, it's not that bad, is it?" Max said.

"Can you repair it?" de Villiers asked.

She laughed. "Sure, I can repair it – we'll just dig out the rubble, hope to salvage some undamaged electronic components. Then I'll use the industrial forge I just happen to have in my pocket to knock up a few new aerials."

"Sarcasm isn't helpful, Max."

"Well, I'm sorry. What I *might* be able to do is restore communications to the minehead."

"I'm more concerned about being out of contact with Tierra."

"Can't help you there. But it shouldn't matter, should it? We were expecting to be self-sufficient all winter, and the loss of our comms doesn't affect that. Tierra will send a crawler out as soon as it's warm enough, whether they hear from us or not."

De Villiers grunted an acknowledgment.

"What actually happened out there? What caused that?" I asked into the resulting silence.

He sighed, wrinkles making him look his age. "I don't know. Weng alerted me – don't know the time, it'll be on record. She told me – what were her words? – 'there has been an unusual seismic event.' Eventually got an explanation out of her."

"An earthquake?"

"Don't know," the commander said. "An avalanche, maybe."

"Weng would've known if we'd built the comms unit on an ice fissure," Max said. "And this place was supposed to be geologically stable."

De Villiers rubbed at his beard and got to his feet. "Okay, I can't see any point in endless talk. Anders, you wanted something to do with your time. Go and talk to Weng. Max, borrow Greigor and Abi and salvage what you can from the wreckage. Be careful – I don't want any more accidents. I'm going to the minehead; got to make sure there's no damage there. We've got to keep the coal and oil coming or there's no point us being here at all."

★   ★   ★

I found Keegan first. His blond hair was still wet from the shower, weathermen not being obliged to put in an early shift. I'd only really called in because his door was before Weng's, and I wanted to be sure that the weather couldn't have caused the building to collapse.

We talked in his office – much more a working room than my own stark, cold and bare little cell. His had maps and computer projections, and paperwork all over the desk and the floor. It didn't look terribly organized, but he must have had a system.

He had very little to say. He greeted the news with amazement, and confidently asserted that there was no way that last night's blizzard could have caused an avalanche.

I left him to wake up properly and went on to see Weng.

As I stood before her door, I wondered if I should mention last night's visit. But she answered the door before I decided.

It was clear that, unlike Keegan, Weng had been up for some hours, and that she was already at work. The walls of her office were taken up with maps and charts, all professional and some annotated in a careful hand – a mix of Chinese characters and English letters. A chess set was on one end of her desk, the pieces arrayed mid-game. A small machine on top of her filing cabinet buzzed to itself, a digital readout showing a black jagged line.

She took me in, her eyes expressionless. She looked back to her papers and spoke to them rather than me. "You are here to ask about the event that, at four twenty-seven, caused the destruction of the comms building. You want to know what caused it."

"Yes." There didn't seem much else to say.

She pointed to the machine. "Look."

I went over. "Is this a seismograph? What am I looking for?"

Finally, she set down her work and came over to join me. Another person would have sighed, or somehow expressed impatience, but not her. Maybe she saw dealing with idiots as part of her job.

She deftly manipulated the controls and the display changed – showing, I guessed, the time period she was looking for. "Here."

It was obvious even to me: steady lines, steady and flat. And then, at precisely four twenty-seven, a sudden spike, a mountain of activity.

"My machines are rigged to alarms that woke me. I realized that the seismic shift was very, very close and so alerted the commander. In case there was damage. And the doctor, in case there were injuries."

"So there was an earthquake? An earth tremor?"

She smiled mirthlessly. "Do you know what I do here, Mr. Security Chief?"

"You're seconded as medic, should anything happen to Dr. Fischer. But your main role is as base geologist—"

"I am here to map the continent." Her words were stiff, formal. "To map it below the surface. Every month I go out – with Max or with Mikhail or Dmitri – and drill into the ice and pack the hole with an explosive charge. I interpret the shock waves and so learn how the continent is made up. Find the resources for exploitation."

"So?"

"So I helped to choose the site for this base. Do you think we are placed here by accident? No. I met my brief. Near accessible resources, within crawler range – and *geologically stable*."

"You're saying it wasn't – couldn't have been – an earthquake?"

Her eyes left mine for the first time – the merest flicker of uncertainty. "I am...I am not saying that. Even the most stable places have tremors...occasionally. The ice shifts and cracks in ways we can't predict."

I looked at her carefully. Pride was etched in every pore of her face, a defensiveness ready to snap into aggression. "But you don't think that's likely?"

She stared back at me and said nothing.

"Could the mining operations have caused it? Or the half-tracks?"

Weng shook her head.

"Then what?"

"I've gone over the data many times."

"And?"

"I have mapped the epicenter of the...incident very carefully. Either it was that freak, unpredictable earth tremor, or..."

"Or what, Weng?"

"Or the avalanche was started deliberately."

CHAPTER FIVE

If the avalanche was started deliberately...

I seized the possibility so readily.

So we had a choice of either a freak event or sabotage. I could tell which option Weng preferred, but I wasn't sure.

I left her to her work. My first thought was that I should go back to talk with de Villiers, but he'd gone up to the minehead. I had no way to get in touch with him, and it didn't seem worth making the trek myself – not yet, at least. I wanted to do some thinking first.

I paced the corridors, vaguely heading towards my rooms. It seemed wrong to be hiding myself away at a time like this, but this had just become a criminal investigation and I needed to get things right. Needed to start from first principles and think my way through.

So much for six months of boredom.

And there was another reason to avoid the rest of the crew. If the avalanche had been started deliberately, then one of my colleagues was, must have been, responsible. I didn't want to cause undue suspicion.

I felt a quaver of excitement, of uncertainty, run through me. This was my chance to prove to de Villiers, to all my doubters – to myself – that I wasn't just a 'Company shill' but that I was capable, that the Psych had got the right man.

My chance to win. My chance to lose.

Weng wanted it to be sabotage to salve her ego. I wanted it for exactly the same reason.

I sat at the compscreen in my office; as long as I didn't try to access higher levels, I could use it as a simple workstation. I stared blankly at the screen for a second, before glancing at my touchstones: my puzzle box, my book. Then I began to pour my memory onto the page. First the facts, the things I knew for sure, before I allowed myself to speculate and to set down some of the many questions I'd have to answer.

The destruction of the comms building should not affect operations but effectively isolates us for the next six months. Was that the aim? Or was there anything else kept in there that might have been the real reason for the avalanche?

I thought of Max and her smoking. I wondered what other vices might be shared amongst the crew.

Can we be sure that there isn't a fourteenth person on the base, or that there isn't a rival station nearby? If – if – this was sabotage, eliminate any possibility that it was caused by an outsider. If we can do that, then there are thirteen suspects. I paused before changing the number to twelve: I'd been including myself. *The explosion occurred when all should have been asleep. It's unlikely that anyone has a solid alibi.*

Where did the explosives come from?

What do the surveillance cameras show?

I stared at the screen for a long time.

Weng thought I might be here because of her. She has the expertise and the determination to have done this. She hates de Villiers, and she did not seem overly concerned by events. She must be considered a suspect.

But it was Weng who suggested it was caused deliberately. If she'd been responsible, wouldn't she have told me there was a geological explanation?

And what did she have to gain? What was the motive?

Who can I trust?

Who could I trust?

★ ★ ★

It was time to talk with de Villiers again. He had to be told about the possibility of sabotage. I sent him a priority message: *Have important information. Meet up ASAP.* As soon as he returned he'd get that and – hopefully – come and find me.

I made myself a cup of strong coffee and returned to my desk. I closed my log and opened up the base security schematic. So this was available to me too; de Villiers must only have blocked off my access to personal information.

The security schematic was restricted access. Only de Villiers and I had a right to go in there, although Fischer could also gain entry in an emergency. We'd had similar in the blocks, but the old system was much more primitive – even if it did have to cover a much larger area.

I spent about twenty minutes getting to grips with its intricacies before I settled on what I was after: the base's surveillance records. I'd finished my coffee; it combined with the caffeine tab I'd taken earlier, and I felt pumped, alive. This, I thought, should be easy. All public rooms and corridors in the barracks were covered by tiny cameras, and many of the smaller outbuildings were recorded too. Only the bedrooms were really private. I didn't know who thought it would be necessary to record all this worthless data – it was probably a requirement of the Company directives – but it certainly made my job easier. It was just a shame that there were no exterior views. It wasn't considered cost-effective to coldproof the cameras.

With so many viewpoints, it wasn't practical to run them all at once. I chose to see the vestibule and the comms building itself – they were the obvious ones. I added the rec room and the internal stairway of the barracks and left the rest.

I selected ten o'clock the night before as a starting point. I couldn't imagine that the charges were set before that, when there were still too many people awake for a saboteur to risk discovery. If I found nothing, then I could go back further.

I set the clock running double-time and leaned back in my chair to watch.

★   ★   ★

By the time de Villiers responded to my message by summoning me to his office, the adrenaline and caffeine had worn off. I had the beginnings of a headache and the excitement I'd felt had been replaced by numbed fear.

There was no answer when I knocked on his door. I was standing there, wondering what to do, when I heard footsteps behind me. I was too new to judge identity by the little traits that accompanied a person's walk, but the stride was long and confident, and I guessed it was the commander. I was proved right a second later as he rounded the corner and gave me a nod.

"Anders, kid, what've you found?" he asked as I stepped aside to allow him to enter his door code.

"How's the minehead?" I asked as the door opened. I didn't want to say too much here in the corridor.

"Fine, no problems there. Operations continue as normal." He ushered me in and shut the door before walking around the desk and taking his seat. "What have you found?"

Deep breath. "The avalanche…it might have been started deliberately."

The commander sighed and leaned back in his chair. He rubbed his beard angrily.

"You don't seem surprised."

He didn't say anything for a good while, as if he was searching for the right words. This was a new side of de Villiers for me. Gone was the glibness and the overbearing self-confidence, the humor and the strength he carried with him. He still had presence, though. And control. I could see in him the man the Company had chosen to run Australis.

"I'm not surprised, no," he said.

"Why not?" The tension made me blunt.

Again he took his time answering. "The chances of a blizzard causing an avalanche are…remote."

"But an earth tremor, or an ice fissure?"

"You've spoken to Weng. She must have told you how unlikely that is."

I nodded. "And—"

"I studied Weng's report thoroughly even before the base was built."

"Is there any possibility that there is a fourteenth person hiding on the base?"

De Villiers snorted. "Possible? Yes, of course it's *possible*, Nordvelt. If he's got a warmsuit and food and a safe place to sleep, then he can survive damn well anywhere. But is it likely? Of course not. I can't believe that anyone's hiding here in the barracks – too many people around. The outbuildings? Well, that'd be one mad risk. Most aren't heated, and Abi would have said something if food supplies had gone missing. And we'd notice if anyone had set up a camp in the wastes."

"So you think that it was one of us that did this?" I asked.

"Weng didn't say an earth tremor was impossible, did she?" The commander stared hard at me. "Is there anything else?" he asked.

I hesitated. "Yes."

"Get on with it, Nordvelt. I need to see Fischer and I haven't got time for your pratting about."

"The surveillance cameras."

"Well?"

"I think you should see for yourself, Commander."

He renewed his stare. Then he sighed and turned his attention to his compscreen. I glanced away as he logged on and looked at a picture on his desk. It was of a group of men – men all – standing in front of a vast open-cast mine. They were laughing, de Villiers in the middle, carefree and young.

"Okay, what am I looking for?" He turned the screen so I could see.

"Bring up cameras one, four, thirty-six and...I don't know, pick a number, any number. Set for three o'clock this morning."

"Fine."

The images appeared quickly: the vestibule, the comms building and the rec room were my choices. De Villiers had added someone's office. I looked closer and saw picture frames on the desk, a plan spread across the surface...

"This office," de Villiers muttered. Maybe he was trying to prove that he'd never left his private quarters, that he had slept through the night. "What am I looking for?"

"Just watch. Speed it up if you like."

We didn't have to wait long. At exactly five past three, all the cameras simultaneously went blank.

"What the...?" de Villiers gasped.

"The same thing happened to every camera on the base."

"Is that possible? How can anyone blank all the cameras simultaneously?" His impatience had vanished; now he looked shocked and, maybe, just a little afraid.

"It's possible," I said. "If you have the right security clearance, then you can switch the system off. And it's all hardwired somewhere.

Somebody could have hacked it. There are ways – look, skip on to four-fifteen."

A few moments later, all the cameras snapped back to life and it was as if nothing had happened. Fast-forward twelve more minutes and the camera in the comms building went blank again. The avalanche had hit.

"Plenty of time for someone to get up, get suited up and walk to the comms building. And then get back again," de Villiers said grimly.

I nodded. "Or take a half-track."

"You realize this doesn't prove anything. Could just be an electrical fault, a loose connection somewhere."

I didn't need to say anything.

He looked at me intensely, resting his chin on his closed fist. "Assuming...assuming this wasn't just a coincidence – who could have done this, Nordvelt?"

I shrugged. "Anyone with the right skills. I'll find out. But I know that there are only two people who could have blanked the cameras without doing that hardwiring, without any risk of being seen."

His eyes opened wide as he saw where I was going. Then his mouth set, tight and angry.

"The only people who have the proper authority to switch off the cameras are you and me," I finished.

For a moment the commander was silent, blue eyes boring into me. "Are you accusing me, Nordvelt?" he said.

"I'm just stating a fact."

"I would point out that whilst I, for the last six months, have been living day in, day out, to develop this base and *make things fucking work*, you've just arrived here."

"Yes. I know that."

"So tell me, why should I trust you? Why don't I just revoke your clearance and keep you locked in your room?"

"If I'd done this, would I be here now, telling you all this?"

De Villiers leaned back in his chair and rubbed his beard again. Then he steepled his hands in front of his face and stared over his fingers. "If I find you've had anything to do with this, I will personally see you spend one hell of a long time in prison. Ha, maybe you can share a cell—" He broke off suddenly.

I couldn't look at him. I fixed my gaze at the wall over his shoulder, sat stiff in my chair. "Share a cell with my father? Is that what you were going to say?" I felt numb. I concentrated on my breathing, like I'd been taught. Imagined my pulse, steady and strong. "For your information, my father was released three years ago and is now working as a logistician in Bergen. And no, we're not in regular contact."

De Villiers shifted in his chair. "Right," he muttered. Then, after a long pause, "What do you plan to do now?"

I took my time in answering. I felt like I was made of glass, brittle, faults wanting to shatter. More deep breaths. "The explosives. Where are they kept?"

"You mean to keep investigating?"

"Of course."

"Look, mate – you're a suspect. For all I know, you're going to be covering your tracks, or setting someone else up for the fall."

"Well, that's the problem you've got, isn't it, Commander?" I said. "You can suspend me, you can lock me in my room. But if someone on this base is a saboteur, then you need to find out who it is. I'm chief of security. Who else can do the job? Dr. Fischer? You? Are you prepared to take the time to investigate properly?"

"You think I don't want to get to the bottom of this?" he snapped. "I want to find out what happened as much as you do. More. This is my damn base, so yes, I'm going to investigate. I'm going to do my damn job, Nordvelt. Best you just keep out of the way."

"I can't do that."

His nostrils flared. "Well, I can see we're going to have more trouble with our security chief," he said, low and dangerous. "Don't know what they're playing at, the fucking Psych. I'd hoped your file was wrong, but no, I can see you're as pathetic as your report said." He snarled at me, actually snarled. "Get out. Get out and just – just get out!"

★　★　★

Anger overwhelmed the embarrassment. I strode out of the commander's office, not like a whipped dog but with head held high. *Damn* him, he had no right.

No, I told myself, *he has every right*. He commanded this base. He knew everyone here, knew every inch of the place – inside and out. Of course he suspected me. But it was clear that he had the real motive. He didn't want anyone who mattered to know that he'd been breaking Company rules. Destroying the comms building was the obvious way to do it, would give him six extra months to convince me to keep quiet.

If that was what had happened, I was damn well going to prove it. Then it was just a case of getting through the night shift before I could submit my report.

Resentment drove me straight to the vestibule and into my warmsuit. It only took a few minutes before I was ready, and once more I went out into the lands of ice. It was snowing and I could only see a hundred yards or so, the industrial complex around me oddly romantic with its white mantle reflecting the blue-yellow of the floodlights. I hesitated momentarily before heading for the garage.

The half-track felt surprisingly familiar beneath me, as if I'd been driving one just the night before and not at the Antarctic training camp several weeks ago. Maybe it was because I was relying on instinct rather than overthinking. I got it running and gently eased it forward. As the door automatically rattled shut behind me, I accelerated and headed upslope – back towards where the comms building had been.

A 4x4 and a half-track gradually solidified as I approached, the snow, white on white, reluctant to give me a clear view. Three figures, suited and masked, were talking next to the vehicles. They watched me as I approached and stopped beside them.

"Commander, is that you?" one of them asked. It was Abidene.

"It's Anders," I called back as I dismounted. "What're you doing here?"

"I asked for his help," Max replied. It was her I'd come to see. "And Greigor."

The other figure nodded. I couldn't help imagining that behind the mask was a scowl, a reproof.

"Greig and I do not have critical duties—" Abi began.

"You speak for yourself," Greigor interrupted fiercely. "My work is vital – a lot more use than poking round out here."

Abi ignored his colleague. "The commander is prepared to sacrifice his lunch if it means we get communications back."

"So what are you doing here, Anders?" Max asked.

"I just wanted to ask you a few quick questions."

"I'll make a start on excavating that aerial, then," Abidene said, tactfully removing himself from earshot.

Greigor didn't move. It was only when Max suggested that he help Abi that he stomped off downslope to where Abi had started to shovel away some snow.

I turned to Max. "Why are you bothering to dig out the aerial? I thought it was trash."

"Recyclable trash. We've got the facilities to turn it into something useful again – any metal's worth recovering. But you didn't come out here to ask me about that. What's on your mind?"

My lips were dry. "You must have explosives stored somewhere on the base."

Her head swung round to stare at me. After a second she reached up to unclip her mask and draw it off. Her eyes were piercing, her mouth set. "Take your mask off, Anders. If we're going to have this discussion, I want to see your face."

I did as she asked. Snow melted on my lashes and threatened to refreeze there. "I just want to know what explosives are kept here and what controls are set on their use. And if any are missing."

Max wasn't stupid. There were no stupid people here. She looked at me silently and glanced back to the others – without our masks there was no risk of being overheard. "There aren't many reasons for asking that question," she said. "You might be head of security, but—"

"But you don't know me." Back towards the base, Abi was still scraping away, slowly uncovering distorted metal beams. Beside him the masked Greigor was staring right back at me.

"I think…I'd rather speak to de Villiers before I answer," Max said.

"De Villiers and I have had something of a disagreement."

She looked at me again, her expression unreadable. "You know, with what you're saying, one can't help but draw certain… inferences."

"We need to talk, Max," I went on. "I need to know what's been going on in Australis. I need to know more about de Villiers. I need to know why Weng hates him. But most of all I need to know if any explosives are unaccounted for."

She turned to face down towards the base. I mirrored her, staring at the hunched, ugly buildings, indistinct lumps blurred by the thin snow.

"The explosives..." she said.

"Max, I need your help—"

"There's a charge unaccounted for. We have to give fingerprint ID for every pack removed. But one was taken at twenty past three, and no ID was recorded. I already checked." She looked round at me but I couldn't read her expression.

"How is that possible? The lack of fingerprint—"

"I don't know."

We stared at each other for a moment before the cold forced us to replace our masks. I drew myself together. "Well, I should get back to—"

"You sure you can't help us here?"

"There are things I need to be doing—"

"Like what?"

I gave up. She chucked me the shovel she herself had been using, and I caught it neatly in one hand.

"Work with Abi," she said. "And when that's done, we need to clear and stack the broken bricks."

I thought I heard Greigor snicker as I went downslope to join the cook. I just bent my back to the work and urged the oxygen around my bloodstream, hoping some would kick my brain into action.

CHAPTER SIX

De Villiers followed me back to my quarters after dinner. He didn't bother with knocking, just walked into my private room. I felt a wave of anger at this invasion but I forced it down. It was de Villiers's way. I was learning that – another assertion of his status. And we had more pressing issues to worry about.

"I've put the destruction of the comms building down as an accident," he said without preamble.

"Despite Weng's evidence?"

"Everyone makes mistakes. No blame to her. Nowhere is absolutely safe, absolutely stable." He stood there, hands in pockets, and glanced around the room.

I leaned against the work surface behind me. "But—"

"If it wasn't an accident, then it was sabotage," he said. "And I've worked with these people long enough—"

"Perhaps they were just waiting for the start of the long night."

His head jerked up and his eyes flashed as he stared straight at me. "I know this crew. I know everyone here. Intimately. I trust them. I know them all and I trust them. Unless it was you – you've no confession for me?" His mouth quirked up and he gave a humorless breath of laughter. "Then it was an accident."

"What about the missing explosives?"

"I don't know. I'll find out." He looked older, closer to his real age, when his brow creased like that.

"It's my job to look into that," I said.

De Villiers sighed and fingered the back of the chair at my desk. "So what's this, then?" He ran a hand down the spine of my book. "Fancy yourself a detective, do you?"

"It's just a thing," I said, trying not to show my discomfort.

"An expensive thing. First edition?"

"Second."

He seemed to find that funny, mouth again twitching into a smile.

"Why are you trying to stop me from doing my job?" I asked.

"You don't have a job. You're just here to make up the numbers." He spoke as if he were simply stating a fact. "Look, I've told you – how many times do you need me to tell you, how many ways? It's not that I don't trust you – but I don't trust you. You're the unknown quantity—"

"So you're saying that it was sabotage. This accident idea is bull—"

"I'm not saying anything," he snapped.

"If it was an accident then let me look into it."

He met my challenge evenly, sandy brows like a golden sliver above the coming storm. He stared at me and said nothing, cheeks puffing out slightly as he kept his breathing steady.

"So the official line is that it was an accident," I said, "but you don't believe that. You still suspect—"

"This conversation is over. You've heard me. I expect you to do as you're told." I stared at his back, unable to find words, as he turned to the door. "As for me, I'm going to do my job. Even if it kills me, I'm going to do my job. I'm going to keep civilization running for one more day every day. And if that means being paranoid, then I'll damn well be paranoid, got that?"

"There's nothing to link me with this. There's no evidence."

"You said it yourself. Only you or I could have done this easily. And I know the rest of the crew."

"So you suspect me."

"I'd be a fool not to, right?"

He left with the last word, letting the door swing shut behind him.

★　　★　　★

De Villiers had the motive. I wanted to scream at him, to force the fight and make him…well, just make him understand my anger. But it'd only taken me a few days to learn how that'd go down. So I pulled on some more suitable clothing and went to the gym. The best way to work the mind was to feed the muscles. Sweat out the emotions, leave the brain pure and uncluttered.

The base gym was small but had the standard equipment. I spent a few minutes checking out the machines before I went on the treadmill and started to run. It felt good. I hadn't really been aware of how limited my exercises had been over the last week, how few muscles I'd been using. Initially I shambled along at only a few miles an hour; after a while I was beginning to stretch my legs and feeling relief in motion. Back in the blocks, I'd gone to the municipal gymnasium every two days: running on the pavements was not encouraged, although I did that too. On the bad nights.

I was just thinking about moving on to the weights when the door opened and Dmitri came in.

I hadn't really spoken to Dmitri yet. I knew him by sight, and I knew him to be a mining expert from Ukraine, but that was about all. I wiped the sweat from my forehead and said hello as I sat back on a multigym to do some arm and chest exercises.

He looked at me suspiciously from below a short, dark fringe and settled himself on another multigym facing me. "Anders," he said as he got into position, his accent heavy. He was a big man, strong and with an inch or two on me. His muscles were well defined.

I placed my arms behind the pads and tested the resistance. Someone was used to using a lot of weight. I twisted to reduce the amount I was lifting, and when I looked back, I saw that the Ukrainian was still watching me. I ignored him and started on my exercises. After a second he began as well, using a much heavier weight-set than me.

For a minute or so we worked without talking, the only sounds the rising and falling of weights and our breathing. But he didn't once take his eyes off me. When he did speak it was without a break in his workout. "Why destroy the comms building?"

So much for de Villiers's declaration that it was an accident. "I didn't."

He grunted and continued working the machine.

After another few seconds I paused to increase my load. "What do you think of the commander?" I asked as I restarted.

"He is a good miner," Dmitri replied. Then he too paused to add more weight.

"You work with him often?"

"He comes a lot to the minehead. Talks with me and Fergie."

"Weng hates him."

He pulled a face, then shook sweat off his brow. "Not my business. Not yours either."

"D'you know why?"

"Not my business," he repeated. But he didn't seem offended by my questions. I felt like he was taking my measure, like he was trying to make up his mind about me. "You're not lifting much," he added.

"I'm out of practice. Don't want to pull a muscle." My breath was coming in great gulps now, my speech becoming more and more staccato. Still, he was challenging me, and I felt the need to prove myself. I paused again, wiped my face with my shirt and increased the weight once more. Now I had to strain for every repetition.

Dmitri grinned at me. "You a strong man? You think you can take this much?" It was his turn to increase the difficulty; now he was lifting almost the entire block of weights.

I shook my head. "I know my limits."

"You are a *clever* man." Dmitri was suffering too. I could see it in his face; every pull caused him to crease up, to grimace wildly. "You clever, what did cause…the avalanche…if not you?"

"Don't know," I gasped. "But…de Villiers…says it was an accident." That was me. I was done. I let the weights fall for the last time – I tried to do it gently, but my strength failed me and with a loud *clang* they came to rest. I sat there, leaning back in my seat and breathing heavily as Dmitri grinned. My arms burned as the big man did a few more reps before he, too, set down his weights. He managed to do it with perfect control, with barely a *clink* as the weights settled back into place.

"Maybe we arm-wrestle sometime? You want to spar?" he said.

I looked at his biceps. "I don't think…I'd have a chance," I managed, my breath still labored.

He shrugged and got to his feet. "Leg lifts now," he said as he adjusted the multigym for a different set of exercises. "You?"

I shook my head. "I've done enough. Tomorrow, maybe."

Dmitri sat back on the bench and hooked his ankles around a padded bar. He nodded at me. "Until then, Mr. Nordvelt."

★   ★   ★

When I woke I felt like I hadn't slept at all, my mind fogged with a whiteness that was all-enveloping; only gradually did my surroundings solidify. My bed, my room…and my computer. For the second night running, I'd been awakened by a priority message. The alarm cut through me, setting my teeth on edge, but still I couldn't move. My muscles just wouldn't obey me.

Eventually, I managed to roll onto the floor, the duvet that had been twisted around me absorbing my fall and trapping sweat against my skin. I crawled over to the desk and used the chair to help me climb to my feet. I canceled the alarm and breathed a sigh of relief as silence fell. Wobbling slightly, I checked the time: thirteen minutes past six. I slumped into the chair and wiped sleep from my eyes before opening the message.

"Mr. Nordvelt." It was Weng – voice only, her certain, precise English clear over the airwaves. "There is a situation. Meet me in the vestibule."

"Weng?"

"There is an emergency. Come to the vestibule immediately."

She cut communication. I spent a few seconds staring at a blank screen in bewilderment before I dragged some clothes together and hurried out.

★   ★   ★

"What's going on?" I strode up to Weng, who was fully suited but for her mask. She stood straight-backed as she pulled her hair into a ponytail.

"It's the commander," she said with barely a glance in my direction. She turned to enter the vestibule.

"What's happened?" I followed her inside and she passed me my warmsuit.

"I received a call from Dr. Fischer at five-forty this morning. She was…upset."

"And—"

"Something has happened to the commander. Hurry up. Let me help you."

I slipped off my boots and, as quick as I could, pulled on my suit. Although her face showed nothing, I could tell Weng was impatient. She opened my locker and pulled out my mask and snowshoes, laid them neatly beside me as I stepped into the suit and pulled it up over my shoulders. "Can't you tell me anything? What's happened to de Villiers?" I asked, tense.

"I am unsure. As I understand, the commander was supposed to meet Fischer this morning." The slightest flicker ran across her face and was gone. "He didn't arrive, so she went looking for him. I got a call at four minutes past six. I called you shortly after."

"Why call me?" I pulled the mask over my face and began to wrestle on the gloves. "I mean, you're medical second, but—"

"You're chief of security, are you not?"

"You think this is a security—"

"And we may need a little muscle. Are you ready? There's a blizzard blowing. We'll take the heavy torches."

She hadn't been joking about the snow. It was borne by a strong wind, a gale, coming from the northwest, and was driving almost horizontally. I cursed as I was buffeted, almost losing my feet despite the heavy treads on my boots. But Weng didn't seem at all fazed. Maybe she was just too focused to notice.

"He's over here," she called, heading towards the garage. I followed as best I could, the beam from my torch illuminating her back and a blanket of snow and little else. A few times she disappeared in the whiteout.

Weng hurried past the garage and on to a building I couldn't immediately identify. It looked like a concrete shed, much smaller than any of the buildings I'd been in so far. Too small to be anything but a storeroom unless it concealed more underground. I scrambled to keep up, but I needn't have worried. She went to a corner of the building and stopped, glancing back to check I was behind her. "Hurry up, Nordvelt," she said.

I reached the corner and followed her gaze. A figure lay slumped on the ground, motionless in the lee of the building. Another crouched by it, but straightened as soon as she detected the torch beam shining over her. "Weng? Quickly, quickly – who's that?"

"I brought Nordvelt," Weng said as she strode over to the pair.

"Nordvelt?" It must have been my imagination, but I thought she shivered a little as she looked at me. "We – we need to get him inside. Quickly!"

The shock, the fear – I was numbed. My reactions were automatic. Fischer and Weng had the training; they knew if anything could be done. I had to look into the circumstances. I stared blankly into the snow, torchlight too feeble in the black-and-white world in which we were standing. I don't know what I was looking for: footprints, maybe, or some sort of a struggle.

Fancy yourself a detective, do you? de Villiers had said.

I could see nothing, just snow and ice churned up by the doctor's boots.

"What happened?" I asked.

Neither of them answered. "Can we move him?" Weng asked Fischer.

"We can't leave him here. God, he—" Her voice cracked. "He's so cold." The doctor was crying, I realized, behind her mask.

"What happened?" I asked again. I stood over the two medics.

"He— you sent a message— you know—"

"That doesn't matter right now," Weng cut in. "We need to get him to the infirmary."

"Yes— we need— can you carry him?"

"Nordvelt will."

"Not him—"

"Nordvelt, come here," Weng snapped.

Why was I so sure he was dead? Was it not possible that there was still warmth in there somewhere? It was only hours since I'd last seen him.

"We've got to get him inside, get him warm…" Fischer's voice broke again.

"It's—" I stopped. *It's too late*, I had been about to say. But she was the doctor; this was her domain. I only had instinct, horror, the total stillness of the figure on the ground. She had the right of it. Best do as she said and get it inside. *It. The corpse. Commander Anton de Villiers, deceased.*

I must be wrong, he must be alive – we must get him inside.

If any clues were to be found here, they were buried beneath the snow.

I took a deep breath and crouched down to get a grip on his shoulders.

CHAPTER SEVEN

The commander had been a big man: broad-shouldered and strong, well-muscled. It was a struggle to get him back to the barracks, and we left deep grooves in the freshly fallen snow as we dragged him, deadweight, between us.

Fischer kept insisting that she saw him move or heard him breathe. Even though the masks filtered out the worst noise of the gale, there wasn't a chance in hell that she heard anything as slight as a gasp.

Eventually we got him into the vestibule, the four of us bumping and tripping and wrestling together. I felt a sudden rush of warmth as the outer door swung shut behind us, before my suit noticed the sudden change in temperature and adjusted its program. De Villiers remained cold in my hands.

"Straight to the treatment room," Fischer demanded.

I wasn't going to argue.

It was still early. There was no one moving but us, the motion-detecting lights flicking on as we approached, then shutting down as we passed.

In the tiny infirmary I helped get de Villiers onto a bed, then stood back. Weng and I removed our masks; she looked at me and I realized she knew as well as I did that de Villiers was dead. And that Fischer had to find out for herself.

It didn't take long. As soon as the doctor removed the dead man's mask and saw his eyes, still open, she broke down.

"No…no, no," she cried as she stroked his cheek. His skin was gray and frozen. A teardrop snapped off under her fingers.

I picked up the face mask she'd discarded and set it aside. "Dr. Fischer…Julia…come on," I said softly. "There's nothing you can do for him now."

She turned to me, her mask incongruously blank against her trembling, uncoordinated movements. "Nothing? Nothing…. Who

did this? What…? It was you – was it you? Did you k-kill him…?"
Tears overtook her and she slumped to her knees.

I took off my gloves and knelt by her. As gently as I could, I
unfastened her mask and pulled it off. She didn't resist. Her long,
graying hair came loose and mixed with her tears.

"Julia," I said, "I'm sorry, but he's gone now. I need your help."
She made no response.

"We need – we need to look to the living now. I need to know
what he was doing out there, how you knew where—"

Her head jerked round at that, her mouth set in a snarl of such
ferocity that I swayed back, nearly lost my balance. "Get the hell
off me, killer! You think that matters?" she snapped. "You think –
you think I give a shit about that right now? He's dead, God, he's
– he can't be…" She trailed off into sobs.

"I – I thought you hated him," I said, inappropriately, nonsensically.
She didn't reply, just shook her head and wept.

I took her arm, tried to urge her to her feet, but she just hissed
and raked her nails across my cheek. I stepped back in shock,
touched where she'd scratched and dumbly stared at the blood on
my fingertips. I barely felt anything, just glistening heat.

Weng stood behind me, unmoving.

I tried again; I had to get her away from there, needed her
sensible and rational. Part of me was screaming that this wasn't
the way to deal, but I was struggling to hold myself together; de
Villiers's death put me in charge – me and Fischer. I couldn't do
it on my own. So I whispered nonsense words to her, as if she
were a cat, an animal, cooing her name over and over. I took her
arm, dragging her as we'd dragged de Villiers. Now she was the
deadweight; I lifted her almost off the ground before she slipped
out of my grasp back to the floor.

"For God's sake, Weng, you going to stand there doing nothing?
Help me."

"Leave me," Fischer cried. "Leave me here, leave me!"

Weng came to my side, reached an elegant hand to the doctor
and touched a shoulder. Fischer pulled back. I ground my teeth in
frustration and stepped behind her. I reached under her armpits,
hauling her up against my chest, turning her to the open door.

She dangled from my grip, boots scraping on the floor. I wrestled her to the doorway – and then she pushed up and, as I jerked my head away, kicked back. My knee became a sudden nova of pain. I swore and angrily shoved her forward, using my whole body – chest, stomach, arms – to propel her out into the corridor.

Too hard. Too damn hard.

She stumbled, fell forward. Hit her head on the far wall and slumped to the floor.

And she didn't move.

★   ★   ★

Cold heat ran through me. Sweat on my brow. I couldn't move, not at first. I was waiting: waiting for the others to come, to rush to the body, to lock me away....

Silence. The echoes of Fischer's fall faded quickly.

I swallowed, took an unsteady pace forward.

There was a smear of blood on the wall, where her head had hit.

Weng, so slow to help before, was already at her side, stripping off the doctor's gloves and checking her pulse, a delicate hand running over Fischer's neck.

I crouched by them, trying to stop myself from shaking. I swallowed, twitched away the doctor's hair—

"Don't touch," Weng snapped.

Fischer was breathing. I backed away until I found the door frame behind my shoulder. I stared at her unmoving form, face down on the bare linoleum. I shivered, hot and cold together, suddenly conscious that we were all still suited.

With practiced hands, Weng rolled the doctor onto her back and inspected the wound, a camouflaged smear just into the hairline. "Very well. Get her into a bed."

"We can move her?"

She glared at me. "You lift."

Awkwardly I shuffled to Fischer's side and knelt, knee stiff from where she'd kicked me. She was starting to stir now, her breath coming with half-formed syllables, broken words.

"One hand there," Weng said, "the other – good. I'll support her head. Be careful through the doorway. Straight to a spare bed. Be smooth and set her down gently – don't drop her."

Fischer barely seemed to weigh anything. She'd seemed so heavy, so solid, just a moment ago, and now she seemed more ghost than human. We passed the silent form of the commander. When Fischer was set down on one of the free gurneys I stepped back, and Weng moved round to lift Fischer's eyelids to check the pupils.

"Did you kill him?" she asked, back to me.

"What?"

"Did you kill de Villiers?"

"No! No, no, I didn't."

"A pity," the woman said simply, and carried on with her work.

I shifted uncertainly.

"There's nothing more you can do here. Leave."

"I need—"

"What?" She didn't look round.

I swallowed. "How did de Villiers get out there? How did the doctor know where he was? Why did she call you?"

Weng straightened and went to a bench, selected a wound-pack and switched on a piece of equipment I didn't recognize. "The doctor was outside when she called me. She'd already found the body. I don't know how. I contacted you immediately. Is that enough?"

"Well—"

"Well, it will have to do. Questions can wait until…until later. Now you leave."

"Weng—"

"Go!"

I went.

★   ★   ★

The silence was oppressive. I walked the corridors alone, the shock I'd been suppressing slowly overtaking me. My knee ached, my head ached. It wasn't my first dead body – I still saw my father's aide in my dreams, saw the bloody rents in his chest from the penetrating bullets that had raked through the hall. I shivered at the memory, the spray of blood on the walls like some abstract masterpiece.

But de Villiers's death seemed… I don't know, it seemed somehow more real, more terrifying. Maybe it's because I was older now, and I couldn't just let other people tell me what to do.

Murder. Funny how I was already assuming de Villiers had been murdered. I had no evidence – it could have been an accident, a suit malfunction, could have been… All the 'could-have-beens'. I knew nothing.

But my mind went straight for murder. And I knew the crew would suspect me. I'd suspect myself in their position. I had, after all, just knocked out their doctor. I stood still for a moment, horror taking needle-fingered hold of me. Of course they'd suspect me – an avalanche, a death, a…an accident – all within a week of my arrival.

What I wanted most of all was to go back to bed and pretend this wasn't happening. But I had work to do. With de Villiers dead and Fischer incapacitated, I was in charge. I had to tell the rest of the crew what had happened, but I had no idea how. All I knew was that the commander was dead. I knew nothing of the circumstances. The questions piled up, heavy on my shoulders.

I needed to put my investigation out of my mind – just for the moment. My first responsibility must be to ensure that the base ran properly, that the rest of the crew were okay and that Australis survived. That came first. But still I couldn't stop my mind from throwing up the sharpest questions.

God, I needed Fischer.

I needed time to think.

The doctor's reaction had been so extreme. I hadn't thought she even liked de Villiers, hadn't thought she cared that much about anything.

I shook my head, trying to focus. Focus on the living. I checked the time: just past seven.

I was prevaricating. I had to act. I took a deep breath and went to the canteen. As I'd hoped, Abidene was in the kitchen, preparing breakfasts. The smells of food took me by surprise; it was so ridiculously mundane to see soya-sausages frying, to hear the simmering of pans. I was overtaken by a hunger I hadn't even known I was feeling.

"Anders," Abi said in his soft, lilting accent. "You're here early, my friend. What happened to your cheek? Give me a few minutes and I'll bring something through to you – what would you like?"

"Abidene, I need to talk to you. Can you leave the food for a moment?"

"Can you not talk whilst I work?" His hands moved delicately, like an artist, as he checked pans and flipped eggs.

"It's important. Urgent." I tried to keep my tone calm, but my voice cracked on the last word.

He looked round, surprise and alarm writ large on his face. "Two minutes. Is that okay?"

I took a chair in the canteen, leaned back and closed my eyes. I felt like crying. When Abi came though, wiping his hands on his apron, I stood again and gave him a wan smile.

"What's on your mind, Anders?" he asked.

"Has anyone else been in for breakfast yet?"

"Not yet. The miners will be in shortly, then the rest. Weng eats in her rooms. What's this about? If you don't mind me saying, you look exhausted. Have you been sleeping? I know a few recipes to help you get off – I researched it for McCarthy. I'd be happy to—"

"So I'm here first?" This was perfect, what I'd hoped. But the words wouldn't come.

"Anders, what is going *on*? I have to—"

"The commander is dead, Abi." Brutal. The voice didn't sound like mine. I couldn't look at him.

"You – you are joking?"

I stared at the table.

"De Villiers? He... What happened?"

"I'm working on that."

"So – so what do we do? Does Dr. Fischer know?"

I touched my cheek. "The doctor – she – she had an accident. She's okay," I added, "Weng's looking after her. Myself, you and Weng – we're the only ones who know. I have to tell the crew."

"My God."

"Yes."

"What happened to the doctor?"

"She...she fell," I said awkwardly. "Bumped her head."

"I will make sure to visit her," he said, his voice shaking barely at all. "Take her some food, if she can eat. She'll need something, even if it is just a friendly face."

I stared at the table. I couldn't stop my mind working – couldn't stop thinking. I remembered Abi's face when de Villiers had been giving his speech during my first meal in Australis. I thought of Abi trying to hide his annoyance at de Villiers's attempts to take over the cooking of the barbecue. Of the conversation I'd overheard him having with Maggie.

"What do you think of the Company, Abi?" I asked from nowhere.

"What?"

I finally looked up at him. It took an effort, as if my eyes suddenly weighed double. "Do you think the Company's a good thing? For us? For humanity?"

"What?" He shook his head, nonplussed. "I think – why do you ask? I work for the Company, I – I know it has done many good things. I – I am a loyal—"

"It doesn't matter, not right now. Sorry. Just…my mind is all over the place."

He swallowed. "Was there anything else? I should get on before the miners arrive."

I shook my head, not looking at him and barely hearing his words. The door to the kitchen swung shut again, and I was alone.

A few minutes later Abidene brought a plate of food and silently placed it in front of me. I controlled my paranoia, nodded my appreciation and started to eat. I was halfway through my meal when Dmitri and Fergie arrived, chatting noisily.

"Anders," Dmitri said when he saw me. "You've beaten us to breakfast."

"I have news," I said, swallowing hastily.

"Oh?"

"Well, what is it, then?" Fergie said. He sat and leaned back as Abidene returned to place a laden plate in front of him. The chef slid another plate before Dmitri, gave me a concerned look and then withdrew to his kitchen.

"De Villiers is dead," I said, anxiety making me cold.

There was silence. Fergie had frozen with fork half-raised. Dmitri was staring at me open-mouthed.

"What?" the Scotsman asked eventually.

"De Villiers. He's dead. We found him outside this morning."

Another silence.

"And here you are, sitting in his chair, halfway through a nice tasty meal," Fergie said at last. His mouth worked silently for a moment as he tried to find the right words. "Puts that avalanche in a whole different light, don't it?" He gave a bitter, furious smile.

I hadn't realized I was in the commander's old seat – a bad mistake. "I forgot about the chair. I'm sorry," I said, trying to keep from shaking.

"How did he die?" he asked.

"That's still to be…to be ascertained."

People are hard to predict. Fischer had broken down, Abidene was practical, Fergie angry and sarcastic. Dmitri looked genuinely upset. He set down his cutlery and stared blankly at his plate.

"Well, if you think you can just take over," Fergie said, "then you're very, very wrong. You're the new boy here; we'd been getting on perfectly well before you arrived." He opened his mouth as if to say something else but settled for shooting me a hate-filled glance.

"I think I am not so hungry," Dmitri whispered. He pushed his plate aside. "I will head to the mine. There is work to be done." He stood, his movements smooth, and strode out, excusing himself to the incoming Theo as he went.

Maybe I should have stopped him, but I had enough on my plate – metaphorically speaking – already. At that moment I was busy shifting to another seat, taking at least that error out of play. Maybe I should have stood, but I doubted my legs could hold me.

Theo raised an eyebrow at Dmitri's back, then came fully into the canteen. "Hey, guys, what's got into the big man? How'd you get them scratches, Anders? What's up?" he asked as he took his place at the table.

"Oh, not much," Fergie said sarcastically. "Our good friend here's just told us that the commander's dead, and he was just sittin' in his chair…."

It was not a pleasant morning. One by one, two by two, the crew came in to eat. And I answered the same questions over and over again: Yes, he really is dead. No, we don't know how – not yet. Yes, I have seniority whilst Fischer is indisposed. Yes, she tripped, hurt her head, Weng's seeing to her – but we'll sort that sort of thing out later. No, I didn't injure her on purpose. Yes, I am having my *fucking* breakfast, thank you, because I'm starving and, just like you, I've had a very bad start to my morning. I'll be running the investigation, yes. Because it's my *job*, that's why. No, I don't think I'm too inexperienced. We'll all get on with our jobs, and this evening we'll have a proper meeting and sort things out.

By the time Keegan came in – the last of the crew to eat – I could barely raise my head. But by that time I didn't have to. Fergie, who'd hung around all morning, was more than happy to relay the news, adding his particular slant to the tale.

"…and so he sat there, in yon commander's seat, as if he's automatically in charge here!"

"Technically he *is* in charge," Max said quietly. She'd received the news with shocked silence. It hadn't put her off her food, though; her empty plate lay before her. "Well, him and Julia."

"If I were Julia I'd be watchin' my back," Fergie muttered.

"You see how things are going wrong since he arrived?" Greigor growled over his food.

"Where is the doc? Does she know?" Keegan asked. And so we had to go through all that again.

Eventually I'd had enough. I found the strength to stand; everyone turned to look at me. "Look," I began sharply, before starting again more gently. "Look, you've all got your suspicions, I understand that. But there's nothing we can do right now except get on with the work. Regardless of who takes charge, the best thing we can do is carry on as normal. We'll meet again at the end of the day and decide how we're running this place without the commander. So finish eating and get to your stations. I've got to go and talk to Weng."

"No."

"What?"

"I said no. No. We need that meeting now," Fergie said.

"We need time—"

"For what? To let you concoct some fairy tale that neatly explains all our problems? Gremlins, was it? Aliens?"

"Look, the commander's barely cold—"

Fergie interrupted me with a bitter laugh.

"This – this is a shock to us all," Max said. "Shouldn't we take a moment to—"

"Aye, we'll need to grieve, to get over the shock. But the living come first. We need to know what we're doing. We need to sort out the running o' the base or we're all gonna pay. Work first. Personal comes later."

"What about—" I began.

"I say rec room, fifteen minutes. Let's get this over with. We can mourn after that."

There was silence for a moment. Then – reluctantly, heavy-breathed – the crew rose and started to trail out of the room.

CHAPTER EIGHT

"What about the others?" I looked around the room. No de Villiers. No Fischer. No Weng and no Dmitri. "If we're going to do this, then everyone should be here."

Fergie stared at me. He turned to Greigor, standing near the door, and got him to put an intercom call through to the infirmary.

"What about Dmitri?" Mikhail asked.

The Scotsman scowled at him. "He went up to the mine. No external comms. You gonna go get him?"

"Why the hell's he gone up there? Nobody could expect us to work right now—"

"His way of coping," Fergie said. His mouth twitched. "You know – you know he liked the commander."

I looked around the room in the resulting silence. Abidene and Maggie, stiff-backed and white-faced on the sofas, Keegan slumped next to them. Max, Mikhail and Theo at the table. Fergie holding court in the middle of the floor, and me off to the side.

Fergie cleared his throat. "Okay. First thing, I think we need to hear Nordvelt's account—"

"I've told you—"

"Your *precise* account of what happened this morning. Exactly what happened to de Villiers? What do you know?"

The door slid open and Weng walked elegantly in. She shared her frown with the room, then came to stand near me. I leaned in to her. "Is the doctor okay? Can you leave her unattended?"

She showed me her datapad. "She's still unconscious. I'm keeping an eye on her – I'll know if there's any change."

"So," Fergie said. "Nordvelt. What happened this morning?"

I drew myself into a cool place and gave my account of the morning's events, stumbling only over Fischer's injury. Then the focus shifted to Weng, but her story didn't add much to mine.

There was a pause when we'd both finished.

"So we need to know what de Villiers was doing out there in the snow at stupid o'clock," Keegan said.

"He must have been going to see Fischer," Maggie said.

"But why outside?"

"How did the doctor know where he was? She can't just have gone searching for him; that'd be ridiculous."

"How can anyone freeze to death when they're suited? He had his mask on, right?" Theo asked.

"All this matters – but not right now," Max said. "Listen, I want to find these things out as much as you do, I want to know what happened—"

"Everything was going fine before Nordvelt came," Greigor muttered. "De Villiers told me to watch—"

"I want to know what happened as much as the rest of you," she repeated, forcing Greigor into silence. "But like Fergie said – we need to sort ourselves out now."

There was an awkward, uncomfortable silence.

"Technically, now, Nordvelt's in charge. But..." She trailed off.

"Don't worry," I said. "I know you won't have that. I'm happy to—"

"Happy?" Mikhail snapped. "'Happy' ain't a word I'd use at this precise moment in time. Listen to this, boy. As soon as Julia's awake, we're gonna have your status revoked. Only reason you're still in this position's because we got no one to remove you. But don't think you'll be ordering us around or anything, 'cause we ain't gonna take orders from you."

I took a deep breath, two, and tried again. "Here's the situation. We're stuck here, with no contact with the Company, for another six months. We can't leave, and no help is going to arrive. The only thing that we can do is to carry on with our jobs."

They stared at me, all of them. I stood my ground, kept my face a stone mask. All were silent. I could see them judging me, weighing up my youth, my lack of experience. I could see the skepticism, their mistrust. But I had no choice but to go on. To try.

"The doctor, when she's feeling better, and I will manage the crew – you – together until the night shift is over. But Fischer and I don't have the knowledge to oversee the mining and drilling operations. So I propose that we are joined by a third person. One of you." I looked to the table, where all the engineers were gathered.

"Who did you have in mind?" Fergie asked.

"I don't know you well enough to make that decision. I want you to decide amongst yourselves. I promise I'll work with whoever you choose." I stared at Fergie.

There was silence for a moment.

"You've nothing to say about the cap'n?" Keegan asked.

"I will be looking into the circumstances of de Villiers's death." I felt so pompous, so awkward, formulaic words coming from all the textbooks I'd downloaded. "At the moment we have no reason to believe it was anything other than an accident."

That was it for Fergie. He couldn't contain himself anymore. "You?" he snapped. "You're the prime suspect for all of this – the avalanche and then de Villiers, and Dr. Fischer...." He hesitated. "Things were fine with McCarthy; we had nae trouble here. Not until you arrived."

"Nevertheless," I said with a calmness I didn't feel, "I am head of security. It's my job to investigate this."

"And I say no. Why should we trust you? For all we know, you're just going to fit one of us up, or destroy all the evidence."

"So what do you suggest?" I snapped. "Do you want to take on the investigation?"

Fergie was taken aback. "Me? Not me. I'm far too busy for that crack. Maybe..." He cast around the room, looking for someone to propose. His eyes slid off everyone, no one seeming to meet with his approval, and he subsided into sullenness.

"I know how it looks, but at the moment all we have are two incidents that might both be accidents."

"And the doctor's injury?" Theo asked. "That an accident too?"

I opened my mouth to defend myself, but Weng beat me to it. "I was there. I saw the incident. I judged it to be accidental," she said, calm as ever.

"De Villiers didn't trust him," Greigor said.

"What?" Theo asked.

Greigor shook his head. "De Villiers, he spoke to me. He didn't trust Nordvelt."

"When did he talk to you?" Mikhail asked.

"Yesterday, just before dinner—"

"De Villiers sent for him, that's true," Maggie said. "We got a message in the greenhouse. De Villiers sent for Greigor."

"To tell him something about Nordvelt?" Mikhail's brow drew up, pulling his cheekbones into even sharper relief.

Greigor hesitated. "Not about that, no. But—"

"He was probably getting a bollocking," Max said.

Greigor colored. "That's no' true. And it's not important. Important thing, de Villiers said he didn't trust Nordvelt."

"What did he say precisely?" I tried not to sound too defensive.

He shrugged and scuffed at the carpet with a foot. "I don't remember precisely," he said, retreating back into a mutter. "We said lots of things. He said he didn't trust you, Nordvelt."

The resulting silence was broken only by the sound of Greigor's scraping and of Theo tapping absently on the table.

"I'm prepared to let Anders continue," Max said eventually.

No one else spoke. Fergie cursed under his breath and stood, shoving his chair back noisily. He seemed of two minds as to whether he should walk out or continue the argument.

"We should have a service for the commander," Abidene said.

"Or a wake," Keegan chipped in. "The cap'n'd have liked that."

"Okay—" I began, but I was cut off before I could get any further.

"You have *no fucking say* in this, Nordvelt," Fergie rounded on me. "Okay, the Company's been dumb enough to appoint you chief of security, but we knew the commander and you didn't. You have *no fucking say* in how we remember him, got that?" he snarled.

I opened my mouth to snap back, then hesitated. He was right. I was the outsider here. This was one thing I could let go. "Okay. Okay. Look, you sort that out between you. I don't want to piss you off, any of you. Just…just decide on a new chief of operations and let me know by morning, okay?"

"So what do we do now?" Keegan asked.

Fergie sighed. Stress etched him gray and old. "I don't know about you, but I'm going to join Dmitri up at the mine. We still need that coal. But…but I guess if anyone needs time off, they should take it."

★   ★   ★

Facts. Data. Information. It was time to get something solid, to get the investigation moving. Once the meeting had broken up I caught up with Max, drew her aside – ignoring the vicious looks Greigor was shooting at me.

"I need your help. Are you busy?"

"What do you need?"

"You might find it…unpleasant."

She smiled grimly. "I'm the janitor. All the unpleasant jobs get passed down to me."

"Not like this one, I hope."

She looked at me inquisitively.

"Come with me."

★   ★   ★

The smiles were gone: we stood over the body of de Villiers, on his bed in the infirmary. His eyes were still open but the skin had warmed. Rigor was starting to set in.

Fischer lay unconscious in the adjacent cot. She moved and mumbled in her sleep.

I reached over to close the commander's eyes.

"What do you want me to do?" Max asked softly.

"I need to know how he died."

She gave a bitter laugh, almost a bark. "Sorry, sweetheart, but I'm not going to perform an autopsy for you. You need a doctor for that."

"I need an engineer." I picked up the mask that I'd set on the bedside table earlier. I gave it to Max. "He was wearing this when we found him. But his skin was frozen. I want you to look at it – and his warmsuit too – and see if they were working when he went outside."

She took the mask in silence and gave it a cursory once-over. Then she looked back up at me. "We'll need to get the suit off him."

I nodded.

It was not a nice job.

"We'll have to deal with the body, I suppose," I said when it was done.

Max stood beside me, his warmsuit in her arms. "This hasn't ever come up before. I don't know…don't know what we'll do."

"You've no storage for – for this sort of thing?" I nodded towards the corpse, now stripped to regular indoor clothes. The loud shirt de Villiers wore had never looked more at odds with his surroundings.

She shook her head. "I guess…I guess we'll have to take it outside. Put him in one of the storage sheds."

"Not very…I don't know…"

She shrugged and looked away, her face hardening. "It's just a lump of flesh," she said. "There's no vermin, no scavengers, to eat it. Barely even any bacteria. It'll be fine until – until the shift's over, until it can be moved. Then his wife can have it, do whatever she wants with it."

I nodded, frown heavy on my face. "Shall we…?"

We left the body and went to the vestibule to suit up. Then we returned and wrestled the commander onto a stretcher. In silence, meeting nobody on the way, we carried him between us.

The blizzard had blown itself out. With powerful lights illuminating the courtyard, the journey was almost comically simple. We laid de Villiers down without ceremony, set neatly against a row of frozen machine parts, and stared down at his body.

We walked back to the infirmary, collected the dead man's warmsuit and mask and took them to the workshop. Neither of us spoke until we got there.

The workshop was clearly someone's private domain and – judging by the confidence in her movements, the very aura of belonging that she radiated – that someone was Max.

She was an artist, a sculptor; I saw that immediately. Amid the workbenches, a maze of installations had been set up. Human-size figures built all from scrap metal; dead robots, a mix of wires and cables and nails and sheet steel, stared at me, light bulbs for eyes. Masks hung on the walls: tribal designs made from the same materials, silver and copper, gray and gold and green. They put me in mind of Mayan grotesques – the pagan gods of an android pantheon. Spare parts littered all surfaces, and a gas ax was propped into the corner, near a service lift designed to carry heavy kit down to the basement. Although part of the barracks, this room had its own outer door, big enough to drive vehicles straight inside. I shivered in the cool air, wondering how much of this mess was being recycled as art and how much was Max's official 'work pending'.

I stood open-mouthed as Max hung de Villiers's face mask over one of the robot heads – that was an image I was sure to have nightmares about.

"This is all your work?" I managed.

She nodded, suddenly coy. "Just a hobby. They're not finished."

"They're fantastic," I breathed. "But – all this metal, do you not have to—"

"Yeah. They'll all be destroyed, melted down before we leave here."

"Doesn't that bother you?"

She shrugged, gave me an etched smile. "Call me Siva. Goddess of creation and destruction." She cleared her throat and changed the subject. "I'll check the suit over when I get a moment. Leave it on the bench there."

I did as she said and turned to look at her. She stared back as if weighing something up in her mind.

"You look exhausted," she said.

I managed a weak smile. "It's been a long morning. I've lost all track of time. What is it, midday?"

"Just gone eleven."

"God."

I watched as she took up a tool from her bench and ran it through her fingers. She seemed oblivious to the dirt and oil that were staining her skin. She looked at me from the corners of her deep eyes, and once again I was struck by her simple beauty.

"What happened out there, Anders?" she asked, voice echoing in the cold workshop.

"I've told you all I know."

"But what about what you think?"

"I think you know that too. After all, why else would I come to you?"

She regarded me. "So why were you really sent here?"

"What do you mean?"

"Was something said in Tierra? Did something come out in McCarthy's debrief?"

"They sent me because you needed a security chief. That's all I know."

"There weren't any hints of...trouble?"

"You tell me. You were here; I wasn't."

"There wasn't any trouble. Only—"

"What?"

"Just Weng and the commander." Her face went rigid when she spoke of de Villiers, her eyes fixed straight ahead. "And—"

"And what?"

"Oh, nothing. Just little arguments – the ones that always come up, you know? About politics and personalities."

I thought of Abi and Maggie talking in the kitchen, criticizing the Company. I was wondering how best to push for details, but she got the next question in first.

"Why you? Why were you picked for this post?"

I shrugged. "No special reason, not that I know of."

"Was anything said to you in your last Psych?"

"My last Psych..." I couldn't remember when my last Psych was. Strange, when the earlier ones were so clear in the memory – the battery of tests, images flashing before your eyes, a fraction of a second whilst the most subconscious responses were measured, measured, measured. "No, nothing was said. Sorry. I've no idea why I was sent here except that – you know, the normal way, application, interviews, tests..."

She seemed happy enough with my answer, turning away and breaking eye contact.

"What about you?" I asked.

"What about me?"

"How'd you come to be here? What's your story?"

"Aw, that story's old and dull, you know? Raised in Kinshasa, fell in love with machines when I was still just a kid. I traveled as widely as possible, to India and China, then Italy, stealing skills and ideas wherever I found myself." She shrugged. "And I wound up here. That's all there is."

"Why did you come here?"

"I told you, I love to travel and I love to learn. And I love a challenge."

She shrugged. "This was an opportunity, a great opportunity, and I love – I was loving it…"

"You got on well with the rest of the crew? With…with de Villiers?"

"Aw, come on Anders, let's not go back there. Can we just – just forget about that for now?"

She looked tired, then, older, skin tight on her bones. "Okay," I said quietly.

"Tell me," she began, "I mean, it's a stupid question, but how are you getting on here?"

I managed a weak smile. "I've not been sleeping well." Not what she meant, maybe, but the first thing that came to mind.

"McCarthy didn't sleep either. Used to complain about headaches."

"I've not had headaches – not yet, at least."

There was silence as we both seemed to be struggling for something to say, not wanting the conversation to end, not wanting to have to get back to the nightmare that this assignment had become. Both knowing we had no choice.

Sharing one last smile I left Max to her work and slipped back into cold corridors.

CHAPTER NINE

First, to the med bay. I needed to check on Fischer – needed to find out what she knew, why de Villiers would have been outside at that hour, and how she knew where he was. But when I got there, I found her still unconscious and Weng standing over her.

"How is she?" I asked as soon as the door closed behind me.

Weng looked up from her datapad, gave me an unreadable look. "She will recover."

That was an incredible relief. I almost staggered with it, a weight I'd not been aware of until then, lifting so fast I thought I might float.

But Weng brought me straight back down. "She is concussed. A minor cranial fracture. I've run the MRI"—she gestured to a bulky helmet-type device, wires snaking back from behind the ears, which was set on a workbench—"and there's no indication of brain damage. She should heal without any long-term effects, but she will be off duty for some days."

"I need to talk to her."

"No."

"Weng, I need—"

"No."

"You don't under—"

"No, Mr. Nordvelt, *you* do not understand. You will not talk to her. No one will talk to her. Not for several days."

"Weng—"

"I have injected her with a sedative to aid her natural healing. She will remain unconscious for at least twelve hours. Then I will re-examine her and judge her condition. In the meantime I shall examine *this*," she said as she held up her pad to show me the pink-gray image of Fischer's brain, "and make sure that I haven't missed anything. Because concussion is a serious condition, Mr. Nordvelt. She will need close attention for at least two days. You will not speak with her before then. And possibly not for some time after."

I stared at her but saw nothing beyond her cool implacability, heard no hint that she was telling me anything other than simple truth made awkward by her formality. I gritted my teeth, controlled my temper, exhaled steadily. "You will let me know if there's any change?" I managed.

"Of course."

I stared at her for a moment longer, then turned and left.

★   ★   ★

What I really wanted to do now was walk. It had always been my escape, my refuge – to wander the blocks and let humanity buzz around me. Of course that wasn't an option, not here and not now. In any case I had too much to do. I needed more data.

So I went back to my room, my office.

Seal the door. Sit at the desk. Scan biometrics. Access CCTV records.

It was no surprise to find that certain sections of the footage had been blanked.

The odds of an equipment failure in the moments leading up to the destruction of the comms building were slim. I mused on the statistical significance of the CCTV going down again on the morning of de Villiers's death.

I sat with my chin propped on the back of my hand, frowning at a screen that showed me nothing. The conclusions…they were inevitable.

I went through the night's footage again, making notes on my pad. *03:26: Footage blanked system-wide. 03:51: Footage returns to normal. 04:41: Footage blanked. 05:31: Back.* Over an hour's worth of material missing. And nothing noticeable, nothing but silent empty corridors, in-between times.

More data. More input. Give me more.

I tapped my stylus on the desk.

I went to de Villiers's quarters. The door opened easily to my security override.

His office was physically identical to mine but there were little signs of his superior rank. The director's chair he'd installed behind the desk – I'd not really noticed when he'd been occupying it, but it was clearly a cut above mine. I sniffed at the indulgence, and at the fountain pens in a neat rack behind his photographs. I had a momentary flashback to staring up at my father's desk when I was a small child.

I went round to the other side and saw that one of these pictures was of a younger de Villiers with his arm around a pregnant woman – his wife, I guessed. The other showed the commander too, this time with a group of people all grinning at the camera. They seemed to be standing atop one side of a great open-shaft mine. The sun shone down on them. Mine workers, old colleagues. There was a note scribbled on a corner: *Limpopo, 20.*

A filing cabinet sat in the corner; I tried one of the drawers. It slid open easily, revealing a row of neat folders, all perfectly organized and tagged. I looked at a few of the headings: *Personnel; Plans; Projections.* All very proper and correct. I'd have to go through them all – but later, not just yet.

I went to the door to the commander's private room, took a deep breath and tried the handle. The door swung open. So he'd not been lying when he said he had little time for security. That or he'd not been the last person in his quarters.

The room inside was identical to mine in layout but felt so much warmer. Yellow, orange and black, the embodiment of sunset over the veldt; the walls were draped in fabrics, throws over chairs and the bed and a rug too. I thought of my own quarters and shivered.

He had a desk with a compscreen. There were more photographs, more family, more old colleagues. I studied the faces but recognized no one but de Villiers.

There was a bottle of pills by the bed. I recognized the label as that of a common contraceptive. The blankets were ruffled and slumping to the floor.

I could see nothing unusual, nothing out of character in a warm, lived-in room. Still, I wished they had such things as evidence-scanners on the base. Or even someone trained in old-fashioned forensics. But then I reckoned that I'd find fingerprints from most base occupants here. I'd learn nothing that way.

His datapad was lying on the blankets. I took it up and went straight to the last thing de Villiers had been looking at.

A message. Priority one.

As soon as it arrived, an alarm would have sounded, waking the commander and demanding his attention.

The message appeared to be from me.

De Villiers
We need to talk. Meet me behind Maggie's greenhouse – NE corner – at 05:00. Be there if you want your control of Australis to last through the winter.
Nordvelt

I stared at the screen, read the message through again and again.

De Villiers went outside in the middle of the night because he thought I was going to blackmail him. Or at least that was how it looked to me.

Fischer, expecting to see him that morning, must have come here and found this message. She'd gone searching for him. The far corner of the greenhouse – far enough away to freeze a man, not far enough to be worth taking a vehicle. She'd have found his body on the way and called Weng, and Weng in turn had called me. That would make sense.

Fischer had read this message. I had to presume that no one else had. At least that explained why she'd been so fierce towards me, why she'd struggled so in the infirmary. What she must think…but then she couldn't talk, not for a little while. I had a day's grace.

I took one last look around the room. Its warmth seemed to have fled. I took the datapad and hurried back to my own space.

★   ★   ★

My mind was shot. Exhaustion; I needed to refocus, to get all the questions in my head into some sort of order. I knew I hadn't sent the message that lured the commander to his death – it could only be that someone was trying to set me up. I wanted someone to share this with, to confide in, but I had no one. In the absence of a confidante, I chose to put headphones on, play some visualizations and pretend I was in the Pennines, running, running, towards nothing and away from nothing.

But when I got to the gym, I found I wasn't alone in seeking relief through physical activity. A sparring session was underway between Theo and Mikhail. Keegan and Weng were watching as the oilmen fought, Theo's heavy muscles tight against Mikhail's greater reach. Sweat spun off Mikhail's headguard as Theo got in a glancing blow – but then the fight stopped and all four people turned to stare at me.

"You decided not to go out to work today, then," I said as I dredged up a smile.

"No, we're up there right now," Theo panted, ripping at the Velcro of his gloves and rolling a blue gumshield out on his tongue. "What the hell are you doing here?"

"I came for a run."

"A run? When there's—"

"Ease up, Theo," Keegan cut in. "We're all in shock. No need to take it out—"

"You can shut the fuck up too, stoner," Theo snapped, turning away.

"So how did de Villiers die?" Mikhail asked. "What did you do?"

I didn't reply.

"Did you knock him out like you did the doctor? Leave him in the wastes to freeze?"

"I didn't do anything."

"This isn't helping," Keegan said. "For all we know it was – it was all an accident."

"Yeah, right."

Weng was silent. I wondered what she was doing here; it didn't seem in character for her to be in the gym, in company. But then fear can make even the strongest of us seek out our fellows.

"So you wanted a run, huh?" Theo said. "Tell you what, Nordvelt – why don't I give you a different kinda workout?"

"What do you—"

"You want a bout? Reckon you can stand with me toe to toe?"

"I don't—"

"Yeah, thought as much. What d'you think, Mik? Want to be his second?"

"Reckon I could do that," he said as he turned to Keegan, got him to help remove his equipment. "What do you say, Nordvelt? You up for it?"

"I don't—"

"Good man." His headguard came off and he shook the sweat off his blond hair before turning and grinning at me. No humor in his expression.

"I don't—"

"Don't you worry, dude – here, you can use my stuff. Let's get you ready."

I looked in turn at the four faces staring at me – and then Mikhail was in front of me, laughing as I staggered when he shoved the guard over my head. The inside was slick with sweat. Moisture trickled down my cheek. "You sure you want this, Theo? Don't look like he'll take much of your time."

"Maybe it's all a ruse," Theo said. "Reckon he might be punking us?"

I gritted my teeth. I was tired and I was angry. "I'm no boxer," I said. "But if you want—"

"You know the rules. Nothing below the belt. Fight until you call quit. Mikhail will ref."

I held up my hands, let the smell of unwashed bodies roll through me as the blond thrust the gloves onto my hands. I grunted and flexed my fingers against moist padding as Mikhail tightened the straps around my wrist. He found a clean gumshield and eased it into my mouth.

"How long do you reckon he'll last?" he said. "What do you think, Keegan? Bet you a beer he won't go beyond three minutes."

"You're on," the Englishman said. "Go on, Nordvelt. I believe in you."

"Yeah, come on, killer. Show me what you got." Theo grinned before pulling his gumshield back into his mouth. He bounced on the spot and brought his hands up to a guard as I stepped forward, clumsy and uncertain, onto the mat that was laid out at the end of the room.

I paused, took a moment to stretch out and compose myself. I'd boxed before – in the orphanage and in the blocks – but I'd never been any good. I'd given it up as soon as I could. I looked at my opponent. Theo was moving easily, white singlet patched with sweat. He still wore his crucifix, a dance of gold between skin and vest.

I raised my guard and stepped up to face him. Even as I was asking myself why I was doing this, how I'd let myself be pushed into this, Mikhail had stepped beside me.

"You ready? Weng, keep time. Okay – box!"

Theo laughed at my guard. Scowling, I raised my hands higher, and the American came forward with a few testing blows to my arms. I felt them, for sure, but the sensation was distant, the padding in his gloves numbing the impact. I stepped in and replied in kind – a tentative jab that he easily absorbed.

"That it, Nordvelt? You got to have more than that," he mumbled, blue protection over his teeth making him into some kind of monster.

"Quit talking and get fighting," Mikhail said. "There's a beer on this."

Theo grunted and stepped in; I caught a hard blow just above my elbow and swayed back to a straight right aimed at my chin. But the movement unbalanced me and I was helpless to prevent the subsequent left clipping the side of my face. Angry and embarrassed, I threw a haymaker, forcing him to skip back and break again. I shook a bead of sweat – my own or Mikhail's, I couldn't tell – from my eyes and stepped forward, rights and lefts aimed at Theo's stomach.

I was on the mat. Hadn't even seen the blow that had sent me to hands and knees. Hadn't felt it, just knew that my cheek was on fire, the room slow to come back into focus.

Mikhail cheered. "You had enough yet, Nordvelt? Ain't no shame in quitting."

"Don't listen to him, Nordvelt," Keegan said. "Come on, get up – you can have him."

"One minute," Weng said.

Theo let me get to my feet. I returned to my guard and watched his eyes above my gloves. Suddenly he dipped a shoulder and instinctively I went with it—

It took me longer to get up this time. And this time I felt it, pain rapidly shrinking to numbness along my cheekbone.

"Watch the feint, Nordvelt," Mikhail laughed.

"One minute thirty."

"Don't be so damn stubborn, Nordvelt," Theo mumbled. I looked in his eyes. The humor had gone. He seemed – he seemed almost afraid, as if he'd realized that now he could only lose. There was little honor in beating such an overmatched opponent.

I struggled up, legs uncertain beneath me. I gathered myself and we danced through Weng's two-minute call. Theo seemed more circumspect now, keeping his guard high and letting me waste my energy on blows that were easily deflected. He moved lightly for a big man, and I didn't know myself why I was still trying. I had nothing to prove, I told myself; I had no reason to go through with this. Only pride and anger.

I pushed forward now. Theo backed off, looking for his moment, stinging my arms with the occasional straight but otherwise content to wait—

"Two minutes thirty."

I don't know what made him take his eyes off me, the merest flicker towards Mikhail or maybe Weng, but I saw it and I swung hard. A left backed by a right jab – and I scored, my first clean blow glancing off the side of the chin, all my frustrations behind the punch—

Keegan cheered. But Theo merely took a pace or two away, then came back at me hard. A flurry of punches, first into my guard, but when that wavered they fell into my gut, then again into the side of my head. I staggered back, but this time I kept my feet.

"Finish him, Theo!" Mikhail yelled.

I could do nothing but try and hold myself upright, desperately attempting to re-erect my defences.

"Ten seconds," Weng said.

Theo had all but abandoned his guard in his attempt to break me down. Through the narrow gap between my forearms I saw his chin exposed – if I could just get in a good jab—

I saw my moment and lashed out—

Theo's fist crashed into my skull and I was down again.

"Time," Weng called.

"Yeah," Keegan shouted. "That's—"

"What are you talking about?" Mikhail turned to him. "Down three times in one round – that's a knockout. You owe me—"

Dizzy and close to retching, I clambered to my feet. Theo watched me. I couldn't read his expression as he held out his gloves for me to bump. "You want any more?" he asked.

I shook my head, afraid that I'd be sick if I tried to talk.

"You got guts, Nordvelt," he said beneath the sound of Keegan and Mikhail's argument. "I'll give you that one. No frickin' muscles, though."

I spat out my gumshield. Weng stepped onto the mat to help with my gloves and headguard. I stood unmoving, let the room drift back into focus. She lifted up my eyelids, fingers cool and delicate, and checked me over. She seemed satisfied that I'd suffered no real damage.

Still, she escorted me back to my quarters, leaving the others to continue their argument. She checked me again when I was sitting on my bed, got a couple of pills out of a medipack and made me take them with a swig of water.

I don't know if it was something in the painkillers, or if it was just the cumulative effects of a long, tough morning, but I was asleep almost before Weng had left the room.

CHAPTER TEN

I woke late next morning, sleep a heavy blanket that had to be heaved off. I'd just had time to stare at de Villiers's datapad, sitting accusingly next to my compscreen, and get a shower before the fire alarm shrieked.

I dragged on my drab clothes and hurried out into the corridor: the noise was far worse here as the klaxon reverberated off metal walls. All the doors had closed automatically, but they opened to my biometrics and after a few minutes I found myself in the rec room.

Weng and Abidene were already there, standing before the viewscreen. I could see from their mouths that they were shouting to each other, but I couldn't hear a word. I hurried over to join them. The screen was flashing red and black – *Fire* came and went. As I reached them, Weng touched the screen and the message was replaced by the control panel. She shouted something but I couldn't understand what. But I got what I needed from the display: the fire had been detected in Dr. Fischer's room. At least she was safe in the infirmary....

Unable to communicate with the others, I ran back into the corridor and the wall of sound.

The alarms cut out just as I entered the stairwell. The sudden silence almost made me fall, but I caught my feet and I hurtled onwards, leaping down half flights. I reached the domestic level in only a few seconds.

The doctor's office was silent and untouched. There was no fire here. I opened the door to her private room, half expecting a cloud of smoke to roll out over me. I ducked back – but there was no inferno, no roar of noise. No heat. Just a sweet-smelling haze.

"Hello?" I called. There was no reply. I peered round the frame of the door.

There was no fire – at least nothing I could see. The room seemed normal save that various papers had been torn up and strewn around. The duvet lay twisted and tangled on the floor.

There was smoke in the air, but it was thin and white and was lazily spiraling up to the extractor in the ceiling. I caught a breath of it and recognized the distinctive taste. I exhaled in relief, sending eddies into the cloud. The panic I'd been feeling began to fade.

"Is anybody here?"

A small sob and a sudden gust of smoke came as a reply, on the floor on the far side of the bed, but sounds of feet haring down the corridor made me draw back. I held up a hand to stop Weng and Abidene – and Keegan too, and Max. They crammed into the outer doorway.

"It's okay," I said to them quietly.

"Doctor Fischer," Max gasped, "is she…"

I looked back into the room and saw movement behind the bed, a head wrapped in a turban-like wound-pad rising—

I blinked, thought for a moment that the fumes had affected me. It was Fischer – yes, it was Fischer, but her cheeks were red from crying, her eyes bloodshot and vacant. I'd never seen her look worse, not even in the horror of her distress. Like some weeping Hindu sculpture.

I took a breath, coughing briefly as the smoke reached out to me. I felt light-headed. "She's there," I said. "She – I think she's okay. But I thought she was still in the—"

"She discharged herself last night." I saw Max sniff the air, and understanding came to her eyes. "Let me talk to her," she said.

I nodded and let her and Weng pass into Fischer's room. Max rounded the bed and crouched down next to the doctor. I stayed in the doorway, and Abidene and Keegan came to stand behind me.

"Stupid bloody woman," Keegan muttered to himself.

Max was speaking to the doctor, soft words that meant very little. "It's okay, Julia, shh, it's okay…"

I turned back to the others and gestured for them to back off. "Go and tell the others it's a false alarm," I said to them.

They left, Abidene in silence and Keegan swearing under his breath. I went to follow them, then glanced back. Max was helping Fischer onto the bed, taking the joint from her unresisting hand. The janitor glanced at me in silent communication. *Nothing you can do here now. Leave it to me. We'll talk later.* I nodded and made my way out into the corridor.

★   ★   ★

Fergie had been chosen as chief of operations. We met in the dining room: it was warm and – at the moment – private.

I was glad it was Fergie. He'd made it clear that he'd pushed for the job so that he could watch me, and I was fine with that. Now he could see that I had nothing to hide and was doing the best I could.

"So," Fergie said once we were seated, "what are we here to discuss?"

"How are things going in the mine?" I asked.

"Fine. Nothin' to report."

"Do you know if de Villiers had any plans to change anything? Or to expand?"

Fergie shrugged. "He was always talking about chasing strata or setting up a new extraction point. I know he was planning to develop the iron mine. Whether he had any actual strategy or if it was just a long-term ambition – that I don't know."

"We'll need to go through his files."

"Aye. Best if we do that together." He gave me a heavy look.

"Look, Fergie—"

"That's Mr. Ferguson to you, lad."

I stopped and drew a deep breath. "Mr. Ferguson, then. Look, I know you don't trust me, but I need you to run the industrial side of the complex."

"Okay. I can do that."

"Just keep the mine running. Make sure all the factories are working as they should—"

"You don't have to spell it out for me, Nordvelt. I'm not an idiot, and I know a lot more about this than you."

"Okay."

"So you're still proposing to investigate the commander's death?" Fergie said.

I nodded. "It's my job."

"I can't stop you. But I want you to share all your findings with us, got that? Maybe we should work together, or with—"

"I work best alone."

His mouth creased into a humorless smile. "Oh, the lone wolf detective, is that right? That what you are?"

"I just work best alone."

"I bet you do."

Silence fell between us.

"Is there anything else?" Fergie asked at length.

"I need to know where the drugs are coming from."

"Wha – what drugs?"

I was hardly taken in by that clumsy attempt at surprise. I glared at him.

"What are you talking about, Nordvelt?"

"Don't give me that bullshit. I know what cannabis smells like. I should've realized earlier. They weren't just cigarettes you were smoking up at the barbecue, were they? They were joints. God, de Villiers must have thought I was an idiot. Where'd they come from, Mr. Ferguson?"

His face ran through a variety of expressions: anger, disgust, stubbornness, anger again. Finally he seemed to realize that he'd already waited too long to reply and settled for a sullen silence.

"I need to know, Mr. Ferguson."

"No. No, you don't."

"You don't think, as head of security, that it's my business?"

"I don't give a damn," he snapped. "This's nothing to do with the commander's death. It's irrelevant."

"How do you know that?" I asked. "How on earth do you know what's relevant and what isn't? Unless you know the name of the killer as well."

"How do you know there's a killer?" he shot back. "Could've been an accident, that's what you were sayin', right? Maybe it was a suit malfunction. Maybe the commander tripped and fell. Ain't that possible? Or are you the damn killer and all these questions are just for show?"

"There is—"

"There is what?"

I didn't want to tell him I'd examined de Villiers's datapad. Didn't want to tell anyone until I'd had more time to think about it myself. We sat in silence for a moment, staring at each other across the table. My face was like stone.

I cleared my throat, broke eye contact. "Did you decide anything about a…about a gathering for the commander?" I asked, as if the last few moments had never happened.

Fergie shifted uncomfortably in his seat and grunted. "Dmitri, Keegan and Abidene will sort something out. Not for a day or two, though. Let things calm down a little first."

"I still need to get an autopsy done."

Fergie's mouth fell open. "You – you'd ask Julia to do that? Now? God, Nordvelt, that's just…just cold."

"As soon as she's capable. We need – we *need* – that information. If de Villiers was murdered, then we need to know."

He stared down at the table. Eventually he nodded.

"Okay. That's good. Let's get to work, then."

★   ★   ★

We went together to de Villiers's rooms. With Fergie looking over my shoulder, I accessed his compscreen, my biometrics providing limited access. I didn't tell Fergie I'd already looked round. I didn't mention the datapad.

On de Villiers's desktop we found plans of the local geology, with mineral deposits marked and heavily annotated in de Villiers's own hand. Fergie took those. He forwarded to himself all the notes that the commander had made on the mining operations, and told me he'd go through them with Weng.

The block de Villiers had placed on my computer access remained and I was unable to look into his private files. I didn't even try. I didn't want Fergie to see how little the commander had trusted me.

There was a record of a disciplinary meeting he'd had with Greigor; simply an aide-memoir for de Villiers to add something to the official record. I asked Fergie about this but he just shrugged and shook his head.

"Look at this, though," he said, showing me a paper copy of a message de Villiers had sent.

I took it. A monthly update from Tierra. All figures and lists. "What's—"

"Look at the projections. There — look — see how much coal he's being asked to pull out?"

"And that's...?"

Fergie shook his head at my ignorance. "That's a third more than we got out last month. In order to meet those targets, we'd have to push right to the wire."

"Why'd they demand something that extreme?"

"Dunno. We'd have to go through all his comms to see what'd been said before — this is just a snapshot, right? Maybe they were expecting him to fail. Maybe some politician's makin' promises we have to keep. I just know this is a massive ask."

It might also explain why de Villiers had been relatively unfazed by the destruction of the comms building. No chance to report failure, no more impossible demands. And a little breathing space to work to this new target.

For form's sake we went into the commander's bedroom. I couldn't help but stare at the place where de Villiers's datapad had lain upon his bed. We spent a silent minute in a pretence of a search, then left.

Fergie and I parted after that. He went to see Weng. I went to see Max.

★   ★   ★

"You were right."

I'd found the janitor at her workbench, examining the circuitry within de Villiers's warmsuit. Another of her android statues was watching over her, heavy, angular and lumpen: sheet metal and pistons. Its torso seemed to be wrapped with vehicle tracks.

Max beckoned me over. "Look...here," she said.

The damage was obvious, even to me. Between the two skins of the suit, a section of the electronics had been burned out.

"This wasn't just a part of the heating mechanism," she said. "It was a control node. The suit would've gone cold in an instant."

"So de Villiers had gone outside without a working suit," I said, matching her detached tone.

But Max shook her head. "No. Couldn't have. If it had been damaged when he left the barracks, he'd have known immediately that something was wrong. He'd have gone back and changed into another."

"So what...?"

"It must have blown when he was already outside. Too far away for him to get back in time."

I nodded grimly. It made sense. "Any chance that it was an accident – a malfunction?"

"Look here." She pulled the inner lining back across the burned circuits. "See the stitching there? It looks like someone slit the lining open and then roughly stitched it closed again."

"Mm. Can you tell how it blew?"

"I reckon that the killer inserted a small charge – a minute amount of explosives would have done it. Or maybe something as simple as a battery. Anything that would have overloaded the electronics. The suit simply shut down," she said.

"Whatever did the damage, how would it have been triggered?"

She shrugged. "It could have been set on a timer. Or a remote detonator. It wouldn't have been hard."

I sighed and felt my legs sag. I leaned against the bench and breathed deeply. I'd known it was no accident – felt it in my bones. But to have solid evidence at last – it was still a wrench. At least that meant I wouldn't have to ask the doctor to perform an autopsy. "Who could have done something like that?"

"If you're asking me to point the finger, I've no idea. If you're asking who had the technical skill – well, it's really simple. I could. All the engineering staff – Dmitri, Fergie, Mikhail and Theo – we all could. But it really is so simple. There are plenty of technical manuals on the Australis database. Anyone could have done it."

"So we can't narrow down the suspects."

"Sorry."

"Not your fault." I felt frustrated, angry. I desperately wanted to *do* something, to be able to act. "Anything else?"

She wrapped her arms around herself and leaned back against the workbench. She shook her head, looking down at the floor. I felt the sudden urge to take her in my arms, to keep her safe, but the android statue was looming over her, its expression suddenly seeming to me to be heavy, possessive and jealous. "Murder," she said to herself.

I shivered. I half reached out to her, unsure myself what I was trying to do. But I dropped my hand as I saw the look in her eye, the readiness to recoil.

We stood uncertain for a few seconds before she cleared her throat and stood straighter. I did the same and the moment was gone.

"What now?" she asked.

I took a deep breath and let it out again slowly. "Get on with your duties, your regular duties. I'll think more about this and get back to you." I turned to leave. I had just about reached the inside door when she called to me again.

"Anders."

"Max?"

"I – I don't trust you. You know that, right?"

"Are you telling me or yourself?" My face felt frozen; the words sounded like they belonged to someone else.

"I can't. How can I? I mean, look at the evidence—"

"There's no damn evidence."

She said nothing.

"There's no damn evidence – just that this happened after I arrived. Might as well say that the killer was waiting for the night shift to begin."

She wouldn't meet my eyes. "But I know the rest of the crew."

I couldn't think of any way to respond. I opened and closed my mouth, leaving a thin trail of breath in the chill air. Then I shook my head and left.

⋆　　⋆　　⋆

In the corridor I paused for another deep breath. I wasn't quite sure what I was feeling. It shouldn't bother me, what she'd just said – it was hardly news. But it did. Because – because I liked her. Maybe she'd said that because *she* liked *me*. And maybe that was just self-delusion. I'd never been good at reading emotions, at least not in my personal life.

I wanted to be angry, wanted to be hurt. I wanted to be able to rail against the injustice – but I couldn't. I marched onwards. Max was doing the right thing – making sure things were clear between us. It didn't change a thing.

I bit my lip, a small penance for my sins. A small act of self-loathing.

Work. The only way I had of coping. And it was time for a proper chat with Weng.

As I stalked down the corridors to her room, I couldn't shake the feeling that I was being followed.

★   ★   ★

Weng stared at me fiercely as I sat in front of her desk. The chair was still warm; I guessed that Fergie couldn't be long gone. In front of her I saw the plans that we'd found in de Villiers's office. I nodded at them. "Anything interesting?" I asked.

She made me wait before answering. "They are all plans I prepared myself. De Villiers had annotated them."

"To what end?"

"He was planning to add new mineshafts. To reach richer mineral deposits."

I nodded. It was as I'd expected. I looked back into her eyes again, met her gaze evenly.

"I have work to do," Weng said. Her tone was neutral, under strict control. But it was clear she didn't want me here.

"Why did you hate de Villiers, Weng?"

She shuddered. It was only momentary, the slightest of reactions. She had fastened her eyes back on mine in an instant, her expression unchanged. Again she took a long time to answer. "That's none of your concern."

"Weng, when we first met you asked me if I had come to Australis because of you. Then you said it was a pity that I'd not killed de Villiers. It's clear to everyone here that you hated the man. Tell me why I shouldn't suspect you of the murder?"

"Why should *I* not suspect *you*? Maybe I was wrong, maybe you did injure the doctor deliberately," she snapped back. "Maybe that's what I should tell the rest of the crew."

I sighed, ran my hand through my hair. My eyes fell on the chess set she kept on one end of her desk. The pieces had moved since my last visit. "You play a lot?" I asked with a nod to the set.

She hesitated. "I…used to."

"Not now?"

"The destruction of the comms building robbed me of opponents."

"You played over the net?"

She nodded.

"You have no opponents here?"

"No one is good enough. They prefer poker." She sniffed. "Only…"

"Yes?"

"De Villiers. I played him. Before…"

I could see the indecision in her eyes, anger battling restraint in the way she grimaced, half opening her mouth to speak then closing tight again. I knew I'd have to be careful, to give the gentlest of pushes. Too much and the shutters would come down hard. "I'd be glad to play you," I said. "But I'm afraid I'll be no competition."

She looked at me. Then she reached over to move the board between us, memstored the position and set up a new game. She gave me white.

"I remember the day I arrived," I said as I moved a pawn. "In the rec room. De Villiers came—"

"I remember," she said as she answered my move, and the next few, without hesitation.

"He tried to humiliate you." I took one of her pawns with a knight.

Her scowl deepened. She castled, fingers nimble and precise.

"He did that for my benefit, didn't he? To prove to me that he was in charge, that he was the boss here. Don't you think?"

"Yes." Her voice was barely more than a whisper. Her hair almost kissed the table as she looked down at the game.

"Cruel."

Silently we moved pieces. I was already losing, I realized, my position cramped and my options limited.

"The engineers liked him," I said. "He had their respect." Again I moved my knight.

She said nothing.

"He could be charming, couldn't he?"

"I don't want to talk about de Villiers, can you not see that?" She broke, broke hard, and in the split second that she was looking up at me, I once more saw the fierceness, the wildcat that she kept so carefully caged, that I'd seen only once or twice since we met. She stared hard at me, mouth half-open before she swallowed and visibly reined herself in.

Silence. Just the tick of her equipment, the seismometer in the corner and the air-conditioning overhead. Slowly she lowered her head back to the game.

"Weng," I said quietly, "you're going to have to tell someone what happened between you. When the long night is over, someone from the Company is going to want to hear your story. Is going to *take* your story. You know what I mean – truth drugs, Psych tests. You know what'll happen." I paused, wishing I had those things available to me here. "Weng, I promise I won't tell anyone what you say—"

"They all know anyway!" she almost shouted. "I hate them, hate them all…I hate them all…" She trailed off.

I sat in silence, waiting until she was ready. I knew she would talk now.

"He told me I was beautiful." Her voice was barely more than a whisper, the anger drowned in her pain. She stared through the board. "He… We met up with the others in Tierra and stayed there a week before we came out here. He told me I was beautiful." She pushed a pawn to the sixth rank, attacking my bishop.

I sat in silence. I waited.

"I knew about his family, but it was easy to forget. I could ignore all the photographs in his quarters. I could fool myself that they meant nothing. But he didn't care for me, not really. He used me. And then he tired of me."

"He started a relationship with Fischer?" I prompted. Her last move looked like a mistake and, barely thinking, I took the pawn.

Now Weng looked up at me. Tears fell from her cheeks and landed unheeded on the board. "Fischer? Yes, Fischer. And all the rest. They'd seen me walking around, happy, and not one of them had – not one of them had thought… They were laughing at me. Laughing at me! The poor, naive little peasant girl, only fit to be eaten up, to be…to be *used*!" She broke down, crying properly now. But she recovered herself quicker than I'd thought possible. She wiped her eyes and threw her hair back from her face. She ignored the loss of her pawn and switched her queen to the opposite flank.

She looked at me again, her expression challenging me to make mockery. When she spoke again, she was back in control. "I went to McCarthy. I made a complaint against de Villiers. But he told me that no rules had been broken. Do anything you like as long as the oil keeps flowing, the coal keeps rolling out. Keep the lights on in Brasilia. Let them power their stupid televisions for one more day...."

"Why did you think that I was here because of you?" I asked.

She wrinkled her nose as if I was asking something inconsequential. "After going to McCarthy, I wrote to his superior. I complained about both McCarthy and the commander. No rules had been broken? That man – that man, he broke rules every day, every single day, and McCarthy did nothing!"

"You thought I'd been assigned to look into your complaint?"

She nodded. We fell into silence.

After about half a minute, I cleared my throat. I wasn't quite sure how to ask this. "Weng..."

She looked up at me, her expression neutral, her posture dignified.

"Weng – did you kill Commander de Villiers?"

She smiled grimly. "No, Mr. Nordvelt, I did not."

"Can you tell me what you were doing two nights ago?"

"Yes."

"What were you doing two nights ago, Weng?"

"I was sleeping."

"Alone?"

She curled a lip back to reveal her teeth. "Yes. And you have lost this game, Mr. Nordvelt."

"What?"

She looked at the board and I saw it – the pawn move that had opened up the diagonal for the bishop, the queen ready to sweep down upon my king.

I smiled wryly at her. "You realize I'll have to check the CCTV?"

"CCTV can be fooled."

I looked at her. Did she know I was bluffing? That I'd already established the footage had been blanked? But I couldn't see anything but defiant pride in her expression. "What do you mean by that?"

"Don't put your faith in machines. Don't put your faith in people. I'd say that you should have no faith at all, Mr. Nordvelt."

CHAPTER ELEVEN

And then my compscreen was hacked.

I'd returned to my rooms for some quiet time, to think, to plan, to reflect. I also had to log de Villiers's death and Fischer's accident and Fergie's new status. Even in this mess, in the chaos and isolation and in the darkness, procedure mattered. To the Company, at least.

I missed the message at first. I switched on the machine and scanned my fingerprints. Then I set the combi-maker for coffee. It was only when I returned to my seat that I found it.

I'm watching you.

Black on a yellow background: impossible to ignore. The usual interface icons were still visible as grayed-out features behind the text. I stared at the screen for a long, long time.

I felt numb, battered. I should have been angry or afraid, but I just felt…numb.

Had the hacker needed access to my room? This wasn't my office; this was my bedroom, my sanctuary. I cast around but couldn't see anything else wrong, nothing out of place. The ruffle in the bed where I'd not made it properly, my book, the rosewood puzzle box by the compscreen, and the memcard still jacked in to the screen's side.

If somebody had been in here, they might have accessed anything. The thought left me cold, although there was nothing dangerous on the card, only personal items. But it would be a violation.

De Villiers's datapad was on the work surface where I'd left it. It didn't look to have been moved, but – but the sweat was cold on my brow. If anyone took the datapad, if they'd seen the message I'd supposedly left for the commander…

I paced the floor once, twice. I had to do something with the damn thing. Had to get it out of there. Had to talk to Fischer – I was working on the assumption that she'd seen the note, and…and she must be convinced to keep that to herself.

I took a long, deep breath and cradled my coffee. I sat and tried to remove the hacker's warning, but it was beyond me – I just didn't know how to begin. But at least the interface icons still worked, and I was able to cover the message with open files. I brought up the CCTV logs – no surprise to see them blanked for just a few minutes earlier in the afternoon. So was the hacker also de Villiers's killer?

The anger I'd been barely aware of, so preoccupied had I been, surfaced unexpectedly. I wanted to punch something. Wanted a fight. I wanted to call Theo and go the full twelve rounds with him – to let him beat me to the canvas and keep getting up until I was nothing but blood and bone.

But I had work to do.

I added my notes to the base log as quickly as possible. And then I needed to be elsewhere, doing something definite rather than just sitting and chasing my thoughts round in circles. My mind wasn't working properly. I had to get out.

I almost walked into Greigor outside my office. He mumbled an apology and said something about getting an item for Maggie. We made no eye contact and strode off in different directions.

I needed to know my turf. I'd been putting it off, but now, filled with a restless urgency, an undirected anger, I stalked through corridors, through all the public rooms. I wasn't expecting to find anything in particular, especially not in places as well frequented as the rec room or the canteen. I just felt I had to go there, to stare into corners, to consider and discard impossibilities, to *know* every space.

The base was quiet. The engineers were out, at the mine or at the oil platform. The support staff kept mostly to their offices.

The upper floors revealed no secrets. I went down to the basement, past the laundry and into the storeroom beyond.

This was a large space, its footprint nearly as big as the whole building and with the base generator at the far end. As far as I knew, only Max had real reason to come down here. I looked down rack upon rack of spare materials: battery packs, sheet metal, wires and cabling...

It was, in other words, the perfect place for a stowaway to hide. I hoped – I needed – to find something or someone.

My footsteps echoed around the large, dimly lit space. I walked slowly now, my anger lost in the gloom. The generator growled gently in the far corner. The floor was smooth concrete, the walls breeze blocks. My breath hung in the air.

I made my way across the floor, skirting machine parts, spare tools and stacks of boxes. I wondered if this was where Max got the parts for her sculptures. I looked with interest at a dump of surveillance equipment: scanners and cameras and fittings.

I saw nothing out of place, no sign that anyone had been hiding down here. And the more inescapable the realization that I'd found no one to blame, the more the frustration grew.

The air was becoming warmer as I approached the far corner of the chamber; the generator, fueled from an oil tank which in turn was fed directly from the refinery, released ambient heat into the room. It wasn't until I was about ten yards away, when I was beginning to sweat, that I saw that I was wrong. The generator should have been carefully insulated to reduce wastage, but part of the cladding had been ripped clear. The metal of the engine was exposed, and the cladding itself rolled away to build a little insulated extension. A still had been built in the warm. It looked like it had been fashioned by a medieval alchemist; a dark, viscous liquid was gently simmering through glass pipes and beakers, becoming steadily lighter as it went. Eventually it dripped into a large metal tub.

I went to the tub and sniffed at it. The oil-alcohol smell was so strong that my eyes started to water.

I fought down the urge to kick it over, to smash the equipment to pieces. I settled for slamming my foot into the cladding, shaking my tears into the brew.

Breathing heavily, I stood and thought for a few minutes, finished my search of the basement, then went back upstairs.

★   ★   ★

I checked my suit carefully before I went outside. I had left this too long; I should have visited all the external buildings the day I arrived. How would I know if anything had been moved or altered? But no use worrying. I visited the garage, the cold store, walked around the coal shed and the oil tanks. Spent an empty moment by de Villiers's corpse.

Snow crunched beneath me as I crossed to the mineral sheds, where iron bars were stacked, ready to be dragged by crawler trains back to the coast. A giant truck crouched in the corner of this warehouse, evidently the way that the ingots were shunted here from the smelting plant. But none of these buildings were heated, and nowhere did I see any sign of an interloper.

I had hoped to visit the mine today, and the derricks that pumped up the oil. But it was already getting late, and it had been a long day. I decided to make Maggie's lair my last port of call.

The hydroponics lab was the largest building in the complex, at least in terms of its footprint. It looked like a massive row of conjoined greenhouses, just like the Company hothouses that you saw on the shuttle into London. All told it covered about a quarter of a square kilometer. I entered through an airlock – a proper one, not like the vestibule into the barracks – and waited for about a minute before I was allowed into the building beyond.

It was like being in a tropical paradise. I felt a moment of overwhelming heat before my suit adjusted.

Rows of large planters stretched away from me on either side. Each of them was around a meter from base to top, and made of aluminum or some similar metal; they terminated in a clear plastic lip, another foot or so high. Inside those I could see liquid swirling gently, and in the liquid grew plants.

On the nearest benches, a cereal was growing, green and unripe. Beyond that I could see half-grown bushes, and fruit plants, and…and many different kinds of vegetation. More than I'd ever seen in my life, and many more than I could identify. A small machine crawled along the floor. It seemed to be scanning the plants. It paused by a specimen, then reached out an extending arm to snip off a particular twig. It caught the item and fed it into its body. Then it trundled onwards, blades at the ready.

Over all of the planters hung great artificial lights, long strips linked to the ceiling by slender wires. They were all on, but seemed to be filtered slightly so the light that shone down on the plants was a sort of blue-yellow.

There was a noise behind me; I spun round, adopting some sort of ridiculous crouch as if I were a gunslinger.

It was Greigor. Only Greigor, stepping round a row of planters, carrying a can in one hand. He raised his free hand in greeting, but there was no smile for me. I'd never seen him smile, not at anyone. Just those deep brown eyes looking down on me.

I began to breathe again. I hadn't even realized how on edge I was, how paranoid this affair had left me.

"Mr. Nordvelt," Greigor said, his tone light – disingenuously so if his expression was anything to go by. "What brings you here?"

I straightened slowly. "I came to see Maggie."

He nodded. "She'll be in her office. Far corner."

Before I could reply, he'd stalked past me in the direction he'd indicated with his eyes. I hesitated before following, unsure if he was leading me or not. I didn't try to keep up – I let him pull away a little, in fact. I wasn't sure of much, but I knew I had little inclination to talk to him – not before I'd found out more about his background and why de Villiers had seen fit to issue him a reprimand.

Around me the vegetation still amazed. I encountered two more of the little gardening machines before I came across the professor.

"Making the Antarctic green?" I said by way of a greeting. Greigor was a few dozen paces away, pretending to study some kind of shrub.

Maggie smiled and wiped her hands on her already-besmirched lab coat. "Anders, hello! Welcome to the future of Antarctica! Are you here for the tour?"

"Just looking around, thank you." I wanted to smile back, but Greigor's presence was a sour note in the air.

"You're welcome here anytime, you know," she said. "I spend a lot of time here, just me and Greigor and my little machines, so I always like to have visitors."

"I need to ask you a few questions, I'm afraid."

"Come on, let's go to my office. We'll have a coffee and a chat."

"I'd rather see where you grow the marijuana," I countered, a little sharper than I'd intended. I didn't dare look to see Greigor's reaction.

Maggie froze for a moment before turning to face me properly. She gave a rueful smile. "How did you find out?"

I shrugged. "How else can you obtain drugs in a place like this?"

"I'll show you the plants, of course. And it's hemp, by the way, not marijuana. Officially, at least. I confess I've tried to subtly 'up' the recreational characteristics of the strain. But are you sure you wouldn't like a chat first?"

I couldn't see why it'd make a difference.

Her 'office', as she called it, was half cozy academic's lounge and half laboratory. It was contained wholly within the greenhouse, and resembled it in some ways. Planters again ran down the center of the room. The main difference was that the lab also had places to work, with benches, esoteric equipment and a fume cupboard at one end. The planters were all filled with growth – some tiny seedlets, one a great bush that was threatening to spill out of its container. I wandered along the row and there, tucked away half-hidden at the back, was a single specimen: a leafy plant that had the typical fingered leaves of the cannabis plant. Both leaves and stem were so dark a green as to be near-black. The veins across the leaves were much, much paler and almost glowed under the ultraviolet light that had been set up over it.

I bent forward to look at it in more detail. A great, heady smell of marijuana rose from it. I reached out to stroke a leaf.

"Don't touch that!" Maggie snapped.

I pulled my hand back as if burned, and looked round at her in surprise.

"Sorry, didn't mean to shout. That's a new strain, Greigor's research project – nothing to do with what you came here for. The stem is very fibrous, good for fabrics – but he's transfected genes from the nightshade plant to build on that. It's poisonous."

"Poisonous?"

She nodded. "Very. That's not the crop we smoke, believe me. That's the thing with genetic splicing – you're never quite sure how it's going to come out. Touching it wouldn't have done you any harm, but you might have damaged the plant. It's the only healthy example of that particular variety."

"You didn't make much attempt to hide it from me," I muttered as I crossed back to her.

"Why should I? I told you, this is serious work. Could clothe the world, this stuff. We're fully authorized to do this – the world needs fabrics as much as it needs power."

"But if it's poisonous—"

"Poisonous, yes – not venomous. But you're right, we need to work out how to process the fibers so they're safe. That's a later phase."

"Why this combination? Why—"

"Because they work. They produce something that's tough, durable and flexible. That's science."

"You care a lot for your research."

"It's my life. Come and sit down, Anders. I'll put the kettle on."

The lounge part of the room was walled with books and papers, making it look somewhat archaic. Several large whiteboards were filled with Chinese characters, Greek symbols and acronyms. None of it meant anything to me.

I glanced at the books while Maggie made drinks in her old-style combi-maker. Most were academic works – serious, heavy tomes: *Biodiversity and Growth; Structural Cell Design; A Casebook of Human Brain Analysis…* There were monographs and journals and unbound printouts on many subjects, all impenetrable.

"Why bring all these?" I asked. "Surely you can get all the info on the base computer?"

Maggie paused in pouring the drinks and looked round at me. "Mm? Well…no good reason, I suppose. I like books. It's as simple as that, really. I just like the tactile experience of holding a book. I guess I'm old-fashioned." She smiled at me and finished pouring the drinks. I thought of my own book in my quarters. There was something about the object that transcended the words inside. Yes, I understood that.

Rather than sitting at her desk she invited me to take a battered old easy chair, one of two that faced each other, a coffee table between. She moved a book that was on her chair, and sat. Even in that low seat, her feet barely reached the floor. She set down the drinks and smiled at me pleasantly. "It was a fight to get de Villiers to allow me to bring the books, but just having them here makes me feel a little more at home – do you understand?"

"You know hypnosis?"

"What? Oh, this?" She looked at the book in her hand as if she'd not seen it before: *Hypnosis for Beginners*. There was a note of self-mockery in her laugh. "A hobby, that's all. Good for breaking the ice at parties, you know? Don't worry, I won't make you do anything you don't want to." She laughed again.

We sat in silence for a moment. Greigor had not followed us, to my mild surprise, and only the low hum of the climate control could be heard.

Maggie leaned forward to take her mug, cradling it to her chest. "Well, now you've found out about the weed, what are you going to do?" she asked, serious again.

"How many people here are users?" I said instead of answering. This woman had a way of unsettling me, of disrupting my thoughts, without apparent effort.

"About half the crew. Some are regulars, some just like the occasional joint."

"Do you not feel bad about what you're doing?"

"No. Not at all. Why should I?"

I wasn't sure how to react to that challenge. Drugs were forbidden by Company statute. That was the end of it, wasn't it? I frowned and tried to redirect the conversation. "What do you get out of it? How much do they pay you?"

Maggie almost spilled her coffee as she laughed. "My God, Anders, is that how you're thinking? No wonder you look so serious. This is just an informal arrangement between friends, colleagues. I don't get anything in return, save for a bit of company, some smoke for myself and some grateful friends. Besides, hemp does well in hydroponic conditions. It could become a major crop – it's a very useful substance, you know. It can be refined to produce textiles, paper, even fuel oils. My brief is to *research*, as well as to grow. The Company knew I was bringing seeds to work on."

"But not to grow to smoke with the crew."

"No. You've got me there."

"How did that come about?"

"I'm not a pusher, Anders. I discuss my work with the rest of the crew, and I mentioned that I was having good results with my trials on hemp. Later, I was talking with others and one of them – I won't name names – asked if I had anything we could smoke. I think it surprised them when I said I could get some."

"And since then you've been supplying the base."

"You're determined to make this sound sordid, aren't you? I've already told you – I don't supply, I share with friends."

I sipped my coffee, not quite sure what to say.

"Have you never smoked, Anders?"

"No."

"You should try it."

"Thank you, no."

"Listen, I know it's hard for you." The smile had gone from her lips, her expression serious – but not unfriendly. "You're new here, and you've walked straight into a nest of vipers. There's been sabotage and a death, and you must be feeling the pressure. No friends…"

I wondered if she was mocking me, pointing out my deficiencies, divining my fears. But I could see only concern in her eyes, her wrinkled brow.

"…and enough people who think you must be responsible for the…uncertainties. But you've got to understand – de Villiers knew all of what went on here. He wasn't an idiot. The Company chose well when they appointed him to Australis. He knew how to get the job done, and how to keep the crew sane. He allowed us our habits, our indulgences, because we work better with them. De Villiers allowed it and he was nothing if not a Company man. Believe me, we had arguments about that—"

"You argued about the Company?"

"Friendly ones, debates more than—"

"What did you disagree about?"

Maggie sighed and shook her head. "Look, the basic fact is that about a third of the people here think the sun shines out of the Company's arse. Another third wants a return to nation states. The other lot don't give a shit as long as they get fed and get paid." She shrugged and took a sip of coffee.

"What's to dislike about the Company? They've given us so much, rescued us from the chaos of the Resource Wars…"

I trailed off in the teeth of her expression; amused, condescending – it was a trick for a woman as short as Maggie to look down on anyone, but she managed it without apparent effort.

"Do you really think it's a good thing that the biggest threat in this world is demotion? That 'breach of contract' is a bigger fear than the police?" she said.

"That's—"

"Have you actually read your contract? You know what you've signed up for? Has anyone? They've got you by the balls as soon as you take your first job – and then you're in the system for the rest of your life. 'No activities contrary to Company interests' – you think that's not a catchall for just about anything? Read that section of your contract, Anders – see all the things you can't do. We live in a giant bureaucracy, no room for any dissenting voices—" She bit off her words and gave me a rueful smile. "Sorry. As you can see, it's something…I could spend a lot more time on the subject, let's just say that."

I sat back in my chair, uncomfortable. I wanted to argue, wanted to make her see the ways in which she was wrong – but I didn't even know how to begin.

The tone of her voice, the bored certainty of the words, as if she was saying something indisputable that she'd had to go through too many times before – it took me straight back to my father. The barely remembered days all merging together, just the image of myself as a young child, still unsteady on my feet, hearing him lecture to a blur of other people.

I shook myself back to the present day.

"Who else shares these…opinions?"

"You want to know the battle lines?" She was watching me intently. I'd made it too clear that I wasn't on her side. "Fergie and Abi were my allies. Greigor and Weng – at first, when she still talked – took de Villiers's side."

"De Villiers backed the Company and yet overlooked your… breaches of contract?"

"The Company isn't as pure and holy as you seem to think. De Villiers fit in their system very well. Look, in a place like this, boredom is a much greater danger than…our little peccadilloes. If anything ever got out of hand, you knew he'd be right there to put a stop to it."

I stared at her, my disapproval all too obvious.

She shook her head. "I'm sorry. I'm sorry, but I'm not sure you can understand. You've obviously not mixed with the right sort of people."

"I was brought up in the blocks."

"Which is why your ignorance is such a surprise."

I flushed, just beginning to lose my temper.

She held up her hands. "I don't mean that as an insult. I'm sorry. You see…" She leaned forward and looked at me earnestly. "Everyone here is an expert. Everyone knows enough to stay in control. No one smokes or drinks during their work shifts. Don't underestimate us, Anders. You weren't here at the start. De Villiers's way works."

"Did McCarthy share this opinion?" I asked, sarcasm edging my tone.

"No. But he didn't put a stop to it either."

"Did de Villiers smoke?"

"He preferred to drink."

"Is that his still in the basement?"

Maggie blinked. "Oh, so you've been down to the basement, have you? Yes, that was Anton's. As I said, he liked a drink. Whisky, mostly."

I nodded. "Why would you say McCarthy left?"

She paused before replying, looking at me with her head cocked to one side and a faint smile on her lips. "A combination of ill-health and a personality clash with— well, most of us, really. But the commander in particular."

I nodded, inwardly disappointed not to get anything new about McCarthy's departure. I'd felt sure there must have been more to it than that, but maybe it was time to let that lie. Everyone was telling me the same thing, and a vague hunch was all I'd ever had to go on. "Back to de Villiers – do you know why anyone would want to kill him?"

Maggie sighed. "I know he wasn't always popular. Weng hated him, poor thing, but she wouldn't kill him. Violence isn't her way."

"Anyone else? Did he get into arguments with anyone else on the crew?"

"I told you, we argued all the time, all of us – that's what happens when you get a group like us all together in these conditions. Remember, Anders – we've been here a long time already. It's isolated, it's claustrophobic. Sometimes arguments come out of nothing but the pressure of the conditions. We can't just go and unwind with our friends. We can't go for a walk, not easily. You're either alone or surrounded. No middle ground."

"And you can't think of anyone except Weng who might have had reason to kill him?"

"I'm sure Weng didn't do it."

"If not Weng, then who?"

"Look, I've told you – we all argued."

"No one more than anyone else?"

She shrugged and glanced away momentarily. "Well, Julia…. She argued with him constantly."

"What about?"

She shifted in her seat.

"They were having an affair," I said.

"There's not much else to do here," she said as if that explained everything.

"So what did they argue about?"

She shrugged again. "Pretty much everything. They're – they were, Fischer still is – volatile people. Neither of them suffers fools gladly; neither is afraid to speak their mind."

Volatile people. I thought back to Fischer's reaction in the infirmary, when she'd been unable to deny de Villiers's death anymore. Could that've been an act? A killer's cabaret? I could see Fischer becoming violent, could imagine her rage. The question was whether she'd be the type of person to sabotage her lover's suit and leave him to freeze alone in the dark.

I changed the subject. "What about Greigor?"

"What about him?"

"There is a record…a note on de Villiers's compscreen. The commander disciplined him."

Maggie frowned. "I didn't know about that."

"Care to speculate?"

She pouted. "Not really. But you won't accept that, will you? Greigor is…he can be difficult. A smart boy, really an excellent assistant. But he is…"

"Yes?"

"The effects of isolation are hard to predict. You think the Psych is perfect? Ha, I can tell you stories – oh, don't pull that face, Anders."

"What face?"

"The 'she's committing heresy again' look. God, you really think that a relatively new science doesn't ever get things wrong? Oh, my boy, you don't—" She stopped herself and held up her hands in a gesture of surrender. "Greigor is oversexed. There are – have been – a lot of petty jealousies over the last few months. I'd guess de Villiers spoke to him about something like that."

"More specifically?"

She hesitated. "Greigor sees men as rivals and women as targets. Not me, of course, or Fischer. We're too old for him. And that's probably why I personally have no problem with him."

"So Max and Weng…"

"I'd guess that de Villiers spoke to Greigor about one of them."

★   ★   ★

I shivered as I stepped away from the building, back into the courtyard. Above me stars were shining clearly; away from the artificial illumination of Australis the sky was beautiful. I saw nebulae and galaxies, and I was small.

A wind blew across the courtyard like the exhalation of giants. Ahead of me the smelting plant growled in its work. On the hillside, coal was flowing down the conveyors from the minehead to the sheds.

I made my way back to the barracks. I was tired, and I had things to do before dinner. I headed straight down to the basement to get a selection of the surveillance equipment I'd seen earlier. I wanted to see what a few cameras independent of the security system might tell me.

★   ★   ★

The meal was a subdued affair, with an empty chair at the head of the table. I suppose Fergie could legitimately have taken the commander's place, but there was no question of that happening. He stayed with the engineers, and it was that group that brought what cheer there was to the room.

Fergie was the one who called openly for wine, the real Australis rotgut, leading a barely observed toast to de Villiers. It seemed that I had turned enough of a blind eye to all the rule-breaking for them to drink in my presence. Keegan told us there'd be a gathering for the commander the next night.

I didn't have any alcohol. I felt too tired to sacrifice any more of my faculties. At my end of the table it was only Keegan who drank, and only he who really spoke.

Fischer was back with us, healing pack wrapped tightly around her head: half headband, half turban. She was quiet, just eating methodically and barely looking up from her plate.

Weng was, as ever, silent. Occasionally I caught her glancing up at me with something like fear in her eyes. It must have taken a lot out of her to open up about de Villiers. I guessed she was wondering what I might do with the knowledge.

Fergie was still shooting me suspicious glances from halfway down the table. I caught Dmitri glancing at me as well. I wondered what he was thinking – did he suspect me of the killing as well? At least any hostility was masked; all in all, the crew seemed to be coping well with the shocks of the last few days.

After the meal had finished, as the crew stood for some downtime, I tried to draw Fischer aside, to take her into a side room and ask some much-needed questions. But Weng was watching. As Fischer looked at me with confused eyes, Weng stepped between us.

"The doctor is not yet fit for an interview," she said. She spoke loudly, voice echoing off the metal walls.

I could feel the eyes of the rest of the crew upon me. "I need—"

"I say again – the doctor is not yet fit to be interviewed." The fear had gone from Weng's eyes; she was in her bailiwick here. "She has had a severe concussion. It is my professional opinion that she is unfit to be interviewed. You have no authority to overrule me."

"There is information," I began. "There are things I need to know—"

"Why don't you just back off, Nordvelt?" Greigor snapped, his accent making even harshness seem somehow seductive. "You've done enough, just let the damn woman recover."

There were murmurs of agreement all around – not one word of support for me.

"Seriously, I really need— there are things I have to know," I tried.

Over Weng's head I saw Theo draw Fischer away, shooting me a dark look as he urged the doctor into the corridor.

"Not tonight," Weng said. "Possibly not tomorrow. I will let you know when she is ready to talk."

I looked around. A kind of solidarity appeared to have grown around the crew. No one, not a single one of them spoke up for me or even gave me a look of silent support. No doubt who was in and who was out.

One by one they trailed past me and out. I overheard someone suggesting that they all go watch a film or do somesuch as a group. Finally I was left alone with Weng.

We stared at each other in silence before she too turned and headed towards the rec room.

They all went through together. I didn't join them.

CHAPTER TWELVE

My dreams were labyrinthine: de Villiers, laughing at me, hacking into the base computers. Then it was Max. Then both were dead, their faces distorted in rictus – and still they laughed at me. I tried to flee but I was trapped in a maze, watched, always watched…

"What do you think?"

Strapped to a gurney, imprisoned and yet oddly calm…just an all-consuming light in my eyes…voices both near and distant and all around me…

"Should be straightforward," a woman said. "Preliminary results—"

A pain in my brow, a sense of pressure…

I woke with the taste of crude oil in my mouth, an iron dryness in my throat. I was glad to be awake, to wipe the sweat off my face.

I didn't feel rested. I felt thin, like I was fading away. Tonight we were to gather to pay tribute to the commander. I wasn't sure I could cope with that.

I got up and had a long shower. I was just walking up to a late breakfast when the barracks seemed to rock. I lost my footing, staggered against the wall. The shock wave lasted barely a second, and for a moment I was unsure if anything had actually happened. A sudden attack of vertigo? The corridor was unchanged. Nothing was shaking, for there was nothing *to* shake. Only me.

Then the door to the canteen opened and Abi looked out. He seemed as bewildered as I felt, and as I met his eyes, I realized that something bad, something serious, really had happened.

My breath became suddenly shallow, my mind blank. Oh, God, where was my training? Panic – I knew that feeling. I knew how to deal with it. Control the breathing. Clear emotions. Focus.

"Check the building," I called to Abi. My voice cracked, overloud in the silence; I cleared my throat. "See if there's any damage, and find out who's here. Ask Weng if she knows what happened."

Abi nodded. "What about you?"

"I'm going outside."

I ran off to the vestibule and threw on my suit. I was out in the darkness before I'd got my mask on properly; the cold hit hard.

The floodlights mounted on each of the buildings illuminated the courtyard well enough but I couldn't see any damage. Garage, coal shed, iron storage, oil tanks – all looked normal. I ran towards Maggie's greenhouse. A few of the glass panes had cracked and I could see some of the lights had failed. The outer door opened as I approached, and a figure stepped out onto the ice – Maggie herself.

"Maggie, are you okay?" I shouted.

She didn't answer, just pointed somewhere towards the south.

I tried to follow her gaze. I didn't see anything at first, but as I got closer to her, I passed the roll in the ground that had been blocking my sight. A flickering red light.

"The oil well," Maggie breathed.

It wasn't too far away – just a few kilometers distant. But I shouldn't have been able to see anything on a normal Australis morning.

"It's on fire," I said numbly.

"It exploded," Maggie corrected.

★　　★　　★

This was now a rescue attempt; Theo and Mikhail had both been working the drills. I sent Maggie running to the barracks to fetch Fischer and the rest of the crew before I raced to the garage and, after a moment's hesitation, chose the 4x4. I ran my finger across the bioreader to get the engine going and was immediately blinded by the glare of the four massive headlamps. The vehicle jumped forward as I fought with the controls.

I wasn't so panicked as to rush straight to the fire: I needed help, and that help was to be found at the minehead. Even if they weren't experts in drilling, Fergie and Dmitri were engineers – they'd know what to do. I'd pick them up in the 4x4 and get to the oil platform as fast as possible.

I was not a good driver. I'd driven these things as part of my training, but never in such a panic. I hurtled over bumps, barely seeing dips and bends in my haste to get up the steep slope to the mine. I ran straight over the revealed section of the radio mast that Max had been excavating at the site of the comms building. Soon I found the conveyor that carried the coal to the storage sheds, and used it to guide me upwards. It was as wide as a road, and a track had already formed beside it.

The mine was nothing like the barracks, or the hydroponics, or anything I'd seen around the courtyard. There was no airlock or vestibule; all there was on ground level was a small control room and a lift shaft. No one there. But on the wall there was a large electronic map of the underground workings. Red lights were flashing, and my stomach began to fill with cold dread.

I grabbed the intercom and jabbed at the buttons but nobody answered. I hesitated, uncertain. Should I go down? Would I just be wasting time? Impatiently I called again.

I was just about to leave when a voice crackled up to me. "Who's that?"

"Max? It's Anders. We've—"

"Anders! We've had a collapse – Fergie's hurt."

I swore, very loudly. "How bad is it? What can I do?"

"Head injury. We need to get him to the doctor. We need you down here!"

I hesitated again, torn between the conflagration at the platform and the need to assist Fergie. "I'm on my way."

"Fourth level, corridor two."

I checked the plans to make sure I could get to them without getting lost, then grabbed a torch from a rack. I ran to the lift, praying that it was still working, that the cable wouldn't snap....

The mechanism ran perfectly. I paced the tiny space, doubting all the way into the depths. For all I knew, Mikhail and Theo needed me urgently – they could have received a lot more than just a concussion.

The elevator thumped heavily to the bottom of the shaft. Too late to worry now; I had to get this done as soon as I could. I hauled open the doors and shone my torch around. It was then that I realized that the plan I'd looked at upstairs was a massive oversimplification. Just stepping into the tunnels was to lose your sense of direction.

The walls were rough-hewn from dark rock, while the floors had been leveled carefully. Rails led both left and right, with a junction in front of the lift. Cabling ran along the walls, and lights hung every ten or so meters. They illuminated a sign: *Corridor One*, with an arrow, and *Corridor Two* in the other direction. Beneath these official notices, someone had added two handwritten direction signs. *Waverley* one way, *Haymarket* the other. A little touch of Scots humor.

I hurried down Haymarket.

It stretched only a few hundred meters, and I began to hear voices above the echoing of my feet. I skipped past a row of trucks before the track ended abruptly in a mass of heavy machinery. I was at the coal face, and had to squeeze to the side to pass the seam's main excavator.

In a shifting pool of torchlight – no wall lights here – I found two figures in their warmsuits wading through rubble and wrenching up steel bars to form a rudimentary lattice against walls and ceiling. They worked quickly, talking almost in code as one held a beam in position while the other lashed some kind of bracing pad onto the end. Behind them a third figure sat on the floor, leaning against a wall. He was half-pinned beneath some sort of metal spider, all legs and angles. Drill bits waved feebly from several of its limbs, and it whined almost piteously. All of the miners were wearing hard hats and I suddenly felt terribly conscious of the millions of tons of rock above me.

"Anders? Anders, we need to get Fergie out of here – before we have another fall!" The figure to the left of the pair had turned her head to look at me, and I knew Max's voice. So it must be Dmitri on the right, and Fergie on the floor.

"What happened here?"

"Earthshock," Dmitri replied, not pausing in his work. "Damn earthshock brought down the ceiling."

"It brought the precursor drill down on Fergie," Max added, not turning from her work. A dustfall drifted over us.

"Are you okay?" I asked, taking a few paces forward to crouch by the Scotsman – but not too close to be threatened by the horribly alive-looking spider-machine.

He looked up at me. "I hurt like a fucker," he grumbled. "At least I were knocked back, didnae get buried. Me hat protected what little brains I have." He was slurring but at least he was making sense.

"Get him to the infirmary," Max said. "We've got to shore up—"

"No time. There's been an explosion."

"*What?*"

"A little quieter, if ye don't mind," Fergie muttered to the floor.

"The oil platform – it's on fire. I was coming to get you – Mikhail and Theo, they were out there—"

"My God," Max gasped.

"Forget about that," I said. "A collapse—"

"A collapse is just a delay, jus' money," Fergie said. "An explosion's people's lives."

Dmitri threw down his plank and crossed to Fergie. With easy confidence he rolled the spider off the man's legs, and together we scraped away some of the debris to let Fergie stand. I helped get him up, and the three of us together started back down the corridor, Max close behind.

"Nice to have an explanation for the earthshock, at least," Dmitri said.

I nodded. We hurried back to the lift shaft.

★   ★   ★

The sky was clear, and on another day, to be hurtling through the moonlight in the 4x4 would've been a pleasure. But we sat in grim silence. All of us could see the fire stabbing its fingers upwards as we approached – and soon we could hear it growling, almost like a tribal chant with its odd percussive bellows, as smoke billowed up to obscure the stars.

A group had gathered by a bunch of half-tracks, well away from the metal platform that formed the base for the huge rig. Steel flashed red and black as the flame eddied. For a moment I dared to hope that both Mikhail and Theo were fine. We raced the last few hundred meters to them, then skidded to a halt. Max and Dmitri leaped out; I told Fergie to stay in the vehicle, but he insisted on clambering out.

"Never mind that now. What're we going to do?" Keegan was saying.

"Is everyone accounted for?" Max asked.

"No word from Theo or Mikhail."

A massive spike of flame was roaring up from the heart of the platform. Heavy black smoke writhed around the structure, always shifting and rising but somehow never clearing from the metalwork.

"Where's the rescue gear kept?"

"You can't go in there!"

"What's the emergency procedure?"

Too many people talking at once. "We don't have time for this," I snapped, and everyone immediately fell silent; the mistrust the crew felt towards me had been swallowed by the emergency. "Fischer – where's Fischer?"

"Still in barracks. She's not fit to be out here," Weng said.

"You, then – Fergie's been hurt, have a look at him. The rest of you—" I paused. "Max, Dmitri – you're the engineers. We need to get the fire out and find the others. How do we do it?"

"We have to go in before the fire goes out," Dmitri said tersely.

"Why?"

"We put the fire out easily – blow up the rig and all the oxygen is gone. The rig was built with explosives ready. But no oxygen, no survivors."

"So we have to go in."

He nodded; tense, professional, steady.

"Will our warmsuits protect us?"

"No way in hell, but there's special protective gear – coldsuits – on the platform. They'll keep us alive."

"Okay. The two of you – with me."

"Hang on," Max interrupted. "We need to close off the pipes that link the rig to the rest of the base. Otherwise there's a chance – if anything goes wrong – that the heat could split them and oxygenate the crude. If that happens, we're all fucked."

"But the chance of it chaining back to base is—" Dmitri started before Max cut him off.

"Microscopic. But do you want to take the risk?"

Fergie staggered away from Weng. He had his mask off, breath white in the torchlight. "I take it you're not gonna to let me go in there?" he growled.

"No," Weng said sharply.

"No," echoed Max.

"Then I'll deal with the pipes. Someone come with me, in case I do somethin' stupid like black out."

"I'll go," Weng said.

"No," Maggie countered. "You need to stay. If Theo or Mikhail are hurt you'll be needed here. I'll go with Fergie." She and the miner hurried to a half-track and disappeared towards the base.

On the rig, a gantry gave an agonized squeal and fell away from its moorings. It disappeared into the heart of the fire, and an arm of flame billowed outwards.

"Looks—" Max's voice broke and she gave a nervous laugh. "Looks a bit hot."

"Well, they say a change is as good as a rest." I shrugged and, not giving myself any chance to reconsider, set out for the rig.

★   ★   ★

The flames filled my world: there was just fire and the black silhouettes of objects in front of it. I felt hypnotized, couldn't look away. My warmsuit was struggling. Adjusting to the heat, it gradually shut down the level of warmth it provided. But it couldn't provide cooling. Once the threshold had been passed, the electronics in my suit just failed, and then the temperature rose sharply as we advanced. My sweat provided an added layer of discomfort. I looked to Max, then to Dmitri. We walked side by side, straight towards the platform, towards the main access center. Like gunslingers heading for the big showdown.

"Where'll they be?" I asked, shouting over the roar of the flame and the screaming of metal.

"Main control room, I hope." Dmitri's tone was grim.

"Where's that?"

"Middle."

Figured. "Do either of you have a plan?"

We were rapidly approaching the platform, where Theo and Mikhail had parked their half-track. Smoke was rising from its seat. There was no escaping the heat now. We paused. As it was doing little more than keeping the sweat trapped uncomfortably against my skin, I unclipped my mask.

"Best keep it on," Max cautioned. "Your sweat's all that'll stop you baking."

It might've been an illusion, but it looked as if the steel of the platform itself was beginning to melt, to buckle. It was a certainty that we couldn't walk in unprotected. "So where are the coldsuits?" I yelled.

"Emergency shelter – can you see it through the smoke? We've got to get there."

Nothing distinguished the shelter from anything else on the rig; it was just another metal shed, dark and dull against the violence of the inferno. About fifty yards away.

"You're sure that's the right building?" I asked.

Dmitri nodded.

"We'll have to run," Max said. "We get there as fast as possible, get inside, and get the door shut. We should be okay when it's sealed."

"Why are you not filling me with confidence?" I muttered. "Ready?"

We all shared looks, nods, and then we ran.

It was like swimming through treacle; time seemed to slow as the three of us sprinted towards the hut. There was a crackling in my ear as the electronics in my mask began to short out. I coughed as the air filters failed, and the taste of burning petroleum and the spit of melting steel began to fill my chest. A crash right beside me made me spin around, but I could see nothing – the earpieces of my mask playing tricks, I realized, as I saw a girder fall to the ground twenty feet away. It landed in silence, it seemed, before a sudden *crump* came three seconds later.

I tried to keep my companions in view but my eyes were watering badly and it was hard enough to stay on course. I kept seeing strange movements, blurred and disorientated, in my peripheral vision, and I prayed it was them; the last thing I wanted was to be alone right now. I felt a sharp pain over my left eye; a piece of burning scrap had burned right through my mask. I brushed it aside, then screamed as a red-hot splinter burrowed into my hand.

I threw myself against the hut, gasping for breath; sensory overload blanked my mind for a moment, and I wasn't sure where I was, why I was here. Then Max's slight figure slammed into the wall next to me, and then Dmitri was at the door, and then one by one we fell inside.

The Ukrainian shoved the door closed behind me; I fell against a wall, the smell of burning plastics still strong in my nostrils. It was suddenly, shockingly cold. Max snapped off her mask and threw it to the floor as it smoked and sparked dangerously.

"Damn," Dmitri said once his mask was off as well. "Hoped they'd be here."

I looked around. I tried to remove my mask as well, but the fastenings had melted shut. My forehead hurt terribly, my hand worse. I tried to push the pain from my mind.

Dmitri had called the structure a hut but it was built like a bunker. It was a bare place where workers could survive even a major blast and wait for help. There was a rack of coldsuits – heavy, clumsy, heat-repellent gear – as well as first aid kits, bottles of fresh water and an emergency radio.

"All okay?" Max asked. Then, without waiting for an answer, she strode to the nearest coldsuit and hauled it off the rack. Dmitri followed, and both began to pull them on over their warmsuits.

I dragged myself over and followed their example, the helmet going straight over my still-masked head. I shook tears from my eyes. Vision began to sharpen again.

"Okay," Max said as she checked first Dmitri, then me, to make sure we were properly insulated. "We go…control room. Dmitri… lead as we know…Anders. Rem…doesn't…debris." Her voice kept cutting in and out, my ears full of static. "We…control room and we…safe…. We get…others…again."

No time to get her to repeat, no time to think. Back to the entrance. Dmitri glanced at us both. He threw open the door.

We couldn't run in these new suits. We walked into the heart of a fire that I could see but neither feel nor hear. Surreal. Destruction lay all around me – shattered barrels, twisted, unidentifiable shards of scrap, burning piles of litter. The only thing I could smell was the acrid stench of my heat-damaged mask; the only things I could feel were sweat and pain. Sounds weren't coming from their sources, the static crackle indistinguishable from the burning around me. I followed the others as close as I could. They led me between pipes that were either bubbling or smoking, I couldn't tell, and soon I could see the jet of flame erupting from the very center of the metal platform that supported the bulk of the above-ground facility. Then we were under part of the superstructure and facing the door to the control room. It was blocked by a pile of blazing debris.

Grimly we walked on – and then both Max and Dmitri stopped and the ground shook violently. I staggered and, massively delayed, there came an awful screaming of metal and a crash that must have been the cause of the shock wave that was still rattling through me. The towers trembled and debris rained down like a deadly swarm of fireflies.

Onwards. We fought, dragged and climbed our way past the blockage, but the control room door had warped and wouldn't open.

Dmitri threw himself against the thick barrier, then he and I took turns. Eventually, on the fourth attempt, it gave and I fell inside.

The others were with me in a heartbeat. We had made it into another refuge, another safe room. It was too hot, though – something had failed. The door, of course – it wouldn't seal now we'd broken through. Dmitri realized at the same moment as I did; he leaned back against it, trying to hold it closed with his body weight. The blazing currents from the fire kept trying to force themselves in. The big man snarled and turned to brace it properly.

A man lay face down on the floor: a nightmare figure, his back horribly blistered, the texture of his suit burned into strange patterns on his legs. His hair had shriveled away, his scalp black. Max hurried over to him as I clambered to my feet.

It was Mikhail. His head flopped to the side, his face streaked with tears. He gave a pained grin and said something to Max that I didn't catch. He was alive. He was conscious. I could hear nothing but static now, but I knew what to do. I grabbed the standard-issue medikit from the wall and scrambled over, snapped the box open and spun it round to Max. She drew out a green-tipped autoinjector and stuck Mikhail in the neck. Then a second – and we'd barely been in the room for twenty seconds. Then Max pointed to a rack of coldsuits and I went to drag one over.

Getting him into it was a nightmare. He couldn't move below his waist. I prayed for him to pass out, for though Max had undoubtedly used a painkiller, his mouth still twisted and retched in agony at every touch. But we had to lift him, to twist and bend his body to get him suited. Without it he was dead. Dmitri couldn't help. It was a constant battle to keep that door shut – already the plastics in the room were smoking from the heat.

Eventually we had Mikhail dressed, the helmet firmly attached to the body. Now we just had to get him out. He couldn't walk. Dmitri and I took him between us, doing our best not to hold him too tight. I was grateful, then, that my mask was broken. I didn't have to listen to his screams.

Finally – too soon – we were ready. Max took a deep breath and pulled open the control room door. The inferno bellowed over us again.

CHAPTER THIRTEEN

I was freezing cold. Then I was boiling in my own skin. I couldn't move; pain roared whenever I tried to turn my head. I gasped as full consciousness suddenly burst through me.

I was in an unfamiliar bed, my vision blocked by curtains on all sides. The infirmary. I tried to get up, to swing my legs round, but my only reward was another shot of pain. I was sweating and shivering alternately.

I tried to remember how I'd got here, and instantly felt my memories swell up: the oil fire. The fire, and then getting Mikhail away. God, Mikhail – how was he? Was he in this room with me? And Theo—

I remembered how the rig had blown as I was being driven back to barracks. Keegan was driving, me by his side, while Weng cared for Mikhail in the back. She'd given him another sedative and finally he was free from pain. The explosion came when we were almost halfway home. Max and Dmitri had done as they promised – they'd extinguished the flames, and now there was only smoking rubble.

Theo was dead. Must've been dead. If he hadn't made it to either of the refuges, then he was dead. The knowledge, the memory, left me numb, an overload of horror blocking feeling.

And I'd been driven home, deafened by the broken mask and freezing in a malfunctioning suit. Lord knew how I'd managed to help Keegan and Weng carry Mikhail into the corridors…

Then I'd blacked out.

I coughed, once, and then was overwhelmed by a great fit. I could taste smoke in my mouth, and when I turned my head my vomit was black. Couldn't even lean to puke on the floor; a dark viscous stain spread next to me on the pillow. I groaned and turned my head back. My lungs felt like they were wrapped in plastic. At least they'd got that bloody mask off me. I felt myself slipping back into sleep, static filling my mind.

Footsteps. I opened my eyes and saw the curtain twitch open. It was Fischer in her white coat, the wound-pad around her head much smaller than it'd been before, more like a fashion statement than a bandage. For a moment I quailed, fearing retribution for the hurt I'd done to her. But she was smiling. A weak smile, to be sure, but a smile nonetheless.

"You're awake sooner than I expected," she said. She came further in to take my wrist and feel for my pulse.

My throat was raw, the taste of vomit still thick. "How's Mikhail?" I croaked.

Fischer gently lifted my head and slipped the pillow out. She dropped it on the floor and pushed a clean one in its place. "He should survive," she said. "Weng did a good job whilst I was out of action. How are you?" She lifted my eyelid and stared carefully at my pupils. "I'll be back in a second."

I was breathing heavily, as if I'd just done a double session in the gym. I let my eyes roll closed. I felt utterly drained; I could barely focus on the doctor when she returned. She was carrying a hypodermic, tapping the needle as she came to my side.

"The…the others?" I panted as she lifted my arm, stuck me and depressed the plunger.

I breathed deeply, the pain receding to an itch, a shadow in my mind. My vision swam for a moment as Fischer opened the curtains. I felt bandages and patches covering my face, my wrist and shins – other places too. A drip had been driven into my forearm. I groaned and tried to sit up a little.

There were four beds in the small ward, and all were occupied. Facing me across the room was Dmitri. The big man was sitting on the side of his bed, talking to Max on the cot next to him. Mikhail was in the bed next to mine; he appeared to be unconscious, most of his body bandaged.

"Anders," Dmitri said. "How are you feeling?"

I didn't know how to answer – didn't know how I should be feeling. My throat still felt stripped, and I was so, so thirsty. My head began to thump and I let it fall back on the pillow. "How did I get here? What happened after…?"

Max and Dmitri shared a glance. "Do you not remember?" he asked, concerned.

"I remember the fire, dragging Mikhail out…after that things are hazy." I paused. "Are you okay?"

"We're fine," Max said. "We're just—"

"Max and Dmitri are just here for a checkup and some minor burns treatment," Fischer said. "You and Mikhail aren't so good."

"Me? What's wrong?"

"Calm down, Anders," Dmitri said. "You got burned, is all. You'll be fine."

"He got burns and pneumonia," Fischer corrected sharply. "Why didn't you *say* your mask and suit were fried by the heat? We could've got you treated quicker. Cooked on one side, frozen on the other, raw in the middle. Idiot." She gave me a smile to leaven her words, but she was still in clinical mode. "You've been very ill – you've slept for most of the last three days."

I groaned. No wonder I felt so disconnected. "Mikhail – how is he?" I couldn't summon the energy to look at the bed next to me, just closed my eyes.

Fischer's voice came from the other side of the sickroom – she must have gone to check on the engineers. "He suffered severe burns," she said. "Rehabilitation will take a long time, but he's out of danger for the time being."

And what kind of life will he have? I couldn't bring myself to ask the question. Instead I opened my eyes again and watched Fischer ministering to Max. I coughed. "Do we know what caused the fire?" I asked.

Dmitri looked at Max, and both looked to Fischer, before the Ukrainian answered. "Explosive on timer," the big man said in little more than a whisper. "Mikhail – he said…said Theo saw something strapped to base of the drill. He went to check and it blew up."

"He would have died instantly," Max said, and the way she looked away told me she was trying to reassure herself as much as she was me.

"Was the body recovered?" I asked.

"Burned to ash." There was silence before she continued. "Mikhail was slammed back against the superstructure by the force of the explosion. But he managed to crawl back to the control room, even with cracked vertebrae. Dragged himself by his fingertips. He was lucky the control room door opened for him."

I looked again at the figure in the bed next to me, unable to find any words.

"We're gonna..." Max trailed off, swallowed. "We're gonna be in trouble, Anders. The Company – the base—"

"That's enough for now," Fischer interrupted. "Nothing you can do about it right at this moment. You two, get out of here," she said to Dmitri and Max. "Get some rest, and if you get any pain or shortness of breath, then call me. And drink plenty of water. The same goes for you, Anders, but you're staying here for a while. I want to keep an eye on you. Get some sleep and try not to worry."

★   ★   ★

"We have ourselves a problem," Fergie said quietly. He was sitting awkwardly on a chair pulled to the edge of my bed.

I raised an eyebrow, wincing at the pain from my burned forehead. "Just the one?" I asked.

"We're going to freeze."

"What?"

"The refinery fed the generator directly. Without it...we're going to freeze."

I didn't know what to say. I couldn't take it in. "We – we only have to survive six months—"

"I need a proper talk with Max. But I don't reckon we have more than a third o' that."

I shook my head. "That can't be right..."

The Scotsman raised an eyebrow at me. He looked old, tired – too tired even to argue.

"Do – do the crew know?" I asked.

"I ain't said nothing, nothing's been said. But they're not stupid. Max must know. The others? If they think about it, they'll work it out soon enough. I mean, Theo's dead, you've been having your nap and Max and Dmitri were totally worn out after going into that blaze. And o' course it took me a day or two to get my head working again. We've not had time to sit together, all of us as a crew, and talk things over. But they're not stupid. If they don't know it's only because the shock's too great right now. Or they're just in denial."

I was silent for a moment. I could see the crew all walking round like ghosts, stumbling like the living dead. "So what are we going to do?"

"I – I don't know...." He cleared his throat and sat up straighter. When he next spoke his voice was louder, more assertive. "We'll find a way. We have to find a way. Don't know about you, but I ain't ready to die yet. It was always my ambition to die in bed with a supermodel – ain't ready to give up on that quite yet."

"Why'd you come to Antarctica, Fergie?"

"Why'd you ask that?"

I shrugged stiffly, forcing myself to sit further up. "I just— I've not got to know any of you. I don't really know who you are yet."

"And now's the ideal time to break the ice? You're a weird one, Nordvelt."

"I just—"

"As if it matters more than a squirrel's fart, I came here because I like a challenge, because I wasn't going anywhere in my career back home, and because...well, because there was someone I no longer wanted to be in the same fucking continent with, if you must know." He looked away.

"I've heard you're not a big fan of the Company."

"What is this, some kind of interrogation? No, I've never been their greatest fan. Dunno about you, but I liked owning my own stuff – remember that, when people could actually own their own things?" he said with bitterness. "I liked being able to make my own decisions, not havin' to chase someone in some mega-office on another continent for permission to wipe my own—"

"So why take their money?"

"What's the alternative? Go out to China or Korea, live as a non-Com? Mate, my language skills ain't that good."

I stared at him for a moment. "So what are we going to do now?"

Fergie sighed and rubbed his chin. "Truth is, we're in a bad way even if we do manage to pull through here. We live to see Tierra again, we got to answer for...for our failure. I hate to think what the Company's gonna do when they hear – they were relying on that oil. Lot o' people gonna be sittin' in the dark in six months' time. No power, factories not working, have to harvest the crops by hand, even. Ain't just our lives at stake here, you know that. They can only cut back so far…" He paused, looked up at me. "We need to find out who did this, Anders."

"You mean you don't suspect me?"

"Of course I do. It'd be stupid of me not to, wouldn't it?"

"But you saw—"

"I saw you walk into the fire to help Mikhail, and I'm seeing you in a hospital bed as a result o' that," he snapped. "Yes, I'm very aware of that. And for what it's worth, thank you." He took a look at the unconscious figure mummified in bandages. "Thank you," he repeated softly. "But if you aren't responsible for…for the incidents, it means that someone else here is. And I find that hard to believe."

I watched Fergie as he ran a hand over his face. He looked exhausted. With me out of action and Fischer preoccupied with her patients, the running of the base had fallen to him. I wondered just what that entailed now. Keeping spirits up, I guessed. Making sure that the crew didn't start falling out over the smallest provocation. At least he looked to have recovered fully from his injury in the mine.

"There is no way that this was an accident," I said.

"Aye, I know. I checked out Mikhail's story. The fire was definitely started by an explosive device."

There was a long pause. I asked him what else he'd been doing for the last few days.

"We held a service for the commander – and for Theo." He stared at his fingers, picked distractedly at his nails. "Abi read some verses from the Qur'an, Keegan from the Bible. Then…then we all went round and said a few words. What they meant to us, you know?"

"What did Weng say?"

"Don't be such a cold bastard, Nordvelt," Fergie said, but there was little rancor in his voice. He just seemed deadened. "She didn't say nowt, as ever. Kept her thoughts to herself." He sighed. "And then we got drunk, cried, laughed and puked. It's what they would've wanted." He gave a weak smile. "Apart from that, we just been getting on with the job. Been tryin' to keep everyone calm, to get the base back on an even keel. Shoring up the ceiling at the mine. Trying to get over the shock."

"It must have been difficult."

"Aye." He took a long breath, and I knew this part of the conversation was over. "But we need to make some decisions. We need to decide what to do. We need a survival plan. And – and we need—" He took another breath. "We need to decide if we're gonna keep up work at the mine. The rig's toast, but even if we all die here, if we leave a big mound o' coal, then at least we might keep the Company running long enough so's they can rebuild this place. Find a replacement crew. Hopefully one without a damn nutter runnin' around."

I let my head sink back into the pillow. He was right, I knew he was right, but I couldn't connect emotionally. My death was staring straight at me. I knew it was there but I couldn't see it. I couldn't feel anything but the dull ache in my brow and a cold, creeping horror.

I cleared my throat, swallowed dirty phlegm. "So…so what do we do now?"

"We need a meetin'. Me, you and Fischer."

"You want to call her? Now?"

In just a few minutes the doctor had joined us at the bedside. She looked tired, bags under her eyes, deep wrinkles on her brow. "Anders. How are you feeling?"

"Better than Mikhail," I said grimly. "What – what're his prospects?"

She shrugged. "What are the prospects for any of us, come to that?"

I thought of the long months ahead and couldn't find any words.

"I'm keeping him unconscious as much as possible," Fischer went on. "Assuming – assuming any of us… He'll have a long, painful time in rehab before he can walk again. He'll need intensive medical care for several years."

I absorbed that silently. The poor man. All his ambitions, his dreams, destroyed in a moment. I thought back to the equinox. He wouldn't be throwing a ball around for years, might never play again. Who was it he'd supported, the West Coast Warriors? I still had no idea who they were.

Eventually Fergie cleared his throat. "There's nothin' we can do about that now," he said. "No point talkin' 'bout freezing either. We'll survive. We'll survive because we have to, right? And we got other things to discuss."

"Okay." My voice cracked. "What have you got?"

"Right." He cleared his throat again and glanced at his datapad. "First up, we've obviously had to suspend mining activities. That means that only Maggie and Greigor are regularly leaving the barracks." He paused. "We could restart the mines, they weren't badly damaged – just have to check the bracing and scan the tunnels for microfractures. That'd be easy enough, but…"

"Yes?"

"But we're *scared*, man. Some crazy's killed two o' us and left Mikhail a cripple. What're they gonna do next? That's what we're all wondering. 'Will it be me?' The barracks is the only place we feel at least halfway safe."

"How do you know de Villiers was murdered?" I asked. Max surely wouldn't have told the crew about the sabotage to the commander's warmsuit.

"I don't believe it was an accident – and neither do you. There are all sorts of rumors going around the base. Most of us think it was you or Weng," he said frankly.

I sighed. "Okay. Let's move on. What're our options?"

The Scotsman rubbed his cheek. A stubbly beard had spread across his face since I'd seen him last; I guessed that shaving had not been high on his list of priorities. "The way I see it," he said, "we can either carry on as if nothing has happened, or we can pull everyone back to the barracks and hunker down here for the next six months."

"What do you think, Doctor?"

"What does it matter if we're all going to freeze anyway?"

"That's not—"

"All right, all right, practical considerations only. Okay. If you want my professional opinion, I'd say it'd be far better for all of us to keep working. Much less chance of us all going down with winter-over syndrome – avoid the mental and physical effects of extended periods without natural light. Regular work and exercise is better than just sitting and waiting to die."

"And your personal opinion?"

"I'm scared too."

"But the miners would be the only extra people inside the base," I said. "And there's no problem of space, what with—"

"With all the dead bodies lyin' around?" Fergie said.

I shifted, the coarse sheet rucking between my legs. "Surely we could work out a routine, a way—"

"Don't underestimate the effects of any big change in a small space. It's not just extra people, it's extra idle people." Fischer smiled without humor. "You think things are tense now? Just wait. Just wait and you'll see punches thrown. In this atmosphere, with all that's happened? It'll happen in a matter of days."

Fergie shifted in his seat. "Okay, so it'd be best to get the mines open again – but that depends on finding out who *did* this. I'm not happy with sending the crew back out to the mine whilst there's a saboteur around. I'm no' too happy going out there myself. There are far too many ways for 'accidents' to happen."

"And we've just got to sit it out," Fischer said. "Nearly six months. God, I wish there was a way off this damn – damn…"

"If wishes were trees, then Bangladesh wouldn't be underwater," Fergie snapped. "We're stuck here and that's the end of it."

"It still seems incredible that one of us could be a killer," I said, half to myself. "We all took Psych tests, didn't we? We've all taken dozens over the years. How could any one of us slip through? How is it *possible* for there to be a murderer on the base?" I turned to Fergie. "Surely de Villiers was right when he told me that no stranger could be hiding here, that no one could be coming from a rival camp?"

"There's absolutely zero evidence for anything like that, no evidence that there's anyone other than the thirteen of us here."

"Eleven of us now," Fischer said in a voice that was barely more than a whisper.

"Psych tests are all well and good," I said, "but can we be sure everyone's who they say they are? I mean – I mean, could someone have taken another's identity at some point?"

"I can't see how," the doctor said. "We had bioscans taken at every stage – every time we got on a transport, every time we logged in to a compscreen…. I just don't see how that could happen. Not without some major conspiracy."

"So we have a choice of impossibilities." I sighed. My head was beginning to ache.

"I suppose…" Fischer began, then hesitated.

"What?"

"Well, I don't have the equipment to do it properly, and I'd have to do some research and prepare, but I could run basic Psych tests myself."

"So you could find us the killer?" Fergie leaped on the idea.

"Maybe. I don't know." Fischer closed her eyes momentarily. "I might be able to eliminate some people, but with the facilities I have here, I'm not too confident. But I *should* be able to prove that everyone's who they say they are, that no one's gone mad, or…you know. That sort of thing."

"What actually goes into a Psych? Technically speaking, I mean," I asked. I'd only ever been on the receiving end of the process.

"There are four aspects. First, a drug to suppress conscious thought. Second is the set of images and questions designed to provoke emotional responses – or not, of course. Third, there's the measurements – the cameras to measure pupil dilation, thermometers, blood pressure monitors and so on – the things that measure pulse rate, arousal, hormones and the rest of the autonomic body functions. And finally the analysis. The last bit's what'll take the time, and will take me most of the work."

"You think you can do that?" I said. "With the equipment you have here?"

"It wouldn't be perfect. Wouldn't stand up in court. But…"

"But it'd be a damn good start," Fergie said. "Begin with Anders – and me, o' course."

I nodded my agreement. I knew my innocence. If there was any chance to prove it to Fergie, then I would take it.

"How long will it take for you to prepare?" I asked the doctor.

She shrugged. "A few days. A week, maybe. I'll have to do it around my other duties – Mikhail comes first."

"There's just one thing," Fergie said. "What if you do your Psych and it comes up wi' nothing, with nobody? Where are we then?"

No one had an answer to that.

★　　★　　★

Fischer discharged me that afternoon, with the proviso that I spend much of my time in bed. I'd lost weight. I tired easily. I hobbled slowly through the corridors, feeling as if I needed a cane.

In my room I stripped down and stood in front of the mirror. A stranger stared back. There were lines on my face that hadn't been there before. My eyes were sunken and dark, and there was a scar on my brow that would be with me forever, unless I had it surgically removed. It was a curious thing, like a fragment of a circuit board – the impression of the burning metals in my mask.

I looked old, and weak. And afraid. My God, but had I only been at Australis for less than ten days? It felt like forever.

I updated my log on the compscreen, doing my best to ignore the message the hacker had left for me. I gave as accurate an account as I could of the fire. I added a note to the official records as well, but I kept that short. *Explosion on oil rig: crew member Theodore Buckland killed. Circumstances unclear. Mikhail Petrovic seriously injured and removed from active duty.*

That was all I could bring myself to put. It was only as I confirmed the entry that I realized I was crying.

I tried again to access the personnel files but de Villiers's block remained in place. I spent hours fruitlessly trying to guess at his password: his wife's name, his children's names, Fischer, Julia – but I'd barely known the man. I had no chance.

I looked longingly at my bed before sighing and turning away. I struggled to draw on some clean clothes before I made the slow, painful journey to Fischer's quarters.

I found her sitting at her compscreen, looking through a paper on Psych testing, making notes with an old-fashioned pen and paper. She looked up at me as I entered. Careworn and tired, she still managed a smile.

"Anders."

"Julia. I'm sorry to disturb you."

"That's okay. Take a seat." She turned her chair to face me.

"I'm sorry to have to do this, but…"

"But you need to talk to me about…about Anton."

"I found the message on his datapad."

"Do you have any idea who sent it?" she asked.

"You don't think it was me?"

"I…I've had a long time to think about it. Yes, at first I thought it was you. I don't know why – I mean, Anton said you'd be trouble, and when I – when I found… Yes, I thought you'd lured him out to kill him. But you're not so stupid, are you?"

I felt my mouth flicker a cynical smile.

"If you'd have done it you'd have hidden your tracks better."

"So tell me – please – what happened that night?"

She looked down at her knees and drew a deep breath. "I didn't love him. I know that, I always knew that. He was…convenient. But still, it was such a…such a shock when he died."

I said nothing, let her draw her thoughts together.

"That night… That morning. We – we'd had an arrangement. We used each other. It was how we worked. He was – we'd arranged for him to come here – my room – at five. He didn't show." Her voice cracked, just the tiniest waver. "It wouldn't have been the first time. I was – I was angry…"

"Because you thought he'd stood you up?"

"Because I thought he was with someone else," she said with a hint of her old acerbity. "Wouldn't have been the first time."

"So you…?"

"I went to his room. I was going to – to shout at him. To tell him that this was the last time. And to – well, I guess I kind of wanted to have a go at Weng, if it was her, or Max."

"You thought he might have been with— sorry, that doesn't matter. Go on."

"You know the rest. I marched in, full of piss and vinegar – I mean everyone knew his access code, right? He hated security, hated that McCarthy kept himself locked away all the time – but he wasn't there. Of course."

"Where did you think he was?"

"In one of the girls' rooms." She shrugged and turned away, but not before I'd seen the tear breaking from her eye. "But – but I saw his datapad on the desk…. I figured there might have been a message from whoever he was with, might save me bursting into the wrong room. Piss and vinegar, remember? So I saw the message, realized where he'd gone."

"You went straight out to look for him?"

"Pretty much."

"Why?"

"Because I'm a nosy bitch. You've read the message, right? If you

– and at that point I had no reason to think it *wasn't* from you – if you were calling Anton outside, it could only have been to tell him something serious or to—"

"It read to me like blackmail. Like someone was trying to make it look like I was going to blackmail him."

She nodded. "Or that. Anyway, it told me where to look for him. I went outside – I – I…"

"You found his body."

She nodded again, auburn hair falling across her face as she wiped at her eyes.

"Julia, I'm sorry to have to ask—"

"Go on."

"Did you see anyone else? Inside or outside?"

She shook her head. "No one."

"No movement? No sounds? Nothing in the corner or your eye?"

"Nothing."

"Did you see any footprints in the snow? Anything—"

"I saw nothing, Anders. I saw nothing. Just – just snow beginning to cover his body – just—" She broke off and swallowed. "Just a dead man by the side of a building, just the end—"

I gave her a moment to compose herself. "What did you do then?"

"God, I barely remember. I called Weng. I must have, right? Because she called you. I don't remember what I said to her, don't remember – I must have got to one of the intercom panels in the outside buildings, mustn't I? I barely remember…. And then there you were, there you both were. God, when I realized it was you—"

"You must have thought I'd killed him."

"I don't know what I thought. I mean – I must have, right? The message… But I don't remember anything coherent from finding the – the body and then waking up in the infirmary with a wound-pack round my head and Weng looking down at me." She tried another smile but gave up halfway through.

I sighed. I could have guessed all this. My brow hurt. "How did you and Anton get together?"

She cleared her throat. "Well, we met about six months ago – before the training in Tierra. It was hate at first sight." She did smile this time. "I thought him an arrogant asshole with an ego twice the size of his brain. He called me a stuck-up bitch. We were both right."

"Where did you meet?"

"He'd been appointed as commander. I was on the shortlist for this position. All of the candidates for doctor met with him and McCarthy—"

"McCarthy was there too?"

She nodded. "The senior staff were hired first. I didn't think too much about it – I mean, not afterwards. At the time I was nervous as hell; I really wanted the job. I'd reached a dead end in Germany – well, that doesn't really matter, does it? But I thought I'd blown it. Didn't get on with either of them, whilst some pretty little tart was charming his pants off. Possibly literally. So I went back to the job-site forums until a few weeks later, when they let me know I'd got the position."

"What then?"

"I started training. Did the Antarctic survival course, then turned up to meet the crew at Tierra. I still didn't like the commander. He was going giddy over Weng, poor girl. I got to watch him at work, with his jokes and grand gestures, and I hated him even more." She sniffed, hauling back a tear.

"So what changed?"

She sighed. "I don't really know. We got here and got to work. He was good at his job, even I had to admit that – he was organized, worked closely with the engineers. Dmitri adored him, poor lamb. Whenever there was a problem, he'd solve it calmly and would somehow get everyone on the same side. He gave everyone enough latitude – you know about the weed and the alcohol. As long as everyone kept working, he'd turn a blind eye.

"The only one he couldn't work with was Weng. As soon as we got here, he lost interest in her."

"She said that de Villiers chose you over her."

Fischer shook her head. "No, that's not what happened. I remember – the first time we – we… Anton had been ignoring Weng. He'd just lost interest in her. I don't think they talked at all. Then one day, in the rec room in front of others – I don't remember who – Anton humiliated her."

"How did he do that?"

"I don't know how it began. I wasn't paying attention at first.

Anton was watching a film with the others, and Weng came up and asked him for a word. Anton told her he was busy and he'd see her later. He said it suggestively – you know, 'I'll see you *later.*' Weng was really upset – you know what a private person she is – and tried again to get him to talk to her right then. She was crying." Fischer bowed her head. "Anton got angry and called her a stupid bitch – in front of everyone. Told her she was just a silly little girl, the patronizing asshole.

"Well, Weng ran out in tears and never spoke to him again. I was furious. I stood up and practically dragged him out of the room and into his office. I shouted at him, told him he had treated her abominably. I told him that he was a disgrace, that…well, lots of things along those lines."

"And what happened?"

"He kissed me," Fischer said with a shrug. "I don't really remember quite how it came about, but he kissed me, grinned that stupid grin of his – what an asshole! But…" She sighed. "But I couldn't help myself. And the next thing I knew, we were in bed."

There was silence for a moment; Fischer took the opportunity to open a drawer and pull out a pouch of tobacco and some cigarette papers. A little bag of buds the color of a summer's lawn slid out of the pouch. She saw my expression. "Don't worry," she said, "I've learned my lesson. I'll smoke outside."

"So that was how your relationship started?" I asked, watching her hands as she rolled her cigarette; she added a healthy layer of marijuana before sealing it into its paper tube.

"Yes. It really was love-hate. Almost the definition of it." She tapped the roll-up on her desk absently. "At times I really loathed the man – I mean, I didn't mind that he had other relationships. I just detested the way that he didn't seem to *care* about the people he screwed with. At first I felt like I'd betrayed Weng – but we all have our needs, don't we? At other times I found myself totally charmed. He was handsome, he was witty, and when he wanted to, he could be pretty damn smart. A little like Greigor, really, but with flair. Our relationship was sexual; that was all."

"The day I arrived…"

"Yes?"

"You – there was something going on—"

"Oh. Yes, that. Yes, he stood me up. Nothing more. We'd had a – an appointment. An arrangement. He'd been…he was going to come and…and see me, that morning. He never showed. No call, no apology. Guess he'd been with one of the others. It was stupid of me to react like that. Must have been awkward for you. I'm sorry, Anders. But this place – when you're with the same people all the time, these little things, they can get so big…"

"Who was de Villiers with?"

She shook her head. "Don't know. And even if I did, I wouldn't say. I shouldn't really have told you about Weng, but you already knew about that. As for the others – that's not my business, and I don't see that it's yours."

I looked at her. She was holding herself tight, keeping herself in control – that was obvious. And although she was smiling grimly at me, there was a great sorrow in her eyes. She was brittle, ready to snap, and I didn't want to push her over the edge. But I still had questions.

"This was the situation up to my arrival?" I asked.

"Until his death."

"You took it hard."

"Yes," she breathed.

"But you didn't love him?"

She shook her head. "Anton was a force of nature. He gave the impression of being indestructible. He told me— no, he *boasted* about all the rules he'd broken in his previous jobs, and how he always managed to come out clean. He never, ever doubted himself. We were all sucked up in his wake; even the people who hated him couldn't help being lifted by him. He could have been a cult leader. He had *charisma.*" She paused, shaking her head. "Maybe whoever killed him did us all a favor," she said sadly. Then she looked up at me, tears on her cheeks.

I had nothing else to say. I thanked her and we both got up. I went back to my room, and Fischer went to the vestibule to get suited up for her smoke.

CHAPTER FOURTEEN

I slept badly again. I was getting sick of it; something was wrong and I needed it sorted. I resolved to talk to Fischer – she had, after all, done a good enough job with my body. My aches had faded overnight, and I barely needed the fresh wound-packs I stuck to my shins and the back of my left hand. My legs were fatigued but bore me well enough; I made my day's plans as I walked out into the corridors. It was time to check the pinhead cameras I'd set around the base.

First, though, I went to the canteen for something to eat, and then to the rec room, where I walked straight into another problem.

Max and Fergie were standing in the middle of the room, snarling at each other like stray dogs. Dmitri was with them; he just looked miserable. Keegan sat on one of the sofas with Fischer, while Greigor, once again finding a way to escape the greenhouse, was alone at the table.

"So you want to let us just – just die of cold?" Max was saying passionately. "You're not gonna let us do anything to save ourselves, just—"

"And what the hell do you want me to do about it?" Fergie shot back. "You want me to magic the oil well whole again? Hell, why don't I bring de Villiers and Theo back from the dead while I'm at it?"

The door swung shut behind me.

"What the hell do you want, Nordvelt?"

Max didn't even look at me. Instead she put a hand on Fergie's shoulder to pull his attention back to her. At the contact, he spun back and knocked her hand away with his wrist.

"Get the fuck off me," he shouted.

"Just shut up and listen—"

"I—"

"We have to shut down all nonessential activities!" she snapped.

"*Everything* we do here is essential! We've got to think of more than just us. What about the people who need us back in—"

"Enough," I said firmly. "One of you – calmly, without getting carried away – please tell me what the problem is."

"We're all going to die, that's the problem," Keegan muttered to the room at large.

Max finally stopped glaring at Fergie long enough to answer me. "The oil. The generator's pretty much full at the moment, but at the rate we're going we only have a month's power, maximum. I've looked into it, done the calculations – I've made a list and checked it twice. If we don't do something, we'll all freeze long before help arrives." She broke for a look at Fergie. "It's no use having a month of full operations if we then spend the rest of the night shift being dead!"

"I'm not even bloody arguing! I'm just saying that we should keep the mines working – and anyway, if you're so bloody clever—"

"Okay, that's enough!" I snapped. "We've a problem. We need solutions, not bickering."

"And who are you to tell us what to do?" Keegan snarked from his seat.

"Yeah, Nordvelt," Greigor spat, "we don' take orders from a murderer."

I ground my teeth, glared at him but got only defiance.

"We've still got the oil tanks," Dmitri said into the resulting silence. "Can we draw fuel from there?"

"Maybe Mikhail could, but he's in no position to help," Max said. "He knew – he knows – much more about that side of things than I do. I'll look into it, but I don't think there'll be more than a few days' worth of fuel in there."

"Okay," I said. "Whether or not you want to take orders from me, you two need to go and think. Fergie, work out a way of rationing energy use – if we keep the mine open, then you need power from somewhere, right? Max, you work out a way of refueling the generator. Please."

Max stared at Fergie; the Scotsman stared at me. For a long time we stood there, and at any second I expected him to refuse. But in the absence of a workable alternative he had little choice. After giving us one last look, as if to demonstrate that he was leaving on his terms, not ours, he turned to the door and left. Max followed a moment later – just long enough for the Scotsman to have cleared the corridor ahead. Greigor went to follow, but Max rounded on him in the doorway. "I don't know where you're going, you little worm," she snapped. "I didn't hear your name mentioned. Get the hell away from me!"

Greigor stared sullenly at the floor. "I was jus' going to Maggie."

"I miss the commander," Dmitri said when they'd gone. "He'd know what to do."

"He wasn't some fucking god," Fischer said. "He was – he was…" She trailed off and shook her head.

The Ukrainian looked so miserable, trapped inside his own world. I thought back to what Fischer had said: *Dmitri adored him, poor lamb.*

I wanted to say something but I wasn't sure what. Especially not in front of the others.

"My God," Fischer said after a moment's silence. "We're falling apart here. This is a nightmare." She was fiddling with a roll-up; her smoking materials were scattered on the arm of her chair. She looked up at me with a black smile. "Take a picture, Anders. Might as well take a photograph, because this is gonna be the last time we see each other like this. It'll be warmsuits for the rest of the shift, inside and out."

"Only if we can keep them charged," Keegan said. "If not, there ain't anything that'll stop us freezing."

★   ★   ★

I'd planted the pinheads in all the public areas of the barracks. Each had a memory of about a week; only a day or two left before they started to overwrite themselves. Independent of the official base CCTV system, they should – must – give me the answers. Or at least narrow down the suspects.

My resolve left me as soon as I found the first one, the one I'd hidden in the vestibule. It took me a second to remember precisely where I'd set the thing, but there it was, nestling on top of a bank of lockers. It wasn't quite how I'd left it.

It had been moved – somebody had turned it around so it was now facing the wall.

I cursed. My first thought was that I'd just set it up incorrectly, but...but surely I couldn't have made such a simple mistake. I took it anyway. Then I proceeded through the barracks, taking the cameras from corridors, from the stairwell, working my way back to my rooms.

Most of them seemed to have been interfered with, moved so that they were pointing at nothing. This wasn't my mistake, not all of them – not possible. Someone had found them and deliberately sabotaged my efforts. But that just raised a new barrage of questions.

How could anyone have known to look for them? Was the murderer so paranoid as to check every room in minute detail? I mean, they weren't invisible, but they were made to be discreet and I'd planted them carefully, doing my best to make them unobtrusive. Had someone been watching me? Had they followed me around as I set them up, or hacked into the CCTV net? I glanced up at the camera as I entered my office. Never had it seemed so invasive.

Although I knew it was a lost cause, I plugged the first pinhead into my compscreen and scrolled back through the footage – to the night the oil rig had been destroyed. And there it was: a gloved hand, reaching over the lens before the camera was gently turned to face the wall. A few cameras hadn't been altered – the quiet corridors, the workshop – but they told me nothing of interest. In the rest – well, sometimes I saw fingers, once a suited arm, and a few times only the camera's movement. In those gloves it was impossible to tell anything at all, even gender.

Only the last camera showed anything else. This one had covered the doorways to the crew's private rooms. I'd set it up so that no one could leave their room without my seeing. I'd had high hopes for that one.

It showed nothing at all. Its memory had been completely wiped.

★   ★   ★

"The commander and me – we were close, Anders." Behind me Dmitri lowered the weights with a *clink*; there was a pause, and then I heard a gasp of effort as he resumed with a larger load.

I kept running on the treadmill, facing the bare gray wall of the gymnasium. "I'm sorry," I wheezed.

"He told me things. Whilst Fergie was out of the way, de Villiers and I would talk over a coffee. This is up at the mine, you see."

"Yes?"

"Yes." He paused again, and when he spoke again, his voice was full of the effort of his exercise. "He didn't trust you."

"He said that?"

"Of course he didn't," Dmitri snapped. He set down his weights and I didn't hear him take them up again. "You think that's what a man does, just goes to his colleagues and says, 'Hey, that new guy – I don't trust him'? No. I could see he was worried, that's what I could see. I saw his face as he stared into the distance. I knew him well, Anders. I know when he's worried."

My shoulder blades were itching. I slowed down the mat, stepped off the treadmill and turned to face the Ukrainian. He was sitting up on his bench and glaring at me, blue vest sweat-soaked and his face flushed and angry.

"You thought that was because of me?"

"Who else would want to take away his command?"

"I wasn't here to do anything like that – and what about Weng?"

He waved away her name. "If she was going to do anything, she'd have done it before you came."

I thought of saying that she'd thought I'd been sent here because of her, but I kept quiet.

"Anyway, he only changed when he'd spoken with you – after the barbecue on the equinox."

"He changed?"

Dmitri glared at me but didn't respond.

"Any idea what he was afraid of?" I asked as my breathing slowly returned to normal after the exercise.

"Are you playing the fool with me?"

I thought back to that meeting with the commander. "He was afraid I'd report him for all the violations he'd allowed on base."

"I knew you were a clever man."

I ignored the sarcasm. "But that only gave de Villiers a motive for destroying the comms building."

"What? He wouldn't—" He paused and began again. "This base was his child. It'd never even occur to him to do anything that didn't help it grow."

"Why are you telling me all this? What do you want?"

He stood, slowly, and took a pace towards me. I stood my ground. He was a big man, certainly, muscles taut from his workout.

"I just wanted to warn you," he said. "I just wanted to say. I liked Anton – liked him a lot. And if I ever find out that you had a hand in his death – well, my friend, I will hurt you."

★   ★   ★

Maybe I was going insane. Maybe none of this was happening at all. Maybe I was dreaming, delusional, dangerous.

I felt so self-contained, so self-possessed. That wasn't right. That couldn't be right. It wasn't normal, surely, to be the eye of the storm: to be the one stable element around which the universe spun (and all the universe had once been compressed smaller than a single atom… Boom!). No, it wasn't right. All I'd learned – all the isolation of my childhood, both before and after my parents were taken from me; all the times I'd stood alone through my teenage years and into adulthood, imperturbable, cold, uncaring. That was my coping mechanism, and that was my madness.

I paced my room over and over and over again, distractions buzzing at the edges of my mind. Like moths, the thoughts touched their winter wings against me, spun away before they could be seized.

This place. This bare gray prison. Soon to be my graveyard, the graveyard of us all – I needed sleep. I needed sunlight. I needed a path but I could see nothing but walls each way I turned.

I took a deep breath and made myself stand still. In front of my compscreen, I reached out to touch the smooth lacquer of my puzzle box, the worn skin of my book. I accessed my memcard – ignoring the message that hacker had left on my compscreen – and put on the music my mother had sung when I was a baby. I let it fill the room, then turned away and forced myself to focus.

None of the attacks had occurred directly. They had all been carried out through sabotage and by using explosives – that was the MO so far. Did that have significance? The culprit could have been physically weak and didn't dare to attack their victim directly. That might implicate Weng, or Maggie.

I thought of Max and her statues. Maybe she'd programmed a robot to carry out the attacks.

The attacks had occurred at night – or at least had been set up at night. The oil rig blew in the morning, but the explosives must have been planted the night before.

I frowned and absently traced the scar on my forehead.

The motive: well, I was in no doubt that a man like de Villiers could provoke murderous feelings. But the other incidents couldn't have been simply to cover up a personal attack. I didn't buy that. No, the real target was the Company. The crew were just collateral damage.

I couldn't stay still for long. I needed to be doing something, needed my displacement activity. I went to the combi-maker and put on a coffee. Then I went back to the compscreen and tapped in random words, desperately trying to figure out de Villiers's password. If I could only access the crew's personal logs – what better place to start looking for clues? But I got nowhere. No shortcuts for me.

If this was a targeted assault on the Company, then I should be looking for an agent of the United Nations. Bad feeling between the two organizations went back years – all about power, of course. As the Company's influence grew, the UN's waned. I couldn't even imagine what politicking went on to get approval for Australis's construction.

I took a mouthful of overhot coffee. Ran my hand over the smooth surface of my puzzle box. Thought of de Villiers. Felt a moment of envy for the man's charisma, his vitality. He was still present in the base in a way I'd never be.

I closed my eyes and pushed those thoughts aside. *Be cold. Be heartless. Be stone.* I'd learned this a long time ago.

First had come the destruction of the comms building. Then de Villiers's death. Finally the nightmare of flame and thick, thick smoke and steel melting in an insane heat as the oil rig burned...and the hideous sight of Mikhail's deformed body. Now, as it all came back to me, my imagination added the reek of burned flesh that my coldsuit had spared me at the time.

Be cold. Be heartless. Be stone. More coffee helped.

Before the explosion someone had again deactivated the surveillance cameras. They had also found every one of the extra pinheads that I had planted, and made sure they weren't going to show me anything.

The explosive store, the vehicle depot, the journey to the oil rig, the delicate task of priming the bomb – it all added up to a calm and deliberate act of murder.

If all this was a plot against the Company it was working. Millions and millions had already been spent on setting up Australis; millions more would be required to rebuild the well. In the spring, the crawler would arrive, hauling the huge tracked oil tankers and expecting to carry all the crude back to civilization. There'd be nothing for them to take. Nor would there be as much coal or iron as planned. The total cost to the Company would be in the billions. Maybe it would be enough to cause the whole Australis project to be canceled.

And that was narrow thinking. I couldn't even begin to imagine the human cost, the lights going out across South America. This was a high cost, high reward endeavor: start with a small crew pioneering this new life and work out practical ways round whatever problems were thrown up. I'd seen projections for the next phase of development – a crew four times the size, the mineworkings extending many more miles beneath the ice sheet. A chance to ease the pressure on the paper-thin veneer of civilization.

Maggie had told me that she'd argued with the commander about the Company. And that Fergie and Abi had taken her side. Of course, that was just one person's word, but I remembered that Fergie had joked about sabotage on the day I arrived – and he'd certainly been quick enough to point the finger at me. I resolved to get deeper into all three of them and work out whether I could seriously consider any of them suspects.

The audio file ran to its conclusion. The resulting silence seemed to fill the room, hanging far heavier than the music had. I shivered and started the recording back from the beginning.

Max had all the technical skills to carry out the attacks. Without even breaking into a sweat. She knew it all – how to manipulate the surveillance system, how to prime the timers on the explosives. But...

The truth was that I was fond of her. I liked her company. I'd already relied on her expertise. I...I trusted her. Besides, every member of the crew was smart enough to learn the little bits of technical know-how they'd have needed to do all this. But I couldn't afford to discount her. Not based on something as fallible as my own opinion.

Greigor. Now he was a shifty little bugger. Full of adolescent bitterness and resentment – and you could tell the others saw it too. He was ignored and patronized, and that provided him with a motive. There was a certain theatricality behind the attacks: the practical necessities of destruction paired with a wannabe artist's escalation of horror. I could see Greigor thinking of himself as an original creator of terror while actually only recycling tired clichés.

But he was just too pathetic, too amateurish for me to take seriously as a suspect. I wanted to give him a good slap, but I just couldn't – quite – see him as a killer.

Fischer was the only person whom I felt I could definitely eliminate from consideration. I'd seen her with de Villiers, when we'd dragged his body into the infirmary. I'd seen her tears.

And what did this leave me with? No one and nothing. I leaned back in my chair and stared blankly at my compscreen. Nothing. I was no closer to finding the culprit, and I could not think of a single thing to do to *get* closer. My hopes were pinned on Fischer's cut-price Psych. Retesting all the crew might – it *must* – provide the answer. Because I had no reason to think that the saboteur had finished their work. As far as I knew, they'd go on until every single person was dead, Australis confined to a footnote in Company history. Or maybe they'd done enough already – operations were suspended, after all. The rig was destroyed. And who'd want to spend the rest of the night shift with only ghosts for company?

I imagined a future group of explorers coming across the ruins of the base, wondering at the perfectly preserved buildings, our corpses frozen as a bitter wind howled through the site.

I'd reached a dead end. I could see no new lines of inquiry to pursue. *Damn* de Villiers. Damn the hacker, whose message I was still staring through. If only the commander hadn't blocked my access to personal files. There was no way, no other way I could see to move forward.

I should really now have recorded my thoughts to my log and thus to the black box. That way, my successors might know what had happened in case of my death. But I really couldn't bring myself to care about proper procedure, not then.

I felt my scar stiff on my forehead and did my best to relax my frown. I could only hope that Fischer was getting on well with her preparations; a fresh Psych test, in front of witnesses, was the only way I could see to demonstrate that I, at least, was innocent.

★   ★   ★

There were too many empty seats at the meal that night. No one wanted to move from their normal places so there were odd gaps. Silence hung over us as we ate. No one had even made eye contact as we'd gathered in the canteen. Fischer was blatantly stoned, gazing around blankly with a thousand-yard stare. Her mouth kept twitching, her face running through a gamut of expressions. She'd look around as if surprised by her surroundings, then smile as if some far-off memory had just surfaced, and then sink her head as if in despair. I was alarmed – we needed our doctor fully alert and aware. I needed to talk to her.

Keegan was stoned too, but not as badly as Fischer. He just slumped in his seat, looking down at the table. He drank glass after glass of water, and when he did talk, he mumbled and was almost impossible to understand.

Everyone in the room had dark shadows under their eyes, and we were all prone to jumping at shadows. When Fischer clumsily knocked over Weng's glass, the geologist stood and glared at the doctor with such rage in her eyes, I thought for a second that they were going to come to blows.

There was no wine served with the food.

When Abidene had cleared up the last of the dishes, there was a move by Keegan and Greigor to rise. Fergie, however, called them back.

"Okay," he said, his voice sounding uncomfortably loud after the quiet of the meal. "Whilst we're all here, we should discuss what we're going to do now."

No one spoke.

"We all know the situation. We're crippled here, and we need to make changes if we're gonna survive. No one is to leave the barracks till we've carried out new Psych tests on every member o' this crew."

A general shifting of seats took place around the table. Surprise crossed many faces, and I grimaced. I hadn't wanted the Psych tests to be announced. Anger swelled through me. I gritted my teeth and watched the faces around me, saw the heavy eyes and drawn lips, saw my own tiredness reflected back at me. *Say nothing. Mustn't say anything. Mustn't inflame emotions.*

"To preserve as much power as possible, we're cutting off all power to auxiliary buildings—"

"What about my plants?" Maggie cried in alarm.

"If you'll let me finish, Professor," Fergie growled. "We're cutting power to all buildings except for the greenhouse and here in the barracks. We are also goin' to look to moving all crew to the lowest level of the building—"

This time everyone spoke up, all the crew at once crying protests and objections. All except for Max, Fischer and myself.

"Hey, this ain't my fault," Fergie snapped back, thumping the table. "*I* didn't get us into this mess! You all know it – all know the facts. Either we consolidate or we freeze."

The murmurs subsided. The crew confined themselves to unhappy glances and frowns.

"Who's responsible for this?" It was Abidene, his quiet voice carrying clear across the table. It seemed as if he was speaking to himself as much as anyone else. "Who brought us to this in the first place?"

No one spoke, but several faces turned to shoot me looks. I was not sure if they were silently accusing me or if they wanted me to have found out for them. I had to disappoint them all. "I'm still investigating," I said, as quiet as Abidene.

Keegan cleared his throat loudly. "Look, Anders, no offense – you seem a nice guy and all – but we should probably keep you locked up for a while."

I turned my gaze on him.

He cleared his throat again and poured another glass of water. He took an awkward sip. "Well, you know – the evidence seems to indicate—"

"What evidence?" I asked. "That all these…things…started happening after I arrived? That's not evidence, that's just circumstance."

"Look, we're all agreed that it must have been someone here in this room that's been doing all this, aren't we? And I know everyone here. Everyone except you, Anders." He shrugged, gave a weak smile. "It's not evidence, I know that, but – well, are we supposed to sit here and wait to be picked off one by one? If Anders is locked up in his room, and things keep happening, then we'll know he's not behind it, right?"

I tried to gauge the faces around the table. There was no help to be found there; hostility and blankness, that was all I saw. Silence lay over us, heavy and cold as a snowdrift. I looked to Max but she wouldn't even meet my eyes. "Are you making a serious proposal? Is this something we need to argue about?" I asked.

"I don't really know," Keegan said with a frown. "I hadn't really thought it through. What do the rest of you think?"

"I think we can do better than some orphanage reject," Greigor said just loud enough for me to catch.

"Yeah, well, fuck you," I said. I was tired, I was fed up, and I was sick of being the target. I stood, causing Keegan to sway back in alarm. "I know I've done nothing but try to help. And I know that this is no democracy and that we have a command structure here. So I say you can all go and screw yourselves. There's no way I'm letting myself be locked up when I've done nothing wrong."

Keegan shrugged and said nothing. The rest of the crew exchanged glances but, again, no one would meet my gaze.

"Right," I said. "I'm going to my room. Doctor, if you'd step out with me? I'd like a word." I paced the corridor as Fischer took her time to follow. When at last she emerged I beckoned impatiently and led the way around a corner and into the infirmary – the nearest door. "What d'you think you're doing?" I snapped as soon as the door was shut behind her.

She looked at me in surprise, her eyes slowly coming into focus.

"You've got to stop smoking that damn weed," I continued. "Look at you! You can barely function."

"I'm not doing anyone any harm," she said.

"What about Mikhail? Think you can look after him in that state?"

"Yes," she said. "Yes, I can. He's stable. He's unconscious. I know what I'm doing, Nordvelt, and I'm not doing any harm. If you don't trust me – well, I've been a doctor longer than you've been alive, and you're just an emotionally stunted little prick. *I know what I'm doing*. Now fuck off and leave me alone." She paced over to the MRI machine and absently poked at the cables.

"Fischer, you're responsible for the lives of the people here. We need you – *I* need you – awake and alert. You can't slack off anymore. Like it or not, the crew needs you to be able to take decisions, to—"

"To back you up?" Fischer sneered. "I'm not stupid, Nordvelt. Yeah, I'm stoned, but I can still follow a conversation. You're just pissed because I didn't back you up, didn't defend you when Keegan said you should be locked up. Well, answer me this – why should I? Did you ever stop to think that I might agree with him?"

"I don't give a damn whether you agree or not. You want to lock me up? Go ahead. Make that decision. Just don't sit there like you don't give a fuck about anything. You're one of the leaders and we need you to lead!"

The doctor swayed back. She opened her mouth to speak, then paused. Her shoulders slumped. "This is a nightmare. I can't do this," she whispered, half to herself.

"Yes, you can. Of course you can. The Julia Fischer I first met could handle anything. What happened to her, hey?" I tried to keep the impatience out of my words. I already regretted losing my temper, but still part of me wanted to yell at her, to purge myself of the frustrations that had been building up in me. "The Company knows you can handle this – you passed the Psych tests, didn't you?"

She smiled grimly. "After all that's happened, I'm struggling to keep any faith in the Psych."

My mouth fell open – shocking words, especially coming from a Company doctor. I stared at her for a moment, then cleared my throat. "I don't—"

"Oh, don't listen to me. I'm tired, I don't know what I'm saying." She leaned back against the bench and ran a hand through her graying hair. I'd never seen her look so old, so small.

My anger had faded completely now. I crossed to her and she flinched at my touch. "Come on, Julia, it's okay. I'm tired too, I'm fed up…I'm sorry. Go and get a good night's sleep and things will be better in the morning."

She looked up at me. "You mean we'll wake up and Anton will still be alive? Theo too?" Her voice fell to a whisper. "I'll wake up and McCarthy will still be here, and you'll be back in your block?"

I felt sick, suddenly cold as if I were suffering from pneumonia again. I sighed, my head bowed in despair. "Just try and cut down on the marijuana. That's all I'm asking," I said, struggling to keep my voice steady.

Fischer just stared down to the floor and was silent.

I left her in the infirmary and went back to my room. I didn't know how much more of this I could take – it was constant now, the stress. I felt brittle, a dead thing ready to break. My only hope was that Fischer wasn't too addled to sort out the Psych test properly. I was desperate to take it – I *had* to take it. It was the only way to prove my innocence.

★　　★　　★

I was at breakfast next morning when the call came in – a crackly voice, Keegan's, on the intercom. "Help…help us," he croaked. His voice was weak, plaintive, and was followed by a noise that sounded terribly organic, like he was throwing up.

For a moment I was frozen. Then I dropped my cutlery and scrambled to the comm panel on the wall.

"Please, anybody," Keegan's voice came again, broken by weak coughs and spitting – the sounds of distress.

I reached the panel, but before I could reply, I heard Weng's sharp tones in answer. "What's wrong? Where are you?"

"Fischer's down – un-uncon…help us," came Keegan's voice.

"Where are you?" Weng asked again.

"Outside – by the greenhouse…"

He must have said more, but I was already running, running towards the vestibule, where I converged with Dmitri and Weng. I shared a fearful glance with the Ukrainian. Weng was too preoccupied with her suit to look at me. "Far side of the greenhouse, nearest the oil tanks – that's what he said." She tugged at her boots.

I nodded and, not waiting for the others, fastened the final seal around my neck, pulled on my mask and ran outside into the darkness. There were no stars this morning, no moon either. But the lights mounted on the buildings were enough; I sprinted across the courtyard towards Maggie's lair. There was a fresh breeze; little snow-eddies danced around me. My boots crunched over the ice. *Far corner, nearest the oil tanks.* I reached the greenhouse and ran along its face, past the airlock and to the end of the building. I skidded round. There, in a pool of lamplight about three hundred yards away, were two suited figures. One was bent double, nose almost on the ground as they threw up. The other lay prostrate on the floor, unmoving.

"Keegan?" I yelled as I ran on.

The retching figure raised a hand but did not – maybe could not – reply. Finally reaching them, panting for breath while Keegan fell to his knees, whimpering piteously. Fischer lay motionless, face down on the frozen ground, vomit dribbling between her lips, a half-smoked joint on the ice by her outstretched hand. Both people were maskless. I recoiled slightly at the oversweet smell of vomit, then knelt beside her. The floodlights made her long hair glow silver, half her face invisible in shadow. I hurriedly pulled off my glove, barely feeling the cold as I reached for Fischer's pulse. It was there, but weak and far too fast.

"Oh God, I'm dying," Keegan wailed before a fresh bout of sickness came over him and he retched again.

"What's happened?" Dmitri called. I turned to see him and Weng rounding the corner of the greenhouse. Upon reaching us, Weng immediately fell to her knees with Fischer between us.

"She's alive," I said.

Weng was still breathing heavily from the run. She nodded and pulled back Fischer's eyelid to check the pupil.

"Can we move them?" I asked.

"What happened here?" Dmitri said at the same time, the shock clear in his tone.

"Get me inside," Keegan sobbed. "Please, I'm dying, get me to the infirmary." He tried to get to his feet but was overtaken by another fit of vomiting and doubled over.

I looked at Weng. "Can we take them inside?"

She nodded. "Kalinchenko, you take the doctor. We'll get this one."

Dmitri seemed glad to be given something straightforward to do. He nodded back at Weng and bent to pick up the body; he lifted Fischer with ease, as if she were hollow. Her head rolled back over the big man's arm, a string of drool like spider silk linking her momentarily to the ground, but other than that she remained frighteningly still.

"Can you walk?" I asked Keegan. When he didn't answer I bent down to take him under one arm and raised him, unsteadily, to his feet.

"You can manage?" Weng asked.

"Yes…yes," I replied, getting the lean figure standing up straight. Keegan's head lolled around and I did my best to avoid the flecks of yellow vomit that spun off his chin.

"Bring both to the infirmary," she said. And without further explanation she went ahead, overtaking Dmitri with his burden as she sprinted back to the barracks.

Before I set off to follow her, I had one last look at the joint that still lay in the small patch of light by the greenhouse. I would have to go back out for that.

CHAPTER FIFTEEN

There was no point in hanging around the ward. Weng and Abi, working as Weng's assistant, didn't need me getting in their way. The rest of the crew were unsure what to do; they knew they shouldn't just stand around and wait for news but they had nothing else to be getting on with. They were waiting in the rec room, pacing the floor or sitting dead-eyed around the table.

Keegan had not been able to make it to the infirmary without being sick again and I offered to clean the corridor. The unhealthy sweet-cloying smell was unpleasant but at least I got a moment alone to collect myself. It also gave me the chance to go back outside and collect the joint and have a more thorough scout around the area. I found a second butt but nothing more. No unexplained footprints, no mysterious notes – nothing but the evidence of smoking.

Once the corridor was mopped and disinfected I went down to my office and checked the security cameras, more in hope than expectation. To my surprise they clearly showed Fischer and Keegan leaving the barracks and heading towards the greenhouse – but then that wasn't suspicious. I knew what they were going out for. I spooled forward to check that nobody had followed them out, then ran back to the previous night. And there it was. A short period – maybe just half an hour – when the cameras had recorded nothing at all. I sat there for a second, drumming my fingers on the table. Then I headed back up to the rec room.

All conversation ceased the moment I entered. The crew stared at me with cold, scared faces. I was getting used to the feeling of mistrust that I was carrying on my shoulders. I ignored the engineers and turned straight to Maggie.

"Can I have a word with you, please?"

"Of course," she said in a neutral tone of voice. But she didn't move.

"I'd like to speak to you alone."

"And I'd rather have people around me," she shot back.

"If you've got something to say to Maggie," Fergie put in, "then you can say it to us all."

I hesitated. "Fine," I said. "I was just going to ask if you could analyze these for me." I pulled out a small, clear bag into which I had put the half-smoked joint and the butt I'd found outside.

All four of them took a few steps towards me, looking at what I was holding up.

"Joints?" Max asked.

"Keegan and Fischer had been smoking them when they…when they became sick," I said, my voice heavy.

"You think there was something in the weed – they were poisoned?" Maggie said.

"I don't know, but Fischer and Keegan looked like they'd had a reaction to something. I think it's worth checking, that's all."

I handed Maggie the little bag of evidence, and she immediately drew out the half-smoked joint and sniffed at it.

"You know," Fergie said, "you were overheard last night, Nordvelt."

"What?" I had been watching Maggie. Now I turned back to the Scotsman and saw suspicion writ large over his face.

"Max followed you," he continued.

I shot a glance at Max, who at least had the decency to avoid my eyes. I looked back at Fergie.

"Max followed you when you went out with Fischer after dinner. She heard the two of you arguing."

"We argued. So what?" I didn't care about this. I wanted to talk with Maggie. I wanted my evidence.

"So everyone you have a problem with ends up dead or in the infirmary," Greigor said.

"What?" I turned to him, blindsided.

"You have an argument with the commander and he mysteriously dies. Theo beats you up an' he—"

"What are you talking about?" I asked.

"The boxing. I hear he teaches you a lesson – and next day he's dead. And Mikhail too – is your ego so small you—"

"That was a friendly bout, just sparring – I never…" I trailed off in the face of Greigor's smirk. It was pointless.

"And now," Fergie said, "now Julia's in her own damn infirmary – just after you were heard arguing with her. Why'd you want her dead, Nordvelt? Was it because—"

"I didn't want her dead," I said, temper finally breaking. "I just—"

"We had no problems—" Greigor began.

"There's not one shred of evidence against me, is there? Is there?" No one answered.

"You're only looking at me because I'm new. Did it not occur to you that the culprit might just have been waiting for the night shift to start? If you're gonna try to destroy a base, you might as well do it when no one can interfere from the outside."

"Yeah, but—" Greigor said.

"I don't want anyone dead," I said over him, "I went out with Fischer to talk to her about her drug use."

"She's not doing anyone any harm—" Fergie said.

"No? She's becoming incapable of making decisions. She's removing herself from this crew and neglecting her duties. She's got a critically ill patient and she's—" I swallowed and took a breath, tried again. "Whatever. Look, that's what I was arguing with her about. I don't want her dead, I don't want her removed from the rest of us. We *need* her! You need her, I need her, the rest of us need her. And last night, at dinner, she was no damn use to anybody." I paused, drawing deep breaths as I struggled to control myself. "It was you that gave the killer a reason to go after her," I said.

"What? What are you talking about?"

"You told everyone last night that Fischer was going to test everyone on base. *You* gave the killer their motive. *You* caused Fischer and Keegan to wind up in the infirmary."

Fergie stared at me in amazement. He opened and closed his mouth. "No," he gasped.

"Or maybe you just gave that information away on purpose, to cover your own guilt," I finished savagely, the last of my rage slipping away and leaving me cold.

"I did – I didn't—" The Scotsman broke off, shaking his head.

"You think Fischer was targeted because of the new Psych tests?" Dmitri asked.

I shrugged.

"No – no, it's not possible!"

We all looked round at Maggie. While we were all arguing she had gone over to the table to better examine the joints I had given her. She was holding a small blade in one hand, and had clearly sliced the half-smoked joint cleanly down one side. Now she was holding an almost microscopic fragment of leaf up to the light, her face a mask of horror. "It's not possible," she repeated weakly.

"What is it?" I asked.

She opened and closed her mouth again.

I hurried over to her side. Fergie, Dmitri and Max all crowded round her as well, but it was me she spoke to.

"You – you remember that new strain of hemp you saw in my lab?"

A horrible feeling began to spread from my gut. "The one that you said was poisonous?"

She didn't need to answer. She was the expert, but the viridian of the shredded leaf in her hand suddenly looked horribly familiar.

★   ★   ★

Max brought me my food. The decision had been made: I was confined to quarters. Finally Fergie, Keegan, Greigor – I didn't know who, the discussion hadn't taken place in my presence – had got their way. We were past proper procedure. Lock me up. Keep me away. The inmates were running the asylum.

Except they weren't mad, weren't stupid. I knew that, and it almost made it worse. I could understand why they wanted me out of the way. It didn't make me feel any less resentful, though.

Max made no move to get up when I pushed the tray aside untouched. She remained seated on the bed, arms wrapped around her knees, staring at me. I stared at my lap.

"Keegan will be fine," she said eventually. "Weng says he'll get over it when he's had some rest. He puked up most of the poison."

"And Fischer?"

Max looked away. "Not so good. She didn't have as good a gag reflex as Keegan. Weng's got her stabilized...but stabilized doesn't mean 'will definitely get better'."

"How bad is it?"

She closed her eyes momentarily and leaned her head back against the wall. "God, all those machines that Weng's got her hooked up to… Julia barely looks human right now." She shook her head, then cleared her throat. "Her liver and kidneys are starting to break down. Her only chance is to get to a proper hospital. And that's impossible."

I stared at Max, horrified. Maggie had said the plant was poisonous, but I hadn't ever imagined that it could be this bad. This whole situation was a nightmare. "God," I whispered. "Does that mean…?"

"Weng's decided that her only chance is to put her into a coma, like Mikhail. They'll retard her metabolic functions as much as possible and try to keep her alive until help comes from Tierra."

"Can they do that?" I asked, desperate for any sign of hope.

Max nodded, but her eyes were still grim. "There's just one problem. They have the knowledge to put her into a coma, but they don't know how to get her safely out again."

"So…"

"So Fischer and Mikhail are as good as dead until we're rescued. It's just lucky Weng's as well-trained as she is, or Fischer would be as dead as dead." Max sighed. "Anyway, that's the situation. Thought you'd like to know," she finished in a monotone.

"What's Fergie doing now? And the rest of you?" I asked.

"Just…just trying to get back to some sort of normality, I suppose. Trying to come to terms with… It's all very raw, you know?" She shook her head. "We had a look in Fischer's room. Her personal weed supply had been thoroughly doctored with the poisonous stuff. She must have just not noticed the difference. I'm not sure she even knew about Greigor's experiment."

"So Keegan went out with her, they found a quiet place to smoke, and they shared from Fischer's supply."

She nodded. "That's what we think."

Silence fell again.

"You must be doing something," I said.

"Yes, yes, of course we are," Max said, exhaustion pouring as frustration from her lips. "We're trying to survive, Anders. We're shutting down power to all the buildings we're not using – the mine, the garage, the storerooms. We're starting to clear the lowest level so we can move in there if necessary. The basement will be the warmest place in the complex if – when – we lose power, and if we're all in there together, we can share a single heat source. Just the ambient temperature of our bodies will help a little…" She trailed off and wiped a hand across her brow. "We're all just trying to survive, and it's not easy. We've no doctor, no commanding officer, and soon we'll be without proper heating in the coldest place on the planet. And all the time we're waiting for the next…next…"

"So you don't all think I'm guilty?" I asked, a breath of hope creeping into my voice.

Max didn't answer straight away. She looked at me for a moment, then stretched out her legs on the bed before adjusting a pillow behind her. She looked…lovely. Even though her face was drawn, exhausted, she still radiated competence and self-possession, and I found that irresistible.

"I'm not an idiot, Anders," she said. "Fergie's not an idiot. No one here would have been hired if they weren't capable."

Now it was my turn to sigh, to run my hand over my scar, to push my mind away from her body and back to serious matters. "Whoever the killer is, they knew where Fischer hid her marijuana, and that Maggie's new strain of hemp was poisonous."

"Did you know both these things?"

"Yes. Did you?"

Max looked surprised to have her question thrown back at her. But she nodded.

"The saboteur can get into crew members' private rooms – Fischer's, at least – with or without permission. Not that that's such a trick," I muttered, "given the stupidly simple entry codes you all seem to use here. They can also hack into the base's security net and can blank out the security cameras."

"You realize that all this you're saying only serves to implicate yourself?"

"Or you," I said harshly. "Oh, come on," I said as I saw her eyes open wide, "you must have worked it out. The only people I know for certain could have managed all this are you and me. I know how good you are with computers – I know how good you are with machinery. You could have done this, possibly with less trouble than me!"

"*Anyone* here might have done it," she snapped back. "Maggie's a genius, Weng's a genius, Dmitri, Fergie – they all either have the skills or they can learn them. But they have no motive—"

"Neither do I!"

"But they've been here for half a year already, and I know what you said about waiting for the night shift to begin, but still – there weren't any problems before you arrived."

We stared at each other in silence.

"Do you really think it's me, Max?"

She took her time and stared hard at me before answering. "Based on what I know of you, based on the impression of only a fortnight? No, I wouldn't have said you'd be capable of murder," she said steadily. "But I've known the others a lot longer. I don't think any of them are capable of murder either."

"I helped save Mikhail's life."

"I know. I was there."

"I got this from that," I said, pointing at my scar.

"They can remove that, a simple—"

"That's not the point."

She sighed. "Look, yes, I saw you walk into that inferno, and I know what you did to help Mikhail – to help us all. If it's worth anything, then thank you. Thank you. But really that doesn't change a thing. Look—" She hesitated. "I should go, Anders. The others will be thinking that you've killed me."

"Is that a joke?"

"You know, I'm not quite sure myself."

"Before you leave…"

"Yes?"

"Could you look at my compscreen for me?"

"What?"

I explained about the hacker. Max, lips tight, sat before the screen and frowned at the message that had been left for me. Almost immediately she began to open menus and layer information and was soon deep in the arcane world of computer programming, a place with its own language and customs. I understood none of it. "I can't help from here," she said after barely a minute. "It's going to take a system reset. It'll have to be done from the network room – I'll get on it when I have a free moment."

"Do you have any idea who might have done that?" I asked as she stood.

She looked at me, curiously reticent. "I should go," she said again. "Just to warn you – we'll be lowering the temperature setting throughout the barracks. Preserve what fuel we can."

"You slept with de Villiers." My God, where had *that* come from? But the words were out now, hanging heavy in the air between us.

Max's face had frozen into a mask. She looked at me; there was nothing to be read there. Even anger would have been preferable. Inside I cringed.

"And?" she asked coldly.

"It's true, then?" It was like scratching an itch; I just couldn't help myself.

"I don't see that it's any business of yours." She picked up the tray I'd left on the table.

"I just…" Just what? I was just bitter and betrayed? Just jealous? Just nothing that I'd admit to myself, let alone share with Max.

She paused by the door and looked back. "Sometimes I *can* see the killer in you," she said, and she left.

I spent a long time cursing myself after that.

★   ★   ★

Over the next few days my only company came at mealtimes, when one of the crew would bring me food. Sometimes they'd sit with me while I ate; others would drop off the tray and leave. I got no information – no specifics, at least. I picked up that Keegan was back on his feet and that there'd been no further attacks. The hours passed slowly. I rested, and I threw off the last lingering effects of my pneumonia. It was somewhat ironic that this was, physically, the best I'd felt since arriving at Australis.

As I felt better, as I grew stronger, I felt increasingly frustrated at my imprisonment. I paced the room for hours. I did press-ups and stretches, exercise keeping me warm as the ambient temperature fell. I toyed with my puzzle box, listened to my music. Tried to read Holmes again, but the words were too familiar to hold my attention. I stared at my scar in the mirror, trying to work out if I still looked like myself.

I took up de Villiers's datapad and read through his files. Although my biomarkers should have routed the device's functions into my personal account, as chief of security I could override it and get into anyone else's. The pads were our personal extensions to the network, so in theory everything on the base computers was available on the pads.

In practice, however, everyone retained all their passwords and kept some non-networked files for datapad use only. De Villiers had outranked me so my override didn't get me past his password. Procedure demanded two ranking officials to override a superior's blocks, and Fischer was in no position to help me.

So I had no access to his personal log but did get de Villier's schedule and his messages. Of course, the message the killer had sent – my name put to a suggestion of blackmail – was top. Below that… Messages from Fischer, mostly, but all the crew seemed to be in regular contact with him. There were a few other names too, names I didn't recognize.

The crew's messages were insignificant. They seemed to be either professional and practical – Dmitri's suggestions for new safety practices while working underground, Weng's geological reports as cold as the woman herself – or thoroughly personal and relaxed. Agreements to meet (I made a chart of de Villiers's movements, as far as I could tell, in the days before his death. I couldn't see any pattern, nothing out of the ordinary), challenges for a gym session – Dmitri again, his need for approval and affection almost embarrassing to read.

The other names – one message was from de Villiers's wife. It took me some time to realize that; she used a different surname, and it was only when I read about 'our son' that I got it. Their exchanges were cordial, even affectionate – but sent as much, I felt, out of duty and necessity and habit as out of love. No clues there.

All the other messages were from de Villiers's bosses in Tierra or Brasilia. He was promising them big things – impressive projections. I wondered if he'd really considered his estimates realistic or if he had been engaging in diplomatic padding.

But none of this helped me find his killer. The information I really wanted must have been in those personal files. I spent hours trying to crack de Villiers's password. Tried the name I now knew his wife used, then the names of all the crew. Tried…desperately tried random combinations of letters and numbers. Shoved my palm into the keyboard, frustrated, moronic. A failure.

Somehow the crew had managed to block off my security access. Couldn't override the lock on the door. Couldn't get CCTV pictures.

And then suddenly I could.

It was Max's doing. I knew that. And I could only think it was an accident, an oversight. My third day of captivity: I was doing sit-ups when the compscreen flickered and went blank. Reels of code scrolled up the screen too fast for me to read. The system reset, I guessed. I didn't pay too much attention, just worked up a sweat as if it would help me get into de Villiers's mind. I forced myself to work until my belly screamed. I lay on the floor and panted for breath, muscles so tight. The reboot finished and the screen returned to its normal welcome screen – without the hacker's message.

Couldn't move straight away.

What had de Villiers cared about? What would he pick as a password?

I rolled onto my front and, aching, got to my hands and knees. Then, with the aid of a chair, I got to my feet. I flopped in front of the compscreen. I wanted a glass of water, but I was out of muscles.

De Villiers. What did he love? Sex. What else? Mining. Maybe his old colleagues? His old…?

I cracked it first time. Or maybe Max had done something with her reboot. Maybe it'd have opened to anything.

Either way, *Debringas* – his first posting as overseer – got me in.

★　　★　　★

I didn't do anything. Not straight away. Couldn't quite believe my luck. I kept glancing at the door as if Fergie would march in at any second.

Max could have done it on purpose. She could've been playing me. I wasn't sure, just then, if I could trust what I was reading. A clever person could lead me down a false trail easily enough.

But there wasn't any point stalling. I'd been desperate for data, and here it was in spades. I had to go to the personal logs.

I read de Villiers's and Fischer's first, but neither contained anything that I didn't already know. The commander's read more like a list of conquests than an objective account. It was filled with phrases like "Weng came to my room tonight", "Saw Fischer in her office", "Spent evening with Max". Apart from that, it mostly described plans for improvements in drilling efficiency, or outlined ideas for ways to expand the base.

In reference to me there was a note of my arrival and of his initial impressions. It seemed Greigor had been right: the commander hadn't trusted me at all. Not that he'd said anything so direct, but the inference was clear. "He seems unwilling to engage with the crew, a cold fish. Why doesn't he want to get close to anyone? I can guess."

After we'd had the first meeting on the night of the equinox: "Convinced Nordvelt will become a problem. Unhappy at some of our extracurricular activities. But think I managed to buy us a little time – maybe we'll manage him but I'll keep an eye on him for now."

And the next: "Why would he destroy the comms building? If he was writing a special report, he'd want to keep communications open. But it couldn't have been anyone else, surely."

The only other comments of any note seemed to concern Weng. "Weng continues to be difficult," one entry began. "Will talk to her next week; until then best to treat her as normal." So he'd known what he was doing. That entry was dated just before my arrival; I wondered if he'd actually had the discussion he'd been planning.

There was also a note of the disciplinary meeting he'd had with Greigor. It was one of the last records and said simply, "Spoke with Greigor RE: complaints. Recommended he do the online sensitivity training."

I frowned at the screen.

Fischer's logs were, if anything, even less interesting. Her notes consisted mostly of treatment records, of which there were few. McCarthy saw her regularly, I noted, suffering from sleeplessness and headaches. On one occasion he'd complained of sleepwalking, said that one night he'd woken in the vestibule, halfway into his warmsuit, with an ice cutter in hand.

Fischer had not attempted to record her feelings.

McCarthy's personal logs reiterated a lot of the previous information. He'd suffered in Antarctica with both his health and his interactions with the rest of the crew. He wrote at length about his arguments with de Villiers. "No discipline," he wrote in successive descriptions of the commander. "No respect for the rules." Over the months his records became terser and terser; I could almost feel his lack of sleep through his words. It was with mild interest that I saw that he'd been hired by the same team that had recruited me. But there was nothing that indicated he had any suspicions about anyone, not even de Villiers. It seemed, as everyone had told me, that his dislike was confined to the commander's personality and methods.

Dragged by the small chain that connected McCarthy and myself, I drifted back to the series of interviews and tests that had led me to Antarctica. It was oddly hazy; less than half a year ago. I should have had some impression of the people behind the desks. I'd been in that room enough times, could still picture the conference table in front of me. But those gathered on the other side had lost definition. They came back as voices only.

"*Lacks experience.*" A woman, disinterested.

"*But his work record shows that he's never been properly tested. The Psych shows a high ceiling. He has potential.*" An older man.

And then being strapped to a gurney, a white light all I knew, as another barrage of tests was launched against me. A new, upgraded form of the Psych, that's what they'd said.

I pulled myself together and pushed away the odd disquiet that had settled on my shoulders. I accessed Fergie's logs.

Craig Ferguson, Scots born, Scots educated, Scots trained. His early records were simple accounts of the mineworkings, interspersed with his feelings and impressions of the people around him. For the first few months he'd seemed content and had enjoyed his work. But there was a marked change once the attacks started. The impression of an easygoing man disappeared almost overnight. It was replaced by a man who appeared paranoid and vindictive. If I hadn't known the circumstances, I would have considered him unstable.

The Company advised weekly updates, but his now became daily. "Comms building destroyed. Explosives causing avalanche...must watch Nordvelt carefully." "De Villiers dead. Can't believe it was an accident – Weng most likely suspect, but Nordvelt...." "Made commander of operations. Can now watch crewmates from better position – must get Nordvelt confined to quarters." "Worried that the janitor is becoming too close to Nordvelt. Cannot trust her to carry out her duties independently." "Nordvelt confined to quarters but crew still divided. Does he have co-conspirators?" "Must keep an eye on Max and Dmitri. Hear them talking behind my back…listening devices planted."

Damn him. Damn that bloody Scot. I looked round me wildly, trying to find the bug that Fergie must have planted in my room. This I was not prepared to tolerate. I calmed myself and began a methodical search, and eventually I found a small pellet-like device stuck to the underside of my table. I threw it on the floor and stamped on it until it was dust. God alone knew how he'd got it in here; maybe when he'd brought food, or – well, it really didn't matter.

I shook my head, my anger spent. I threw myself back in my chair, sighed and leaned back. What was the point? What was the point in even trying to work it out?

I found nothing to help me prove my innocence, nothing to suggest an alternative suspect. Although I could hardly have expected to find a confession in the personal logs.

And then I read Greigor's log. And the anger I'd thought was spent came back, doubled and redoubled.

I got up and moved for the intercom. Then I hesitated.

No point going off half-cocked. There was more to be done here first.

*   *   *

There was something else. Whatever bodge, whatever software patch, the engineers had put on my door to seal me in, the system reboot must have erased it. I didn't realize at first. Whether from boredom or frustration, I had tried my access code a dozen times over the days and got nowhere. This time it worked.

Again I wondered if Max had she known what she was doing. It was possible – it was possible that this was a setup. It would not look good for me to be caught outside my rooms.

My heart was thumping as I sidled along the corridor wall, every moment expecting to be discovered. It'd be a hard job convincing the others that I hadn't broken out to perform mischief.

With my security override working again I'd accessed the surveillance network to make sure that no one was around. I'd made sure that Greigor was in the greenhouse. Still my palms were sweaty and my breath overloud. I reached the end of the corridor and peered round the corner, ears hypersensitive for any sound that didn't belong.

Greigor's room. I paused, waited a moment for my heartbeat to slow, then overrode the lock.

I slipped inside.

CHAPTER SIXTEEN

Fergie came for me next morning.

"Come on," he said without preamble.

"Where are we going?" I asked, pausing in the middle of a press-up.

"The basement," he said. Dark rings circled his eyes, his skin pale and appearing almost brittle. He looked like he hadn't slept in weeks. "We're clearing out in there. You can help us. What's that damn music?"

I jumped to my feet and turned it off, spilling sweat onto the screen. "Does this mean—"

"You're still the killer," Fergie snapped. "You won't be left alone, I promise." He still talked tough but the strain was clearly getting to him. He didn't seem able to look me in the eyes. He stepped back to let me through.

I'd spent much of the night lying in my bed and staring at the ceiling. My mind was working, working, working. Someone had to be told about what I'd found in Greigor's room. Someone had to know. I just had to put it all together myself first and find the right moment, the right person...

I grabbed a shirt and walked out to the corridor. Dmitri was waiting there, leaning against a wall, scowling.

"Three days locked up and no trouble," Fergie said with a note of smugness as he led the way to the stairwell. "Still claim you're innocent, Nordvelt?"

I didn't reply. Dmitri too kept silent as we descended to the lowest level, our footsteps echoing up the shaft.

"So what're we doing, then?" I asked as we emerged into the relative warmth of the basement.

"Moving all this crap up to the workshop," Fergie said, gesturing at the piles of stored material.

"We're readying our move down here," Dmitri added.

Fergie scowled at the Ukrainian as if he'd given me too much information. But he just told us to get on with it and left us alone in the strip-lit chamber.

Dmitri looked at me steadily. He moved over to the nearest stack of material and took hold of one side of a large sheet of steel. "Take the end," he said.

With a sigh I did as he asked. Together we spent the rest of the day ferrying metal to the service lift and then stacking it in the workshop. Thinking, thinking, thinking all the while.

★   ★   ★

I fell back on my bed, totally exhausted. My arms, back and legs ached. I had never in my life put in such a hard day's work. Dmitri and I had been lugging materials around all day, and yet we hadn't even managed to clear the first rack.

I hadn't seen Max since our argument but I was glad to see her appear with my dinner tray. I struggled to my feet to greet her.

"Hi," I said as she placed the food on my table and dropped a bag on the bed. "Are you staying to talk, or are you heading straight back up?"

She didn't reply immediately. She stood, hands on hips, and stared at me, unsmiling. "You had no right to bring up my relationship with de Villiers."

"I'm still trying to find out who killed him," I said, unable to keep the snark out of my voice.

"Don't give me that shit, Anders. You didn't ask me because you needed the information. You asked me because—" She didn't finish the sentence, telling me louder than any words that she knew I was jealous.

I opened my mouth to reply, then closed it again.

"You have no hold on me, Anders. You have no right to interrogate me over my personal affairs."

"I am security chief – I have—"

"That's not why you were asking, though, was it?"

Deep breath. "No. You're right. I'm sorry."

"Not that I'm not flattered."

I kept my eyes on the floor.

"Right. Okay. That's that out of the way. Eat."

I gave myself a mental shake. "There's something I need to show you first."

She raised an eyebrow.

"It's important."

"Well?"

"I need to go with you to Greigor's room."

She blinked, then burst out laughing. "What the hell are you talking about? Go to Greigor's room? Why would we do that?"

Her smile faded slowly as she took in my expression.

"Why?" she asked. "What's in Greigor's room?"

"I think it'd be easier if I showed you."

Max shook her head. "You're locked in here, Anders. Fergie'd do his nut if I let you out."

I grimaced, frustrated. I didn't want to let anyone know I'd already left my quarters – not if I could help it. Then it clicked. I realized I didn't have to.

"The CCTV cameras. I can show you the security footage."

"We removed your access to the CCTV."

I looked at her carefully. I could see no signs of dissembling, no quirk of the mouth that'd indicate a joke. Good acting? Could be. I didn't say anything, just went to the compscreen and dialed up the right images.

"How come you can get access?" she snapped, grabbing me by the shoulder.

I didn't answer. Just stepped back and indicated the screen.

★　　★　　★

I thought I'd seen Max angry before. It was clear now that I'd not seen a thing.

I trailed in her wake, striding, almost running through the corridors. Finally she reached the canteen and, barely breaking step, thrust her way inside.

"Max, what? Hey, Nordvelt – wh—"

"You little turd!" Max snapped, pointing a finger at Greigor. Her arm barely trembled. "You little sniveling wretch! I'm gonna kick the shit out of you, you motherfucker!"

Everyone was scrambling to their feet now, plates hastily pushed away, cutlery falling to the table. Greigor looked totally perplexed, stumbling back as his chair fell with a thump.

"Max, what is this?" Maggie asked. "What's going on?"

"Why the *hell* is Nordvelt here?" Fergie demanded.

Max took another pace forward, eyes still consuming the Argentinean. "This worm, this *thing*, has been spying on us. He's broken into the security system somehow, he's been—"

"It's n-no' true," Greigor stammered. "I never—"

"Don't try and deny it, you little shit. Anders showed me the footage."

I ignored the glances aimed at me, kept fully focused on the rat Greigor.

"You've got recordings of…" She hesitated. "You've got footage of me and Anders… You've got footage of me *naked*. Couldn't have me yourself so you thought you'd try a little voyeurism, huh? Well, I hope you fucking came hard, shitbag."

Now all eyes were on Greigor. He shook his head desperately. The silence lay heavy across the table.

"Greigor, is this true?" Maggie asked, voice shaking only slightly.

"Oh, it's true, don't you doubt it," Max said. "He's got hours of video. Of me, and of Weng."

The Chinese woman, who for months had been seated next to Greigor, gave a little gasp and edged away.

"I jus'…" Greigor hesitated, looking around wildly. "I jus' looking for the murderer, for the *saboteador*, yes? I do—"

"Don't give me that bullshit!" Max said. "Just looking for the saboteur, huh? Did you have any particular reason for thinking the killer would be in Weng's room, or mine, just when we're getting undressed? Did you have any reason to collect these – these videos back in the day shift, way before we had any problems?"

Weng was muttering something under her breath. She looked absolutely horrified, was still backing away. Maggie said something to her in some form of Chinese, but the woman just shook her head, turned and ran; she pushed past me and fled the room. Maggie gave

Greigor one last, furious glance, then hurried out after her.

Max leaned forward, knuckles on the table. "You're going to pay for this, you little maggot." She held his eyes for a long moment before she too swept out.

Now only the men remained in the canteen. All thoughts of eating had been abandoned.

I cleared my throat. "It was you that hacked my computer, wasn't it, Greigor?"

"He did what?" Fergie asked, looking between us.

"He hacked into my compscreen and left a message for me, didn't you, Greigor? He wanted me to know I was being watched. That I'm not really a part of this crew." I felt immune to emotion in that moment; I felt like an automaton, could store my feelings in a locked-off file to access later.

Greigor was still shaking his head but he couldn't keep the truth from his eyes. To his credit, he pulled himself together quickly and straightened. He wiped a lock of his hair away from his face and gave me the full impact of his good looks, his cool Latino eyes. "Okay, Nordvelt. Yes, I reprogrammed your compscreen. I was just doing what the commander wanted me to do—"

"The commander wanted—" Fergie began.

"Just before he dies, the commander calls me in for a meeting—"

"Where he was goin' to discipline you—"

"I told you already, de Villiers didn't trust our new security chief! He told me to keep an eye on him."

"Really?" It was nice to have Fergie's skepticism aimed at someone else for once. "He said that?"

"Well—"

"What precisely did he say to you?" Dmitri asked.

Greigor looked around and saw that everyone was still focused on him. "Well – he say – he said... De Villiers was preoccupied, all through our meeting. I ask him why and he says that he's worried about Nordvelt—"

"What about Nordvelt?" Fergie demanded, sparing me a look.

"The commander, he said that he'd need an eye kept on him—"

"That's what he said?" I asked. "An eye? He didn't say anything about you hacking my compscreen or spying on the—"

"It was clear what he was trying to say!"

"—and he didn't say anything about spying on the women," Fergie said.

"—and it was a good job I did," Greigor said over him, in a rush to get the words out. "Because I know a lot more about you, Mr. Nordvelt. A lot more than you'd like, yes?" He grinned at me, fierce and triumphant.

There was a moment's silence.

"What—" Keegan began, but Greigor cut him off.

"I was right to check you out, wasn't I, Nordvelt? Go on. Go ahead. Tell all these good people what the Psych says about you, yes? Tell Mr. Ferguson, Mr. Kalinchenko, Keegan, Abi – tell us *all* about who you really are, why not?" he snarled.

"This is not about me—"

"You want me to do it for you? Okay, then, that's how it is, huh? Well—"

"*Shut the fuck up, you little shit*," I roared, suddenly breaking like a tsunami. The next thing I knew, Dmitri was holding me by the shoulders, big hands gripping me firmly. Fergie was standing in front of Greigor, shock covering the Scotsman's face. The little rat behind him looked smug, and I squeezed my fists tight, tighter.

"You see? He's dangerous, a killer."

"Shut up, Greig," Fergie said, his voice shaking only a little. "We're gonna deal with this sensibly, right? No fights, no violence."

Dmitri's hands slackened on my shoulders, but he didn't quite let me go. I took a deep breath, keeping my eyes on Greigor. He met my gaze and didn't flinch. I was shaking with anger, cold with sudden fear.

"I reckon," Keegan said into the resulting silence. "I reckon we want to hear what Anders has to say, right?"

No.

"Greigor's saying that there's something that he knows about Nordvelt that we should know too. That right? Reckon we should hear it; then we can work out what to do with them both. Right?"

God, no.

This was a nightmare. A nightmare. Everyone was looking at me. I felt tears pricking my eyes. I was trapped, beginning to panic. I could run, I could refuse to talk, I could *knock Greigor cold*...

"You might as well tell, Mr. Nordvelt," Greigor said. "If you don', I will. Sound fair?"

"Anders," Dmitri said quietly, finally releasing me. "What is he talking about? I think you'd better tell."

I speared one final look at Greigor, then looked away. I fell into a vacant seat and leaned heavily on the table. My hand found an abandoned glass of water and I drank.

"Well, Nordvelt?" Fergie said.

I let a little numbness seep through me – a defense, an insulation. Was I really – could I really go through with this? "I...I had a difficult..."

"What's this, now, you're gonna say you had a difficult childhood?" Fergie said. "Well, didn't we all, one way or another?"

"Shut up, Fergie," Dmitri said heavily. "Let the man speak – and you keep your mouth shut too, Greigor."

Greigor held up his hands in surrender, somehow managing to put on an innocent face.

"Go on, Anders."

"I told you – I was raised in Sweden. I was raised in the White War."

Silence. Couldn't look up from the table.

"My father was one of the leaders – of – of the rebellion." Deep breath. "You know how pathetic that was – not a real war, just an idiotic group of malcontents refusing to adapt to the new reality of the world, of Company rule. My father was a killer. He was a terrorist. He – he got my mother killed, and he..." I broke off and tried again. "I was five when they caught him."

"I don't see – why should we care about that?" Dmitri said after a short pause.

"You don't see?" Greigor put in. "His father weren't just a rebel, he was a leader. He was rich. Here's the boy Anders, raised in luxury, all the toys his little heart could desire—"

"You know nothing!" I shouted.

There was a momentary silence before Greigor went on. At least I'd taken a little of the gloating from his tone. "All those riches, all coming to the only child – until the Company took it all from him."

"My father was an idiot! A stupid, reactive idiot! I'm glad he was caught, I'm glad I was brought up by the Company—"

"You're saying you never missed that money, those houses?" Greigor asked.

"They're better in Company hands." And I believed it. But I couldn't make it sound like I did. "Listen, long ago I rejected my father and everything he stood for. Don't you think I've been through a hundred separate Pysch tests? Think they'd have sent me here if—"

"And this is the man the Company have chosen to give power over us." Greigor snorted. "They must've been crazy. First a jumped-up *generalissimo* like McCarthy, and now this retarded little runt. Both hired from the same office, you know? When we get out of this bastard wasteland, I'll be there wi' a gun—"

"That's enough," Fergie said. "You've got nothing to crow about, you little pervert. You think you'll have a career after this? Just shut it. We'll get to you in a minute." He turned to me. "Nordvelt. Anything else we should know?"

I shook my head. Couldn't look up at him.

"What about the message you sent de Villiers?" Greigor said.

"What message?" Dmitri asked as I lifted my head to stare open-mouthed at the Argentinean.

"Ask him why he's got de Villiers's datapad in his room," Greigor was saying. "Ask him about the message he sent de Villiers, drawing him out into the snow the night the commander died. Ask him all about that."

I couldn't tell if my heart was beating hyperfast or if it had stopped dead. "You've—" *You've been in my room. You searched through my things.* The words wouldn't come. Of course he'd been in my room. He'd been prepared to plant cameras in private chambers. Just looking in my miserable quarters wouldn't have bothered him at all.

The rest of the crew were staring at me, I realized. I swallowed.

"Well?" Keegan asked.

"After we brought de Villiers's body back in—" I cleared my throat. "After I told all you...I went to the commander's rooms and had a quick search..."

"Alone? No witnesses?" Fergie asked.

I shook my head. "I – I found his datapad." I explained about the message that had lured the commander to his death.

"You see," Greigor said, "there's the proof – Nordvelt's the killer and the evidence is in his room."

"So why the fuck didn't you tell us about this?" Fergie said.

"I didn't send the message," I said. "Someone's trying to set me up. But I knew how it'd look…"

"I wasn't talking to you," he said. "Greigor, why'd you no' tell us about this message if you knew about it—"

"I only found it yesterday," he said quickly, "while you were in the basement—"

"While you were supposed to be with Maggie?"

"Hey, I told you, de Villiers told me to watch Nordvelt!"

"So why not tell us as soon as you found it?" Dmitri asked.

Greigor hesitated. "I…I knew he'd just deny it. I wanted more evidence…"

"You just wanted the feeling of power you'd have over him," the Ukrainian said.

Fergie turned to me. "Did you kill de Villiers an' Theo?"

"No. I've not done anything."

"Okay. Okay," Fergie said shakily. "I think…we need time to take this all in. To work out what to do. Nordvelt, I ain't judging, but this all changes nothing. You're still the prime suspect. It's not personal, but you should—"

"I should be locked back in my room, I know. Don't worry, I'll go straight back. I just…" I tried to focus on what really mattered. "I need to know one thing."

"What's that, Chief?" Keegan asked.

"Did…did Greigor ever say anything to any of you about me putting cameras up around the base?"

"What are you talking about, Anders?" Abidene asked.

"I never—" Greigor began, but I cut off his denial.

"Before the oil platform exploded," I went on, as calmly as I could manage, "I planted pinhead cameras around the barracks. To try and catch the killer. With all Greigor's snooping, I'm willing to bet that he saw me doing this. All those times I've randomly stumbled across you in the corridors, Greigor? All those little 'missions' you've been doing for Maggie? How many of them were just an excuse for you to spy on us?"

"Listen, I—"

"But someone moved all my cameras. So I need to know if this little weasel told anyone else about them. I need to know, Greigor."

He shook his head. "I don' know…I may have…"

"He didn't say anything to me," Keegan said.

"Nor me," Dmitri added.

Fergie and Abi were shaking their heads, expressions grim, angry, confused.

"Whoever moved those cameras," I said with a humorless little smile, "has got to be a strong candidate to be the murderer."

"Max! I told Max, it was Max!" Greigor yelled.

"Yeah," snapped Fergie, "because we're gonna believe everything you tell us now, ain't we, rat boy?"

★　★　★

Keegan and Dmitri escorted me back to my quarters. I handed them de Villiers's datapad and ate a cold meal alone. Nothing had changed, not really. All I'd done was give Fergie a new suspect, a new problem, another person to keep locked up.

Max came to see me an hour or so later. She slung a bag on the floor and sat on my bed, looking glum.

"So what happened?" I asked.

"I beat the shit out of the gym punchbag, then went and welded something," she said.

"Feel better?"

"Not really. Did a bad job, it fell straight apart. Kicking the bits around helped, though. You know the worst thing?"

"What?"

"I was thinking that at least this'll get me a proper alibi for the sabotage. If anyone's suspecting me, then at least I can say, 'Look, I was asleep all along,' and point out Greigor's network. But I can't do that. He only recorded – or saved, at least – the—"

"The interesting bits. Yes. I know."

"You've watched it?"

"No, no – I only looked at enough to get an… I mean, he saved short sections. I didn't have to watch them, the titles were enough—"

She glared me into silence.

"I'm sorry."

She sighed and made a gesture for me to forget about it.

"Have you spoken to the others?" I asked.

She nodded.

"Did they ask you about the cameras I'd set up?"

"What? Oh, yeah, it's true, Greigor told me about them. I think he was trying to impress me."

"So—"

"But I told Maggie. And she probably told everyone else. Sometimes there's just nothing to do but gossip."

"Damn."

"Sorry."

I took a deep breath. "Is Weng okay?"

"Maggie's spoken to her."

"And?"

Max shrugged.

"So what happens now?"

"Well, I try and find a way to heat the base with coal – without poisoning us all with the smoke. We abandon everywhere except the kitchen, the infirmary, and the basement, and we wait for help to arrive from Tierra."

"I meant about Greigor. And me."

"Neither of you are to be left alone. You help us to survive, and then we hand you back to the Company."

"I didn't do this," I said. "I didn't do any of this."

"About your father…"

I went cold. "What about him?"

"You know, I was going to ask why you didn't tell us. About your past. But then I realized that I wouldn't have told you if I'd had that in my family," she said. "Yeah, I know Fergie and me, and most of us really, we grumble about the Company. No room for initiative, the endless committees and all that – but really we all know how awful life would be without it. I come from the Central African Zone, for God's sake. You remember how devastated the area was after the Resource Wars? All those petty dictators fighting for their piece of the pie? I'd never have got beyond the city limits without the Company. I certainly wouldn't have got to travel like I have. Hell, chances are I'd be dead." She shook her head. "It's hard to imagine anyone wanting to fight against the Company, let alone be willing to kill to end it."

I nodded and stared at the floor. Then I got up and went to the compscreen, put my music on. I turned to face Max on the bed but couldn't bring myself to look into her eyes. "This…"

"Yes?"

"This is my mother."

"The singer?"

"She was – the Evening Star, they called her. Jasmine Burroughs. Angel of the North."

"I've not heard of her, I'm sorry."

"She was never big outside England. This was her only album." I paused to listen, caught as my mother sang descending soprano, voice swooping as a harrier upon the melody. "This is all I have of her."

Max was silent for a long minute as the guitar played: urgent, sorrowful arpeggios over a wide, angry bass. Above it all was that voice, crying for freedom, for the wild places, for the search for solitude away from the human hive.

"So what happened?" Max asked as the track faded out.

"My parents met through her music. He was a fan, rich enough to push her career. I was born into that money. And then the Company began its advance into Sweden, and… Look, you have to understand that I was a baby – I don't remember anything, not really, just impressions."

I could feel her eyes on me.

"I don't even remember their faces. I was only five. My mother – my father killed her, you know? He dragged her into his war: rebel meetings in our drawing room, moving between countries, often at just a few minutes' notice. I remember him practicing his speeches – I wasn't allowed in his study – never even saw his desk before the security teams shot their way in. I remember – my mother didn't smile. I don't remember her ever smiling – she must have, mustn't she? But in my mind she's always pale. And thin."

"I—"

"And when the Company mercs closed in we retreated into the wilderness. I don't remember – don't remember…" I swallowed. "I don't remember anything, not really, just going from refuge to refuge. Sometimes we'd stay in great country houses, sometimes we'd sleep in tents, in snow-shelters, burying ourselves under pine branches for a little extra warmth...and all the while their trackers were closing in.

"I don't know how she died. Some say my father shot her, some that she was gunned down by the hunters. Some say she was shot trying to flee, others that she killed a dozen men before she took a bullet. I never wanted to know. I still don't." I could see every one of those tales in my mind, and a hundred others. I pushed them away. I'd rather remember her voice.

"So there I was," I said. "My mother dead, and my father... Do you know how it feels? To be told that your childhood hero has...is really a monster?"

Max was silent.

"I was moved to my grandparents. In England. My father's parents. And they tried, they tried – they tried to love me, to care for me, to do the right thing. But how can anyone look at their grandchild without seeing their son? They were...they were afraid of me, I think. Afraid of getting anything wrong. Of getting it wrong *again*."

I ran out of words.

"Anders...Anders." Max sighed and leaned back. "You make things so hard, Anders. When you talk like this – with that look on your face..." She trailed off. When she spoke again her tone was cooler, calmer. "When you talk like this, I really feel for you. But for all I think Greigor's a contemptible little shit, I can't see him killing anyone. I just... Why? Why would he blow up the rig? And being able to hack into computers isn't the same as knowing how to plant a bomb or sabotage a warmsuit. It doesn't make sense."

"And it makes sense for me to have done it?"

"I don't know who you are," she said simply. "If I'd had your upbringing, I'd probably be just plain nuts. These attacks make no sense, so why not look for a madman? Look, Anders, we've already had this conversation. Goddamn. God*damn*. I just know that – that I feel safe with you. I like you." She banged the back of her head against the wall, frustration on her lips. "You want a drink?"

"What?"

"Where's my bag?"

I passed it over to her.

She pulled it to her and reached inside. "I'd have preferred to have a smoke," she muttered half to herself, "but taking you outside would probably not please Fergie too much. Get some glasses." She pulled out a bottle like those that had contained the wine at my first meal at Australis.

"You'd drink with me?" I asked, surprised.

Max unscrewed the cap and took a sniff at the contents. Her eyes opened wide; even I could smell the spirits from across the room. "Anton's private stock," she said. "He liked his whisky. Hurry up with the glasses."

I found a couple of tumblers and took them over to the bed. Max poured the liquor. It caught the light and refracted strange, shifting golden shadows onto the bedclothes.

She took one of the tumblers and held it up to me. "Here's to the prime suspects," she intoned. I raised my glass to her, and we each took a sip. Tears immediately leaped to my eyes and I choked.

"I said it was de Villiers's private stash, but I didn't say it was *good*," Max croaked.

"God, that tastes like…like…God, what the hell is that?" I managed.

"Rocket fuel, that's what it's like." She wiped her eyes and took another sip. "You realize Fergie's probably got the room bugged. Cameras, listening devices, whatever. Man's getting paranoid," she finished in a mumble.

"You're okay with that?" I asked, too surprised to tell her that I'd already found and destroyed a bug.

The janitor finished her drink in one big go, gasped and held her glass out for me to pour her another. "You listening to this, Ferguson?" she called. "Just a quick message to tell you to go fuck yourself, you perverted little…*Scotsman!*" She began to laugh, and, after a moment, I joined her.

★   ★   ★

I woke up before Max and left her sleeping while I went into the wet-room for a shower. I stood unsteady and heavy-headed in the booth, eagerly anticipating the hot water pouring over my skin, washing me clean. But nothing happened. There was no flow; the shower control panel was dead. I frowned at it blearily, slapped it a few times, but there was nothing.

I leaned against the wall and swore quietly to myself, then staggered back through to my compscreen. I hit the power and scanned my thumbprint on the reader. Then I got up again and jabbed at the combi-maker for coffee. The room was silent. I couldn't even hear the climate control, the usual background to life here on the base.

I sat back down. The screen hadn't activated. I hit the power again but got nothing. I scowled at the machine and hit that too; the only response was from Max, who grunted and rolled over in her sleep. So I got up and went to the door, intending to check the compscreen in my office. But the door wouldn't open. I did exactly what I'd tried the other day, when it had opened without any problem, but now there was nothing. The door panel looked inoperative. Not one of the LEDs was lit. I went to the combi-maker for my coffee, but that seemed as dead as the door.

I was half-asleep. I was still half-drunk. I was scared, and I was cold, and I couldn't face this. I glanced down at Max. I should have woken her, should have found out what was going on – if Fergie had just shut the power to my room, or if there was a bigger reason.

I had goosebumps on my arms. I shivered and hugged my bare torso. I so, so wanted just to crawl back into bed with Max and pretend I'd never got up.

And so I did. Coward that I am, I slipped in next to her, put my arms around her and cupped her small, soft breast in my hand. And I pushed the fears from my mind and tried to shut my brain off from the outside world.

CHAPTER SEVENTEEN

Another crisis meeting in the rec room. Another session filled with frightened faces and paranoid stares. There was no amazement this time, no shock, just cold fear. It seemed that we'd passed the stage for accusations; now we stood in silence. Me, Max, Fergie, Dmitri, Weng, Maggie, Greigor, Abidene, and Keegan. It was the first time I'd seen the meteorologist since he'd been admitted to the infirmary.

We looked at each other but nobody wanted to speak. Just trying to all get together had been an effort. The doors had sealed shut and we'd had to force open each one. And with no internal communications each person had to be found individually. It had taken time, all of us in ones or twos, sealed together but apart, as if we were trapped in some horror movie. No automatic lights – instead we held torches which showed either too little or far too much.

Fergie cleared his throat, then winced as he was immediately in the spotlight. "Y'all know the situation," he began. I'd never known him talk so quietly. "We've lost computer functions. We have no door locks, no biometrics, no combi-makers, no compscreens…"

"Wh-what about the equipment in the infirmary?" Abidene said – the first time I'd heard his calm voice struggle.

"On an independent system," Weng answered. "Precisely in case of…this."

It seemed that everyone relaxed slightly. I hadn't realized that we were holding ourselves so tightly.

"But we will need to arrange some form of power boost," she went on. "The systems aren't designed to run for more than a few days, let alone six months."

"I'll see what I can do," Max said. She sounded exhausted, stretched to the limit. "I'll put it on my to-do list."

"Make it a priority," Weng said. "If you don't want them dead—"

"What do you mean by that?"

"Well—"

"You think I'd—"

"That's enough," Fergie said. "We don't need arguments, not right now."

"I thought it was just a power-saving measure at first," Keegan said half to himself. "I thought you'd just switched off the electricity – a bit weird you'd not told us, but…"

No one spoke. Eye contact was impossible in this environment of constantly shifting light.

"How?" Keegan went on. "How did this happen?"

I wasn't sure whether this was a genuine question, but Maggie answered anyway. "With a hammer," she said. "With a hammer and a flare gun." She sounded as numbed as the rest of us. "Someone went into the network room, smashed up the computer facade with a large hammer, then fired a flare into the hole they'd made. It burned out everything."

"More than that," Fergie said. "They then went outside and severed the network hub that runs to the other buildings."

"And then finally they dug out the black box, took it into the smelting plant and crushed it under an ore hammer," Max finished.

Everyone's eyes seemed to visit me briefly, uncertainly. Some glanced at Greigor too. Or at least I thought they did.

"I think we're supposed to disappear here," Maggie said in a hollow voice. "Australis destroyed and our bodies too. Who'll know what happened? It'll be like the *Mary Celeste*. And the killer will find a way to get off Antarctica, set up a new identity somehow and be free. Without the data from the black box, the Company will never know what really happened."

I glanced around at my colleagues. They all looked ghastly, odd shifting shadows ebbing over their faces, as if they were already specters. Keegan looked sick. I thought Max looked puzzled, but the torch that was on her shifted before I could be sure.

"That's only part of it," I heard myself say.

Everyone was now staring at me.

"We've lost all our computer files. All your personal logs, all records, everything that could be used to catch the killer. Or could be evidence…of *any* wrongdoing." Heads turned to Greigor.

"Hey, I never—" he began before Maggie cut him off.

"So, what are we going to do?" she asked. "I don't know about you, but I'm not too happy about the idea of just sitting around and waiting to die."

Again I surprised myself by answering. "We carry on with Fergie's plan," I said, my voice barely wavering. "We hibernate. We clear out the basement and live down there, shutting down all power except to the infirmary and the kitchen, and the greenhouse."

"There's no point in saving the greenhouse," Maggie said bitterly. "Without the computer I can't maintain the crops that we've been growing. My robots have deactivated. The heating system's already failed. We'll have to abandon the greenhouse as well."

"How does that leave us for food?"

"Not good. There are some grains and fruit that are just about ready to be harvested. If we get them, we'll have…?"

"About two months' normal rations," Abi said. "We can stretch that out, but two months' normal rations are all we have."

Keegan slumped into a seat, his face pale. He moaned quietly. Dmitri and Fergie shared a glance.

"Can we all survive until the night shift ends?" the Scotsman asked. "Can we cut right down and starve ourselves to eke it out until help arrives?"

"Possibly," Abi replied. We all waited for him to say more, but his mouth remained grim and closed.

"Who's doing this?" Keegan wailed, before burying his head in his hands. He still looked ill, his skin disturbingly yellow in the poor light.

"I have an alibi for this one," I said with a bitter smile. "I had… company all last night."

There were no secrets left for me; now everyone turned to Max. I had expected her to nod, to agree, but instead she just frowned and would not meet my gaze."Anders…" she began slowly. "Anders, I'm sorry, but I can't give you an alibi. I – I was drunk, I couldn't swear…I wouldn't know…"

My head dropped. Goddamn, *I was telling the truth*. I'd been telling the truth since the very beginning. Why was there never any proof, never any evidence? "I – I never left," I mumbled. "I woke briefly in the morning but that was after the power went." I looked back to Max in desperate appeal.

She looked away.

I broke. "I didn't do it," I cried. "I didn't get up, not until the computers were already broken!"

No one spoke. They just stared at me, and that was far, far worse.

I leaned against de Villiers's stupid pinboard and this time no one moved to pick up the fallen papers.

It wouldn't have been hard for Max to tell the rest that she knew I'd been with her all night. I mean, it was the truth – I'd never left my rooms. I watched Max, but still I couldn't read her expression. I could see nothing but the anxiety and the fear and the deep, deep cold that rode through us all; and that once more I was alone. Alone and hated.

Maybe she *had* set the system reset on purpose – to let me out, to read the personal logs of the crew, to give me the rope to hang myself...

"Does it really matter?" Dmitri said into the resulting silence. "At this point, does it really matter who's done this? Now we must survive. We need every hand to get through this."

"Why should we feed a murderer?" Maggie replied, her face tight with anger and fear.

This time I didn't even have the energy to deny it.

"Even if Anders is a murderer," Dmitri said, "I am not. I won't allow anyone to starve. We survive until rescue comes. All of us."

I felt rather than saw a general shifting of feet around me, an uncertainty in the air. I took a deep breath. My head hurt and my legs ached. "I didn't do it," I said again. "I'll work with you. I'll help you. When we get through this, I'll take another Psych test. I'll take any test you like."

"But that ain't gonna come soon enough, is it?" Keegan said. "I mean, without Fischer and without the computers, we can forget about doing our own test here. Any Psych you can take's gonna come a bit late."

Silence fell again.

"Okay," Fergie said eventually. "This is all well and good. Now we need to work out what we're going to do."

"Survive," Dmitri growled.

"We know what we have to do." Abidene took a half pace forward.

"Maggie, Greigor and I will go to the greenhouse and salvage what can be salvaged. The rest must continue to clear the basement and find a way to keep warm for the next five months."

"I—" Max hesitated and cleared her throat. "I need to go to the workshop to knock us up a good, efficient coal brazier. And check on the infirmary's power supply."

"May I make a suggestion?" My voice was still cracked. "We shouldn't work alone – none of us. We should stay at least in pairs—"

"Yeah, because I've never seen a horror movie before, dumbass," Fergie said. "Of course we go in teams. We're not stupid. We all stick together. And we keep our suspects apart," he added with a glance at Greigor.

"Hey," Greigor protested, "I was sealed in my room las' night."

"So was I!" I snapped.

"Only if Max thought to lock the door. Weren't too busy fucking a killer."

"Hey, I—" she began, and I think only the intercession of Dmitri and Abi prevented her from hurting the little rat.

Max wasn't mentioning the system reboot. I wondered if she'd forgotten I was no longer a prisoner or if she was deliberately keeping that to herself.

Fergie turned to her. "So we work in teams. You need to go to the workshop. Who d'you want with you?"

"Keegan," Max said with barely a pause.

"Okay," Dmitri said. "Maggie, Abi and Greigor to the greenhouse. Max and Keegan in the workshop. The rest of us – the basement."

"We need to check Fischer and Petrovic," Weng said. "They need to be maintained."

"We'll all go," Fergie growled. "You, me and him," he said, jerking a thumb in my direction. "That way we can all look after each other – can't we, Nordvelt?"

*　　*　　*

The next few days passed in a haze of exhaustion. The work seemed endless, constant lifting and carrying. There was barely any time for thought, let alone talk. Even moving through the barracks was a mission; every door had to be wrestled open and then wrestled closed again behind us – all to conserve precious heat. Now the ground floor was almost as cold as it was outside. Had the computers been working we could have worn our warmsuits permanently, but now the small battery packs that powered them couldn't be recharged, and so they were reserved for essential use only.

All this technology. The planners hadn't thought we'd need anything as basic as fur-lined coats. Even the primitive gear worn by the very first Antarctic explorers would have been so very welcome.

It was a little better – survivable – below. I spent my nights locked in my room, cocooned in blankets, all spares dug out of storage. Max had found – or made – some old-style bolts, and she fitted one across my door. That was enough. Funny how the simplest ideas last through the centuries; for all our electronics, it was plain mechanics that we were falling back on. I gathered they'd done the same with Greigor's door, but I barely saw him. Our paths only crossed when the work shift had finished and we sat together for a silent, inadequate meal. Nutritious mush, packed with vitamins to stave off scurvy, beri-beri and whatever else.

No one smiled and no one laughed, not at dinner and not after. Small arguments became large. I spoke to nobody beyond what was necessary, and nobody spoke to me except to order me around.

Life became painted in shades of amber and gray. Battery-lamps were retrieved from the minehead and hung around the barracks. Shadows mocked our efforts, our own forms twisting grotesquely around the walls. The floors became scuffed and stained as beams and plates of metal were set down or dropped.

The service lift was as dead as the rest of the building. I felt like a pit pony. Clearing even part of the basement for habitation meant the endless moving of sheets and shelves of prefab steel: three flights of stairs from the basement to the surface. There were buckets of bolts, loose cable by the mile and great reels of wire and mesh. Sectioning off an area to trap our body heat meant holding heavy panels in place with muscles that were barely getting fed, while Max wielded the rivet gun or the arc welder dangerously close to the flesh.

We hardly spoke. No communication was necessary. We just did the jobs that needed to be done.

I stopped feeling hunger after the first week. I stopped feeling human at the end of the second. There was no hot water and the cold was too cold; we began to stink. We were animals, weak and helpless. We worked in silence, timeless as every day became the same. Sleep was a blessing.

I was only allowed outside once, to help Max and Dmitri fetch the large brazier that Max had knocked together. But while the fresh air made me feel awake, the sky was as black as ever. I could see no stars, no moon, nothing to tell me whether it was day or night.

Eventually the basement was clear enough for us to start moving beds downstairs. Weak as I was – as we all were – it took a long time to negotiate the stairs. Fergie cursed fluently every time we dropped the pallets, his imprecations becoming a constant background as we all focused on nothing more than the next few feet, the next few steps.

Another week and we moved into the basement. Max had carefully drilled holes in the walls, next to the pipes that had once fed the generator, to allow a jerry-rigged chimney to pass out of the building. The brazier was installed in the center of the sectioned-off area and we crowded around it and watched the coals smoldering beneath a crude hood mounted on the ceiling. The generator now served only the infirmary. We huddled under whatever blankets and duvets and sheets we could find. We wore all the clothes we had. We shuffled around like troglodytes and we prayed for time to pass.

★   ★   ★

Physically, Weng seemed to be coping better with conditions than the rest of us. Maybe it was because she was so slight to start with; she didn't suffer from the painful muscle wastage of Fergie, Max, myself and especially Dmitri. Mentally, however, she was suffering.

It was in her eyes, in the times we spent playing chess, when the body was broken with exhaustion but the mind was still too active for sleep. Sometimes in those eyes I saw the cold fury, the ice-passion of self-contained, calculating rage. But other times she seemed to barely be there. She would stare through the board as if she were in a different land in a different time. She looked like a child at those times: a lost, scared little girl. She still won every game.

Once, before we thought to play, the loathsome pariah Greigor had gone to talk to her. She didn't respond. Didn't object to his putting an arm across her shoulders. But when he tried to pull her in for a hug, she suddenly seemed to wake, and she shoved him away with a little screech. Greigor, who once stood so tall, was once so handsome, slunk away in the half-light.

Lost children, that's what we were. All lost children, pale echoes of people.

I had no idea of the time. Day and night meant nothing anymore. The night shift was all there was. I'd lost track of how long we'd spent here, of how long I'd been meekly submitting to restraint and suspicion, tied to my bed when sleep overtook me. Greigor was left free, but I couldn't bring myself to complain.

Weng and Keegan separately kept track of days, the arbitrary twenty-four-hour units of gloom in which we existed. Maybe some of the others did too – Abi must have, because he had to ration our food.

I'd tried to talk to Max, but she was always working, worn snappy and short. Eventually, I learned to leave her alone, not knowing whether we had a relationship or even if she thought I was a killer. And the less we spoke, the more difficult it became to form words. Silence begot silence and we lived in our individual heads.

There wasn't much to do down there. We had chess and we had cards, but the games became more and more desultory, default activities drained of any real enjoyment. Poker caused too many arguments among a crew already stressed and frayed. After the first month, chess was too much for most of us, the intellectual depths ungraspable. The few books that Maggie had brought from her library were too technical. We were left to play patience games, taking turns with the cards.

Fergie had developed scrubby ginger stubble, while Abidene's beard had grown bushy and unkempt. We seemed to be shrinking. Dmitri, the biggest of us, seemed top-heavy, stumbling around the basement as if in a state of constant near-collapse. There was nothing to do but wait and sleep. The cots were arranged at the generator end of the basement. They'd originally been set in two rows, but it hadn't taken long before they'd been edged into a crude horseshoe around the brazier. The table had been brought down from the rec room; it sat at the open end of the horseshoe, completing a rough circle. A set of the mine lamps ran on minimal power, providing enough illumination to see the coal dust and ash hanging in the air around us.

Only Abi and Max and Weng had jobs anymore; Max was still trying to improve the heating and ventilation systems, while Abi managed our rations. Weng had to make sure that Fischer and Mikhail survived along with us.

The passivity sickened me. I couldn't take the waiting, the static fugue of existence, anymore. I hauled off the many covers that were piled over me and swung my legs to the floor. Every movement was painful now. At least there was no risk of diseases or malnutrition; Abidene and Maggie had plenty of vitamins to draw on. The pain was simply from a lack of calories.

The only thing we had in abundance was water. I took a long drink, trying to assuage my emptiness.

Max was awake, crouched by the brazier. She was trying to direct a small fan into the grate. I got unsteadily to my feet and staggered over to her. In the firelight her face looked shallow, haunted.

"Hey," I croaked. "What are you doing?"

She didn't look round. "Moving air will make the coals burn better, and, if I can get it right, keep the smoke going up the flue rather than poisoning us all," she said.

I felt a sudden surge of anguish. "Max—"

"Don't," she cut me off. "I'm sorry, but – I've too much to do. Maybe – if we get through this – maybe then we'll work out who's to blame. But I'm too busy for any more bullshit now. Too tired. Too cold."

I felt rather than heard Weng sitting behind us, on the edge of her bed. On the other side of the fire, Fergie shifted beneath his duvets.

Above the smell of coal and the acrid taste of the air I caught a whiff of body odor. I wrinkled my nose.

When I looked at her again, I saw that Max was watching me carefully. "I didn't do it, Max," I said in a whisper that I'm not sure I even meant her to hear.

"You still deny it?"

"Of course I do." I was crying. I hadn't been aware until a drop landed on my hand. I wiped my cheek, and when I looked at my arm I saw I was covered in coal dust, filthy. I felt a sudden wave of revulsion at myself. I wanted to be clean; I so badly wanted to be clean.

Max sighed and turned back to her work. "We're nearly out of coal," she said. "Find someone else and get some more."

I stared at her for a moment, then stood. I watched her for a second more, swaying slightly, before turning away.

"I'll go too," Weng said from behind me. It said a lot about our collective states of mind that no one objected, pointed out that Weng was far too slight to defend herself.

I led the way to the stairs, snatching up the empty sack we'd been using to carry the fuel. Together we put our warmsuits on before going out into the unheated upper levels.

★   ★   ★

There was something eerie about walking these corridors now. It wasn't right to say they were abandoned; there were still enough reasons for us to go up and out. But now we'd turned off even the mine lamps and relied on our heavy torches. There should have been rats, or cockroaches, or some other symptoms of decay, but nothing moved. The only sounds were of our feet. I trailed my fingers over the wall, expecting to feel the icy chill, but my gloves registered only the smooth texture. Our breath froze in the air. The empty sack I carried brushed the floor.

"I need to check on Fischer and Petrovic," Weng said.

"Right."

We stopped at the door, unlocking it manually and shouldering it open. I held it closed as Weng crossed to the figures on their beds. This room still had power, and I was momentarily blinded as Weng turned on the lights. The heating was working, and for a moment I felt a rush of warmth before my suit adjusted to the ambient temperature. We took our masks off, both of us. I felt unsettled, uncomfortable; only a month underground and it was this room that seemed abnormal, our subterranean existence the natural order of things.

As my eyes adjusted, I turned to the casualties. They looked so peaceful, Julia and Mikhail, as if suspended in time. The doctor had a faint smile on her lips. Only her pallid skin seemed wrong. That and the tubes running from her nose and mouth, and the drip plugged into her arm.

If only the room was larger. If only we could be here without multiplying our energy use. If only our presence didn't endanger the patients. Then we could have stayed here, in the light, if only in shifts.

Desires hurt too much so I focused on Weng as she examined Julia and Mikhail. She checked all their vitals before she replenished the drips with the nutrients that served as their meals. She changed catheters and bowel bags – an unpleasant business, keeping people alive. I had not seen this before, not seen this side of Weng, this caring, gentle woman. She didn't seem to notice the smells, the mess that caused me to turn away. When I looked back and met her eyes, they seemed softer than usual. Maybe that was just a trick of the light, but still it was enough to make me try and start a conversation.

"Are they okay?" I asked.

"They're as expected."

I took that as a yes. "How are you bearing up?"

She had been apportioning saline solution to add to the drip, but her head shot round in response to my question. She froze for a moment, the shadow across her face distorting her features. For a moment she looked haggard, like a witch. Then she straightened, and for the first time I really noticed how thin she was. Her breasts had shrunk and she looked disturbingly androgynous. "I'm fine," she said, her quiet voice carrying clearly through the silence.

I couldn't think of anything else to say. Weng returned to her work, then came back to stand by me. I moved to open the door for her, but she held out a hand to stop me.

"You didn't kill anyone, did you, Nordvelt?"

I was taken aback. "N-no," I stammered. "No, I'm not a killer. I've had nothing to do with any of this."

She held me in her eyes – dangerous eyes that seemed to swim in and out of focus, seeing and not seeing.

"Do *you* know who the killer is?" I asked.

She shook her head gently, not looking away.

"We should get the coal," I mumbled after another pause.

She nodded, but still did not move. She was standing so close, so close to me now; I could feel her breath on my face, could smell the sweat on her skin. I could see the dirt encrusted on her face, see how ragged her hair had become. What once was strong and lush was now brittle and split. And all the time I was looking at her, she was watching me. She saw nothing better in me.

She reached out a hand to touch me. She laid her hand on my chest as if trying to feel the bones through the thin skin of my suit. Then she raised her hand to trace the scar on my forehead. And then she lowered it – all the same hand, her right – down to my crotch and she stroked me.

"De Villiers abused me," she whispered as if she were in a trance. "I went to McCarthy and he did nothing."

"Weng…" I was sweating, my back pressed hard against the door.

"I was going to kill de Villiers. I planned it all, I worked out how to murder him without anyone finding out it was me. It was the perfect crime."

"Weng, please…"

"I told McCarthy how I felt. He made Fischer give me sedatives."

"Why are you telling me this, Weng? What are you doing?"

Suddenly, without warning, she grabbed the back of my head and pulled me forward and kissed me. I should have pulled away. I should have fought it, but I was so surprised – and despite her skeletal form, it was hardly unpleasant. But then she started to bite my lip. I jerked away, blood running down my chin. I grabbed her shoulders and held her at arm's distance. "Weng, this isn't right. What's got into you?"

She looked at me for a moment with the light of madness in her eyes. In a second that seemed to run in slow motion, the passion drained from her. Then she was crying. Crying like a little girl. She dissolved into sobs and threw herself at me.

What could I do but hold her?

After maybe half a minute, she pulled back and wiped her eyes with a dirty hand. I could almost see her regaining control. "We should get the coal," she said with only the slightest tremor of emotion.

I nodded. We left the infirmary, my lip still stinging from her bite. Madness. I didn't know how to fit her story into my mind – I believed her, had no doubt that she'd planned de Villiers's death in the silence of her own private quarters. But I couldn't see her actually going through with it. Her confession was of hatred, not murder. And I could see no reason for her to destroy the oil rig.

Opening the vestibule door took most of my strength. We were all so weak, so fragile; without computer assistance, the mere effort of pushing open a door as heavy as that of the main base entrance was a struggle. I stood for a moment, panting, before I attempted the exterior door. Weng watched me in silence as I took a drink of water, declining with a gesture when I offered her my bottle. She dropped her head every time I looked at her.

Getting the second door open was even more of a struggle, but I managed unaided. My legs could barely sustain my weight. When I felt the heavy metal unseal I paused to pull my mask over my face. And together we went out into the darkness beyond.

Was this daytime? I could see stars as the breeze darted around me, and for a moment I wanted to just lie down on the ice and sleep. I was aware of the emptiness. I felt it somewhere deep in my soul, felt like I was drunk on it, giddy, and I may have laughed. Then, the moment I wondered if Weng had heard me, the high turned back in on me. It became paranoia, became an agoraphobia that chewed at my belly as if it wanted to burst out of me and explode into the eternal night.

All the lights that illuminated the courtyard that was Australis base had been extinguished. Our torches glowed feebly – so small, so insignificant. I struggled to control my breathing, swallowed, swallowed again. This was the sort of place in which religions were born. I drew a deep breath and let Weng go ahead, then shoved the door closed behind us.

Weng led the way towards the workshop and the smelting plant – not that we could see the buildings, or anything beyond the limbus of our lights. I followed her closely.

"You can have me," she said quietly, the mask transmitting her voice above the whip of the wind.

"What?"

"Max is closed to you. You can have me."

"Weng—"

"I'm used anyway. If you want me, you can have me."

I almost laughed. To be having this conversation out here in the frozen wastes, pack ice sighing beneath my feet; what were we supposed to do, just throw away our suits and get to it? And the masks – it'd be like making love to a locust, some alien insect... I shuddered and desperately searched for some way to respond.

"I'm going to be too busy defending myself against a murder charge to have anybody," I said.

She didn't seem to hear me. "After McCarthy sent me to the doctor...later, a few days later...I told McCarthy he could have me if he helped me destroy de Villiers. And do you know the funny thing?" There was an echo of madness in her laugh.

We fought the entrance to the coal store open and staggered inside.

"What's the funny thing, Weng?" I followed my torchlight to the edge of the giant mound of coal and dropped the sack on the ground before kneeling by it. Slowly, laboriously, I began to shovel lumps in with my hands.

"He didn't even hear me." She gave another mad laugh. "It was late – or early, maybe. Everyone else was in bed, but I couldn't sleep. Even with the sedatives." Her voice had taken on its own dreamy quality, and I knew she was lost in her memory. "I wandered the corridors, and I came across McCarthy. I remember so well. He was walking away from me, towards the stairwell. I called to him. I was desperate – it was in that time..." Her voice faded a little. "When the hurt was so clear, the pain a burning needle in my brain. I called to him. He didn't seem to hear. I called again. I told him I'd be...I'd do anything if he got rid of de Villiers for me."

I paused in my shoveling and looked back at her. She was invisible in the darkness, her torch pointing at the ground a few meters away from where her voice was coming from. "What happened?" I asked softly.

"He walked away. He didn't even acknowledge me. Just went into the stairwell, murmuring to himself – a name, he kept saying a name, 'Francis'. McCarthy left...just left. I – I was...I was crying a lot at that time. I kept expecting him to say something to me, to come to me to talk – maybe to...maybe to...to fuck. But he acted as if nothing had happened. Like he didn't even know I was there. Though he and I were closer than you are to me now."

"He was sleepwalking?"

"I realized that later…" Her words came from a distance, as if she were talking to herself. As if I was a walk-on in a lucid dream.

The sack was full now – or at least as full as I could carry in my weakened state. I stood and tried to swing it onto my back. I couldn't. So I dragged it along the floor, just not caring anymore. I was far more concerned for Weng.

"Come on," I said. "We've got the coal. Let's get back downstairs."

Weng looked up at me as I shone my torch at her. She'd taken off her mask. Her eyes reflected like a cat's, so clear that I could even see myself, the suited, masked figure who could have been anyone.

And then it hit me. I knew. I knew who the killer was.

CHAPTER EIGHTEEN

I stood there swaying in the ice-cold wind. My warmsuit protected me from the chill but couldn't stop the despair from washing over me – and I embraced it. Ahead of me, Weng was making her way back to the barracks, her torch casting a light that seemed mere fodder for the darkness.

I switched my own torch off. I didn't want to see. I dropped the sack.

I took long, slow breaths. Nothing changed, except that Weng was a little further away. Abstractedly, a phrase came to me: winter-over syndrome. They'd gone to great lengths to explain it to me in my training. Winter-over syndrome. It was the reason Weng had been behaving so oddly, I was sure. *An observed danger of long periods in Antarctica, winter-over syndrome is caused by stress, social isolation, and a lack of natural light. It can lead to cognitive impairment, hallucinations, insomnia and depression.* I could hear the voice of my instructor. I could hear *everything* in that moment, in that great emptiness: all the words I'd ever heard crashing through my brain all at once and somehow, magically, coming together in harmony, as the pure note of the Antarctic gale.

I knew who the murderer was. And I wasn't sure I could live with the knowledge.

Weng hadn't noticed that I'd stopped. She wasn't supposed to leave me alone – no one alone, under any circumstance. But she'd been so wrapped up in her own mind that she'd never really been with me. Maybe this was all a dream to her; it felt enough like that to me. Maybe she was still imagining me by her side, still talking to me. She showed a strength I wasn't sure I had in me when she forced open the barracks door and disappeared inside.

I turned aimlessly and wandered away from the barracks, not paying any attention to my surroundings. I was in true darkness now, like I was walking through the void. Cocooned as I was in my suit, all I could feel was the gentle buffeting of the wind.

I was heading out to die.

And so I had a new sense of purpose. I oriented myself on the hills that surrounded the base, which showed up only as a deeper black against the sky, and started my last journey.

I walked slowly and steadily, following the stilled conveyor that marked the way to the mineshaft. I was protected from the winds here and I moved through silence. As I walked I thought again of the events that had led me to this. They brought me no joy. I felt like I was one of Max's androids. All the wires were plugged in but there was no life, no light behind the eyes. A juddering pace was all I could manage, a mere simulacrum of a human being. I wanted out. And my exit would allow the others a little more food, a little more heat, a few more blankets. It was fitting that I should leave on my own. As I'd arrived, and as I'd always been.

After a little while I reached the ruins of the comms building. I didn't stop, just carried on upwards. I wasn't sure why I was going to the minehead; it wasn't as if it had any special place in my heart. It was just a destination, a place to go. Maybe I too was losing my mind. Maybe I'd lost it long ago, long before I'd come to this damn wasteland.

It didn't concern me that I would soon cease to be, but it did bother me that nobody would know *why*. That I would go to my grave – should I ever get one – with nothing explained, no one the wiser.

Theo never got a grave. That thought was enough to banish my doubts. And my death should reassure the others that the killer was gone. Remembrance of me didn't matter. Didn't matter at all. I had no family to be heartbroken, no lost loves, no true friends. Mine really had been a wasted existence.

As I reached the entrance to the mine complex, another memory from my training surfaced from my subconscious, bursting open like a bubble.

Paradoxical undressing: the phenomenon where someone in the final stages of hypothermia will voluntarily remove all their clothes, as if they were burning up, before death. In the past such happenings have been wrongly taken as a sign that the victim was murdered.

I should have taken off my warmsuit. All I was doing was

wasting battery for those who might still need it. I really wasn't thinking clearly.

I entered the minehead and almost fell; no longer protected from the wind, I had to take a few stutter-steps to keep my feet.

I took off my mask and let it drop. I looked all around and saw nothing. I didn't try to wipe away the tears from my eyes.

There was no special place I wanted to be found, no special way I wanted to lie. Here was as good a place as any: a middle point, somewhere my body would be found eventually, not lost in the wilderness forever – but not right on their doorstep. Now I took off my gloves, my fingers becoming numb almost immediately. It made unzipping my suit difficult, but I was in no rush. The cold slipped wraithlike into my chest, down to my belly, my groin.

I removed my boots and lay down on the ice. There was a rail under my shoulder; I shifted a little so my head was propped against it. After a moment's thought I sat up and tried to write a message in the ice. Just – I didn't know what. I could make no impression on the surface anyway. I shrugged and lay back. It didn't matter.

I stared upwards for a moment, then closed my eyes and opened myself to oblivion. Time passed, and steadily I lost the feeling in my fingers, my toes, my legs. I don't know if I could have moved if I'd tried.

I almost felt content. Almost felt happiness. Death was good. This was the way it should be. My thoughts drifted, my mouth curled into a smile. The worries I always carried with me slowly emptied into the clouds above. Death was kind.

I didn't hear the sound of the engine until it was almost on me. I should have picked it up earlier; it wasn't as if there was any other noise to cover it. A half-track. By now I'd become familiar enough with its low, growling voice. I groaned. Not now, no, no, not now. I screwed my eyes tighter shut, to deny the reality. Maybe it wasn't really there, maybe I was just hallucinating...

I could see light through my eyelids. I wanted to cry, or to shout, or to rage, but...well, there wasn't any point, and I didn't have the energy.

"Nordvelt!" A male voice, familiar, but I didn't want to let myself know whose it was. "Nordvelt, what the fuck're you doin'?"

Anger, alarm. My moment had passed, I knew it. Why, why had they wasted more of their precious supply of power for someone like me? I'd have wept if I'd had the energy.

"He's here! I've found him!"

More voices. Questions. Words. All assaults, transgressions against me. I didn't reply, didn't move. I felt hands upon me. Felt myself raised, lifted, carried.

My moment was gone. My death had been stolen from me.

★   ★   ★

I lay on my bed in the basement, unmoving. I'd been shoved back into my warmsuit and buried in a mountain of blankets, but still I felt numb. Couldn't feel my face. Couldn't move, didn't want to move.

I drifted away. Slowly the basement faded from my mind, to be replaced by an office – a meeting room. Bright and well lit. I gazed into the light that poured through the windows. We were high up; birds circled in the sky, and I had to shade my eyes from a low sun that even the self-tinting windows couldn't filter.

"Mr. Nordvelt. If you'd take a seat?"

I looked around, startled. Around the long conference table, three figures had appeared, and I knew them. Not their names – they were too high up in the hierarchy for me to be given anything but titles. But they were all familiar to me somehow.

I took a seat at the far end of the table, facing them across the vast extent of wood. I was wearing a suit and tie, and they were examining papers and shooting me occasional critical glances. I was sweating.

"Lacks experience," the woman to the left said, her voice flat and uninterested.

"But never properly tested. The Psych shows a high ceiling. He has potential," the woman on the right countered.

It was my third time here. One of the series of interviews and tests I'd undergone for a promotion. I didn't know too much when I applied, only that the post would be in hostile terrain. Details were given slowly, almost reluctantly.

I could not see the faces of my interrogators, not even when the man in the middle stood and beckoned me to him... And the memory skipped, the room shifted and I was strapped to a gurney in something like an infirmary, a laboratory.

"Mr. Nordvelt, you've passed all tests so far," said an unseen man. I didn't recognize his voice, but I knew it was the person who'd just beckoned to me, the one the other interviewers looked to for leadership. "Now you just need to go through this one last procedure."

A light came on, and I wasn't sure if it was shining in my eyes or passing directly to my brain.

"Anders? Anders, wake up!"

I jerked upright in my bed, in the dark basement, and gasped for breath. The sweat was pouring off me as if I had a fever. After the light of my dreams, I found it harder than ever to penetrate the gloom, but I managed to make out Dmitri by my side, his hand on my arm. The rest of the crew were crude shapes in the distance, shadow-wraiths and twisted golems. I blinked and shook my head, beads of sweat falling to the duvet.

"You are okay, yes? You were talking in your sleep," the big man said. His breath drifted lazily in the cold air.

I tried to speak but all I could force out was a cracked sigh. He passed me water and I felt the fire-warmed, brackish liquid spill down my throat, my chin and chest.

I passed him back the bottle and almost instantly I was asleep again.

★　　★　　★

"Are you ready to talk?" Fergie was standing before me, a strange mix of anger and concern on his face.

Hands. I couldn't help staring at the hands around me, could barely take in anything else: just eight pairs of hands. Hands that were cracked, broken, split; nails falling out; wrinkled, sallow skin. I wasn't sure how much of this was real, how much was hallucination. It was getting hard now to tell dream from reality.

This was paranoia. This was madness. This was terror.

I didn't know how much time had passed, whether it was the same day, the same week... I sat up on my bed, tried out each muscle in turn. I didn't even have frostbite. It didn't seem right. I tried to speak, but the words caught in my throat and it took me a long time to force down my panic. Finally, finally, my breathing slowed. I licked my cracked lips.

"Why'd you do it?" Max asked. She was standing behind Fergie, camouflaged in the ochers and umbers of our existence.

Now I looked around me and saw properly. Everyone was there. Weng on her cot, looking a lot better, a lot more focused. The chessboard was set up on the end of her bed. Greigor, unwatched and unrestrained, scowled at me from his. Maggie was at the table with Dmitri, Keegan and Abi. A deck of cards lay on it, but nobody was playing. Everyone was watching me. Everyone was waiting. And though they were all still, light and shadow kept shifting across their faces, making them grin horribly before casting deep frowns over their faces. A pack of demons waiting to rend my flesh.

"How did you find me?" I croaked.

It was Maggie who answered. "Luck," she said simply. "If you'd just gone into the wilderness, we'd never have found you."

I cursed myself for that error. Next time I'd know.

"When Weng returned alone…" Max said, before pausing and shrugging. "We came out to look for you."

"We thought ye'd arranged some sort of escape – you'd hidden a vehicle or something. Or you were goin' to kill us all in one fell swoop," Fergie said with a trace of bitterness.

"So we went out," Dmitri said, "all of us, and split up to search the complex."

"What on earth possessed you, Nordvelt? Guilt got the better of you?" Fergie was definitely angry now.

"A desp'rate man," Greigor hissed. His hair was beginning to fall out. He looked old and vicious.

I shook my head. Opened my mouth to speak but no words would come.

"No' worth risking our lives for," he muttered.

I shook my head again. "I…I'm sorry."

"Just tell us why," Maggie said in a voice halfway between a command and an entreaty.

I swallowed, made myself look in her eyes before turning to Max, then to Fergie, and then to the floor. "I know," I whispered. "I know who's behind the sabotage."

I felt all their eyes on me.

"Who?" Dmitri asked from the table.

I shuddered and took another drink.

"I know who killed de Villiers and Theo," I said, louder this time.

"Well? Who was it, Nordvelt?" Fergie said, cutting across the echoing of my voice.

I stood, trying to stop myself from shaking. I felt like I was burning up, but I needed the fire. I held out my hands to feel its heat.

"Who was it?" Fergie repeated sharply.

Still I couldn't just say the words. "Maggie, you know hypnosis, right?" I asked.

There was a moment of silence, which Fergie again broke, this time with a harsh laugh. "Are you for real, Nordvelt? Are you seriously gonna suggest that Maggie hypnotized one of us to…to kill? Man, Greigor's right, you really are desperate."

"I couldn't do anything like that, Anders," Maggie added, the tremor in her voice such a contrast from Fergie's bark. "I just couldn't. I know a few party tricks, that's all. And I couldn't stop anyone from *knowing* they've been hypnotized."

"I know who's responsible for all that's…that's gone wrong here," I repeated, my voice unstable. "But I can't prove it. We need a confession. A real confession. Recorded. We need a recorder too."

"The datapads are all dead—"

"Nordvelt, if you've got some crazy theory about the saboteur, then ye can damn well tell us," Fergie snapped. "Sit down, Maggie – you don't have to respond to his mad whims. We should all hear who Nordvelt is going to throw the blame at."

"Just tell us, Anders," Max said.

For a moment the only sound was of the coals popping and shifting in the brazier.

I swallowed, my throat once again drier than it should by rights have been. "I did it," I croaked. "It was me. I did all of this."

★   ★   ★

For a moment there was silence. And then, out of the darkness, Fergie began to laugh. It was an oddly mad sound, echoing around the chamber like the wailing of some fantastical beast. He laughed for a long time, longer than reason dictated, as if he'd heard the funniest joke in the world. When he finally subsided, he had to wipe his eyes before he could speak. "Oh, oh Anders, that's priceless! That's just priceless. Why bother teasing us with that buildup just to confess to the crimes we already knew you'd committed? Priceless!"

No one else spoke. Weng alone hadn't changed her expression; the rest of the crew were watching me with puzzled faces.

"Is this your confession, Anders?" Abidene said eventually.

That was a difficult one. I didn't answer directly. "It is the only explanation that fits," I said. "Who better than me? I mean…the message sent to de Villiers to lure him out into the waste, the pinhead cameras, the blanked surveillance…who could have done all that easier than me?"

"You're saying that you did these things," Maggie said, "so why are you talking as if you still have no idea what actually happened."

"Because I *don't*." The words poured out of me at last, the fear and frustration boiling from my lips. "I have *no memory* of any of this."

"But—"

"I know that Greigor knew of the cameras and you all had the skills – *could* all have done it, but who was better placed than me?"

Again the only sound was the crackling of the flames. Max leaned forward to put another lump of coal into the brazier. Everyone was looking at me, waiting for me. But the only words I could reach sounded so weak in my mind, so clumsy and pathetic, that I couldn't bring myself to speak.

I looked around the room. Shadows cloaked the basement, the firelight flickering dangerously. I cleared my throat again. "McCarthy," I said. "It was supposed to be him."

"You're blaming your predecessor?" Dmitri said, a confused look on his face.

"It may've escaped your notice, but he was long gone before anything started going wrong," Fergie added.

"Are you not listening?" I said, frustration bursting from me. "I said it was *supposed* to have been him. You told me – all of you, at some point, have told me that he couldn't sleep, that he had headaches. It's why he left, for God's sake. He sleepwalked – Weng, you told me that. It *should* have been him."

"Why don't you start from the beginning?" Max asked, a hint of steel in her quiet voice.

"I'm trying to," I said. "Look, I was recruited from the same Company office as McCarthy. Greigor found that out in his snooping. The same people interviewed us, I'm sure of that. It was all in the personal files. McCarthy didn't work out, so they had to hire someone else. McCarthy was an old military man; maybe he had the right sort of training to resist—"

"You're saying that you were brainwashed into committing these murders," Maggie interrupted. I should have known that she would get there first.

"I don't know what was done," I said to her. "Brainwashing, posthypnotic suggestion – whatever you want to call it. The only thing that makes sense is that McCarthy, and then I, were programmed to destroy Australis.

"McCarthy was too strong," I said, my voice barely more than a whisper. "And so they got me. Weak, inexperienced – I wonder how surprised de Villiers was to find that they'd appointed someone as raw as me…"

"Why would anyone at the Company want to destroy Australis?" Keegan asked. "I mean, it's their investment. Why on earth would they want to do that?"

"It would have to be an infiltrator, or a group of infiltrators working to damage the Company from within," I said, staring into the flames.

"Oh, more and more plausible," Fergie muttered.

"From where?" Keegan asked. "The United Nations?"

"I think so," I said. "I can't think of any other group with the resources and know-how to carry out such an operation."

"I'm still wondering how you're goin' to prove it, Nordvelt."

"Look, it's the only rational explanation," I said, trying to keep the desperation out of my voice. "Think about it. Everything that's happened since – since—"

"Since you arrived."

"—has been an attack on the station itself." I took another sip of water, tried to wash the coal dust from my mouth. "First of all there was the destruction of the comms building. That was evidently done to isolate Australis, to prevent us from alerting Tierra and to give the saboteur—"

"You."

"—the opportunity to destroy the base without the Company knowing what was happening. Whoever did that was able to shut down the surveillance cameras and gain access to explosives without leaving a trace. I know Max could have done that, and me. We know Greigor could – anyone else?"

"I never—"

"I could." To my surprise it was Weng who cut Greigor off, her tone sharp enough to shut him up.

"Maybe I could too – I'm not sure," Dmitri added hesitantly.

"What is this? 'Let's all incriminate ourselves' day?" Keegan said.

"I could probably have done it too," Maggie said, ignoring the interjection.

"Then de Villiers was killed. I still don't know precisely why – either because as commander he was an obvious way to damage Australis as a whole, or for personal reasons. I know I didn't particularly like him. It was also a good way to throw the investigation off course – so many people here had reason to resent him. Look, there are certain things the attacks have in common—"

Maggie cut me off. "And you think that it was originally planned that McCarthy was to do all this?"

I nodded. "Yes. Yes, I do. Listen. The attacks were all either carried out or arranged at night. That's one thing."

"That doesn't prove—"

"Secondly, I think it's true – you'll know better than me – that a person cannot be made to do something that is totally against their nature, even under hypnosis. You can't make a man commit suicide, for example. I don't know if I *could* have attacked de Villiers directly. The murders were committed through sabotage because that was the only way my psyche could have brought me to carry them out."

"I'm still waiting to hear the proof for all this. I'm still waitin' for the proof that you didn't know exactly what you were doing all along and this isn't some desperate – really, really desperate – attempt to pass the blame along," Fergie said.

I ignored him. "The destruction of the oil well was an obvious way to damage the Company's interests. Theo's death—" I swallowed, hesitated. "Theo's death was just collateral damage." No one spoke. Still all eyes were on me. I felt small and alone. "And then Fischer told us that she could run basic Psych tests. I have no idea if that could have detected the killer in me, but my subconscious obviously didn't want to take the risk of being discovered. Or maybe it was planning her removal anyway."

"So I was just 'collateral damage' too?" Keegan asked.

"How come nothing showed in the most recent Psych you took?" Maggie asked.

"I...the last Psych I took was after my final interview for this job."

"That's not what I asked."

I tried to remember, staring into the flickering brazier. "The...it was different, the last one. I don't remember it clearly – I know no one remembers the actual process, all the sensory stimuli, but...I don't remember the room, the doctors..."

"But you're sure it happened."

"Yes. Yes, I'm sure."

There was a moment of silence.

"What about the destruction of the computer system? And the black box?" Keegan asked.

I sighed. "Think about it. Think what would have happened if all had gone to plan – what still might happen. The base is dead. We're all dead. You see, that's the other thing – why has the saboteur not made any provision to escape, to save his own skin? None of you seem suicidal to me, not Greigor, not Max – you've all got a life to live, a life you want to live. I was programmed to be disposable. I was meant to die here too, I'm sure of it.

"And then in four months' time, or however long we have now, someone at Tierra would send out a team. They'd find us all dead and much of the base destroyed. But they'd never know what happened. It'd be a mystery. No survivors to interview, no computer records. There'd be an inquiry, questions would be asked, but there'd be no one to blame. The Company would either have to start again from scratch or abandon the Australis project. And then what's to stop the UN from doing the same thing again? We already know they've infiltrated the

Company's European division. They could create sleeper agents all around the world."

There was quiet, then. Apart from the crackling of the fire, the soft whirring of the fan and the steady breathing of the crew, there was silence. I turned to Maggie. "You know hypnosis. I need you to hypnotize me."

"Ah," Abidene breathed.

"You want me to put you under, so we can get an account from the part of your memory that you can't access?" Maggie said. But she was shaking her head. "I'm sorry. I can't do that."

"What? Why not?"

She shrugged. "I told you. I can do a few party tricks. That's all. I…I wouldn't know where to begin."

I closed my eyes. Tears welled up. "So – so how will we—"

Coal crackled on the brazier. I couldn't meet their faces, couldn't feel anything but the eyes upon me.

"This is all horseshit," Greigor said into the silence. "No proof, you can jus' about smell the desperation."

"Sounds weak as synthetic whiskey to me," Fergie said. "No proof – nothin's changed."

Silence again.

"Brain scan," Weng said.

"What?"

"We do a brain scan."

"What are you talking about, Weng?" Maggie asked.

"Psychogenic amnesia can be detected in scans of the brain."

I looked up at her, a sudden stab of hope in my chest.

"Psychogenic amnesia? What the hell does that mean?" Fergie asked impatiently.

"You ask me," Greigor said, "Weng and Nordvelt, they got somethin' going on together."

"It's the type of…it's what causes you to not realize when you've been hypnotized," Maggie said to Fergie. "Or with some types of injury. Neurones don't link up properly between different parts of the brain."

"And you can scan me, show that?" I said, my heart beating again.

"I…I'm not sure." She looked over at Weng. "We have the

MRI scanner. But I'm not sure… We've lost the computer, we can't research, can't check your medical records. Can't really be sure what we're looking for, or looking at."

"But there is a chance," Weng said. "We can compare your scans with mine—"

"My books!" Maggie interrupted. "I have – ha, and de Villiers said I was an idiot, bringing actual paper books to Australis! I can check—"

"Wait, wait," Fergie cut in. "You two are actually taking this lunatic story seriously? You think it might actually be possible, what he's sayin'?"

She shrugged. "It's not like we've anything better to be doing, is it? I think it's worth checking out. That's all."

CHAPTER NINETEEN

Collaboration. I couldn't tell you how good it felt. After such a long time with no purpose but to survive – now, finally, we had an aim, something to live for.

Weng and Maggie were energized. They sat together, huddled under blankets and duvets, reading the professor's odd assortment of textbooks and guides – using precious torch battery and scribbling on old scraps of paper. The rest of us got on with living, circulating around them, bemused, uncertain. No one other than the two women would even discuss what they were doing; no one understood either what they were saying or what it might mean – for us, for the group.

Finally, without ceremony, our footsteps echoed upwards to the infirmary. The whole crew went. No one wanted to be left, waiting – not enough trust in anyone but themselves. Shivering, draped with what warm clothing we could find – there was no point using warmsuits for this short trek – we fought the freezing air. It was crisp, sharp and dry.

The warmth and the light of the infirmary bathed us like the afterlife. Immediately I knew I was dirty, impure, and I started to tremble with fear.

What if they found nothing?

The crew parted. Without taking a step, I found myself alone in the center of the room.

"Wh-where do you want me?" I asked, struggling, failing to smile.

"Sit," Weng said, gesturing to a bare metal chair.

The MRI machine was brought from a corner. Dmitri, at Weng's instructions, placed it over my head. I shut my eyes. It rested heavy on my shoulders. I was top-heavy, and my breathing quickened. I fought down a sharp stab of claustrophobia. A hand rested on my back – Dmitri's? I drew strength from it and from the voices, muffled and distorted, that now circled around my head.

A sudden light: even through closed eyes I was aware of it, blue-green beneath my lids. And at the same time a low drone, a taste in the air – static, acrid and metallic. The hum rose in pitch until I was bathed in it, until it was no longer a sound but something I felt in my teeth.

And then there was nothing.

The light went out. The hum died, cut off, sudden enough to make me feel like I was falling – and I was sweating, and my sweat was pooling around my neck and chest—

And then the device was lifted off me and I almost floated up with it.

★　　★　　★

There was a shadow.

There was a shadow in my brain.

I didn't – I couldn't take it in, not properly. Not much was said, not there in the infirmary, as each of the crew – Weng and Maggie, of course, then Fergie with his deep scowl and skeptical Greigor and Keegan and Abi and Max and Dmitri and Fergie and Greigor again – as each in turn stared at the readout. Not many words.

A shadow.

Weng was next to be scanned. A baseline, a contrast – and then, because no one wanted to be left out of this mutual paranoia, the rest of the crew. It was as if we were waiting for the sacrament, a silent ceremony: the sacred donning of the helmet.

No one else had a shadow. That was my blessing alone.

We turned off the lights, left Fischer and Mikhail in peace. Reluctantly we trooped back down to the basement. And if the infirmary was heaven, then the basement was surely hell: even the flicker of warmth there carried the taint of sulfur.

★　　★　　★

"So what does it mean, then?" Fergie asked. The rancor, the anger had gone from his voice. Without it he sounded oddly neutral.

"The occipital and temporal lobes are isolated," Weng said.

"Not isolated," Maggie corrected. "Most functions are normal.

But…well, we're not experts, but it matches the patterns in my books. And contrasts distinctly with a normal, healthy pattern."

"So…so what does it mean?" he asked again.

Maggie shrugged, casting vulture-like shadows on the wall behind her. "All I can say… It's consistent with Anders having memories he can't access—"

"For fuck's sake! Can you not just give me a straight answer? Is he telling the truth or not?"

Maggie gave him an icy look as the echoes of his outburst rolled away. "I can't answer that. All I can say is—"

"Yeah, yeah – all you can say is that it's fuckin' consistent with your textbooks blah blah bloody blah." He fell into silence, chin propped on his hand, scowling into darkness.

No one spoke. I felt like I wasn't really there. I'd been in heaven and hell and now I was somewhere in limbo, waiting for judgment.

"So what's the trigger?" Keegan asked.

"Oh, what the feck now?"

"The what?" Dmitri said.

"Well – right, okay, so you're saying that Anders is right, right? He's been acting under posthypnotic suggestion, yeah? So isn't there a trigger? I mean, I don't know, but isn't there always a trigger? Something that instructs – I dunno, not instructs, but… You know what I'm getting at, right?"

"If he is right – if he's telling the truth…" Max's voice was cold, dispassionate. I looked at her, saw nothing but logic in her eyes. Like a machine.

I shivered.

"If Anders is telling the truth…if this shadow really is a sign of posthypnotic suggestion, you're saying that there should be something to set it off. Something to cause him to kill—"

I winced at the baldness, the naked cruelty of the word.

"He only carried out the attacks whilst he was asleep," Dmitri said. "Isn't that the trigger? Unconsciousness?"

"Maybe," Maggie said slowly. "Maybe. But – what did you bring with you, Anders? What items?"

I shrugged, spilling the blankets from round my shoulders. I fought to hitch them back up again, my fingers unable to grip properly. "I –

I don't know – I mean, just a few personal items... My book. My puzzle box. Clothes. Not much more than that."

"What about your music?" Max asked.

"What music?" Keegan asked.

"He's got a memcard – an album his mother made." She shrugged.

"Mother's boy, is he?" Greigor asked.

"Audio triggers – they can be pretty effective," said Keegan.

Everybody stared at the Englishman.

"And what the hell do you know about it?" Fergie asked.

The meteorologist's eyes were wide. "Hey, I like stories. No need to look at me like that."

"Did McCarthy have anything like that?" Max asked the room. "Anyone know? Because if he was supposed to attack us – if there was a device that caused them to—"

She paused. I couldn't help insert the words *to go nuts* into the silence.

"If there was something, McCarthy must have had one too."

No one had an answer. Maggie turned to me. "Tell us more about how you got these things. The memcard?"

I shook my head. "It's just a standard memcard – I've had it for years—"

"How many years?"

I struggled to think back. "Since I was a teenager. Just something I can keep a few personal items on – music, photographs, my CV..."

"And the puzzle box? What actually is it?"

"Just – it's a puzzle box. A cube around three inches each face, mahogany and rosewood inlay..."

"How long have you had it, Anders?"

I frowned. "I – I've had it forever. It can't be that – as long as I remember..."

"Where did you get it?"

"My...my mother gave it to me..." I couldn't – couldn't grasp it. I could see the thing itself...I could see hands holding it, giving it to me...my mother's fine, thin fingers... The memory wouldn't come into focus, but my heart gripped tight, an almost overwhelming love.

"And the book?" Fergie asked. "I've seen that. Seemed weird for someone like you to have a thing like that, I thought that at the time. I mean, must be worth a half-year's wages for a first edition like that, right?"

"It's not a first edition. I found it – they were clearing out some old lady's house after she died. The workmen were going to throw it away, recycle it. Didn't know what they had. I just thought it was beautiful."

There was silence save for the sounds of the fire burning low and steady and the faint wheeze of Max's jerry-rigged ventilation system.

"Seems like a pretty long story to me," Fergie said. "Everyone knows there's money in old books. No one in their right mind would just recycle such a thing."

"I think we should have a look at these items," Dmitri said.

I felt terribly afraid.

★   ★   ★

Three items. Next to each other on the table, the crew crowded around. All the crew save for myself.

I sat huddled on my bed, unclean, unsteady, barely feeling the cold anymore. I stared at the blankets.

No, no, you're wrong, I wanted to shout. *This is my life, this is all I have.* My mother's music. The puzzle box. The only memories I had of her. And my book – I thought of its smell, the comfort it had brought me when I'd had nothing else.

"So how do we do this?" Maggie asked. "We've no computers. No analytical tools—"

"And no idea what we're looking for," Fergie finished. He took up the book and leafed through the pages, screwing up his eyes in the half-light.

"Here's what we do," Greigor said. He snatched the item from the Scotsman, and before I could even think he'd tossed it onto the burner.

I sat frozen for a microsecond, the horror colder than the Antarctic wastes. Then I shouted something inarticulate and tried to scramble up, to save it from the flames – but I was so twisted in blankets, they caught beneath my feet and I sprawled onto the hard concrete floor. I barely noticed the pain in my knee; I was up again and at the brazier. Heedless of the flames, I reached for the book, its blackening cover smoking and bright yellow flame stroking its edges—

Someone slammed into me, knocked me back to the floor – Greigor, of course. I should have felt the impact but I didn't, was only conscious of sour-milk smell of his rancid body, and the snarl on his lips – hatred, it was hatred, and even with tears filling my eyes and my fingers scorched, it was a hatred I could reflect and give in to. With our shrunken bodies we were like children, all bones and awkward angles, and we fought with a playground fury – rolling, arms swinging, and desperate to hurt, to gouge, to bite—

Hands grabbed at my shoulders, at his too, and the rest of the crew pried us apart.

I half lay, half sat on the floor, and I cried. Proper tears now.

"And this is what I say to this too!" Greigor yelled at the room. He snatched the memcard and cast that too into the flames before he was grabbed again and bundled away.

Max grabbed a set of tongs and pulled the smoking, twisted card from the brazier. The book was gone. Ash.

I cried. My mother's voice. Lost forever.

The room was silent save for the mocking crackle of the flames. I couldn't focus but still clambered to my feet, wavering on unsteady legs. I didn't look at anyone. I didn't even feel any anger. All my emotions seemed to have been leached out of me and I was nobody, nothing. Numb.

Someone cleared their throat.

"The memory chip within the card might have survived," Abi said. "We might be able to recover the contents."

No one said anything. He was wrong. I knew that. It was gone forever.

"And then there was one," Keegan said. I didn't understand what he meant until, through my tears, I saw him looking down at the puzzle box.

No one said anything to Greigor. He stood beyond the circle of the remaining crew members and glowered at nothing.

Max returned to the table and sat. She took up the box and turned it in her hands. "Tell us again, Anders – how did you get this?"

It was a present, a gift, and now it's the last connection with my past...
But no words would come. I shook my head. I couldn't focus.
When I probed my memories, I kept sliding off. Like a blind spot.
A hole in my head.

"Anders?" Max prompted.

"I – I was young...I just remember being given it..."

"By your mother? How old were you?"

I shook my head. "I – I'm sorry – it's the cold, the hunger – I
can't..." Why couldn't I remember? Just the hands giving it into mine,
those long fingers – but then they changed, switched – man's hands,
then. Not my father's – they were too delicate...I frowned, couldn't
focus, couldn't get it clear. I was shivering, trembling.

"So how does it work?" Keegan said.

"Puzzle boxes are designed to open after a series of switches are
pressed – either pressures in specific areas in a specific sequence,"
Maggie explained, "or a series of panels are slid out."

"Can't see any panels on here."

"No. Pressure points, then?"

"Just because it looks like a puzzle box, don't mean it actually *is*."
Greigor. "Here—"

"Stay where you are, Greig," Fergie snapped. "You've done
enough. Just stay back there."

The box was passed among the other crew.

"I can't work this out." Keegan. "Anyone got any ideas?"

"Just burn the damn thing," Greigor said. "We could use
the warmth—"

"Greigor, if you don't shut the fuck up, then I'll damn well shut
you up," Fergie said.

"It looks to have been made in sections – here, give it to me." That
was Max. "If I can find the right tool—"

"No!" I was hyperventilating, my eyes not working properly.
Didn't even realize I'd shouted until I felt a big hand gently pushing
me back to the bed.

I was dimly aware of Max getting to her feet, and then Dmitri was
blocking my view, and then she was back at the table and my nostrils
were clogged with dust and the stink of dirty, dirty humans. I saw her
probing with something long and thin, like a needle.

"No," I moaned again.

"Got it," she said. There was a crunch like a bone breaking, and a section of the exterior lifted partially off the core—

★　　★　　★

I think I screamed.

★　　★　　★

I am in an office. I am being interviewed. There are three people across the table from me. I know…I know them. The names well up in me, fill me for a moment before flooding into my mind. Hannah Robertson. George Francis. Demelza Augustine. One external HR consultant, two operations managers. I am standing. I am nervous. I hold my hands tightly behind my back, my suit heavy on my shoulders. They aren't looking at me, but at the papers in front of them. It is warm. The air smells faintly of pine.

"Lacks experience." That's Robertson. She sounds bored.

"But never properly tested. The Psych shows a high ceiling. He has potential." Francis. He sits in the middle. When he looks down, I can clearly see his bald patch.

Then the questions begin in earnest, the role-play, the barrage of scenarios, my responses instantly challenged, clarified, dissected…

There is nothing unusual in this.

Now I am waiting in a corridor. Tension is gripping my throat. There is something wrong – why is this memory coming now? Why have I not remembered—

Francis is talking to me. He is smiling. His jowls are heavy and I can smell breath-freshener on his words. He is telling me to follow. They want a new Psych test. I've had three already this year – why do they need another?

I don't say anything. I nod, comply, conform. This man will decide my future.

Now I am lying on a gurney "Anders, can you hear me?" *and I am being strapped in, head immobilized.* "This is not a Pysch," *I say.*

"No," Francis agrees, "not the sort you're used to. A new version. Doctor?"

He steps aside and there is a woman there – Fischer? – no, no, it's not her, this one's younger, fewer smiles, more detachment. She doesn't look at me as

*she ties a strap across my forehead, holding me down. She injects me then –
right between the eyes, before I can say anything. Now the smells are sharper
– almonds? Almonds and antiseptic.*

"You're sure?" the doctor asks Francis.

"He'll do," he says, and then—

*A bright light. Brighter than a thousand suns, it skips my optic nerve and
burrows straight into my brain—*

★   ★   ★

My scream was still echoing around the basement.

★   ★   ★

For a moment I felt peace. A kind of peace I'd not felt for months,
maybe years, and I had an irresistible desire to hold it to me, to remain
in a kind of half sleep in which I was warm and comfortable and
nothing could ever, ever touch me. But I couldn't. I was lifting
irrevocably towards full consciousness, and soon I was back in the
gloom of the basement. I was lying on my bed, surrounded by the rest
of the crew. I opened my eyes – or maybe they were already open, and
I was only regaining my awareness – and saw the others all watching
me. I sat up slowly and scanned their faces. Fergie looked shocked, and
maybe a little sick. So did Dmitri, and Keegan. Max and Greigor were
staring at their feet. Abidene was wearing a grim expression. Weng was
as dispassionate as ever.

"What happened?" I croaked.

"That's what we were goin' to ask you," Fergie said.

"You—" Maggie stopped and swallowed. "When Max pried open
the puzzle box, you collapsed. I—" She shook her head.

"Water," I gasped. Dmitri forced a bottle into my hand, spilling
lukewarm liquid over my blankets. I drank urgently. My face was
bathed in sweat. The slight movement of air from Max's ventilation
system chilled it instantly. Hot and cold, as if again I had pneumonia.

"What happened, Anders?" Maggie asked.

"A…I think…a memory. I think it was a memory."

"A memory of what?"

Riding out on a half-track…climbing up towards the minehead…. Taking off my rucksack and pulling out a bundle – a bundle of wires wrapped around three strips of explosive…burying it next to the comms building…

…stalking through the corridors, the empty, echoing corridors; reaching up to turn aside a tiny pinhead camera…

…outside again, warm and strong inside my suit, the base black box carried easily in two hands…. Heading for the smelter, setting the box onto the ore smasher and stepping clear…

It took some time before I could say these things to my colleagues.

★   ★   ★

Later, some unknown, unmeasured time later, I was sitting at the table, picking listlessly at some of the nutritious mush Abi had prepared. Weng and Fergie came downstairs, their twin clouds of breath merging and dissipating slowly.

"Fischer and Petrovic are fine," Weng announced. She went over to sit on her bed. Fergie came to sit across from me. Between us the puzzle box lay in pieces. The wooden sides removed, neatly arranged. The electronic device that had lain inside had been carefully removed. It still made me sick to look at it.

"So is he safe?" Fergie asked the room. "Is he still gonna kill us all?"

All eyes now turned to me. I could only look back helplessly.

Keegan gestured at the collection of chips barely half an inch across. "Maggie…you think this thing—"

"It broadcast a high-frequency tone, beyond normal human hearing." It was Max who answered. "That was the trigger. It was – I'm pretty sure there was a sensor made to detect the sounds of breathing, that would go off when Anders reached a specific point in his natural sleep. It'd happen every night, but the locked-off part of the mind would control whether he actually did anything or just went back to sleep."

"So…?"

"I've deactivated it. He should be safe."

"Willing to bet your life on that?" Fergie grinned humorlessly.

She hesitated, then nodded. I glanced round to the others – to

Greigor, to Weng, to Dmitri and Abi. I saw nothing there. Just…just deadness. No emotions, no energy.

Fergie took up one of the wooden panels and turned it in his hands.

"So what now?" I asked.

"What d'you mean?"

"Is – this enough for you?" I could hardly bring myself to ask the question. "Do you believe me? Do you – do you trust me?"

There was silence. I'd – we'd both been speaking softly, but I suddenly realized that no one else was moving. Everyone was listening, waiting.

Then, almost infinitesimally, Fergie nodded.

I hadn't even realized I'd been holding my breath.

"But there's a lot more we need to know," Keegan said. "I mean, Anders has told us fragments – there's still a whole account to give, a lot more that we need to find out."

I shook my head. "I – I've tried…I just can't remember – I mean, I know it must be in my head somewhere, but it still feels like I'm fractured, things still aren't—"

"You'll need specialist medical care," said Weng. "Drugs we don't have here. Knowledge we cannot access. It is possible that your memories will rebuild themselves in time. But there is nothing we can do to speed the process. Not here."

Fergie stood abruptly, a look of grim determination on his face. With an odd kind of formality, he spoke. "Anders. I'm sorry. I'm sorry for blaming you for all this." He reached out a stiff, unsteady hand to me.

I took it, and we shook. I gave him a weak smile. "You've nothing to apologize for. You were right all along."

"Yeah. I was, wasn't I?"

"So what do we do now?" Dmitri asked.

"We survive," Max said. "We cooperate and we survive."

"Four more months…"

"We either work together or we die," I said, and I realized for the first time just how much, how very much I wanted to live. "I don't know about you, but I'm going to do everything I possibly can to see the sun come up again."

EPILOGUE

Survival came at a cost. The changes occurred so gradually that we barely noticed them, but just occasionally I would catch sight of my reflection and see a stranger there. The flesh had melted away from us all: that was immediate and obvious. Abi and Maggie kept the worst effects of starvation at bay, and none of us suffered from diarrhea or dehydration. But I was bald now. All of us were, as our bodies stopped diverting precious energy to hair growth. Abi's beard went first, then mine, then Fergie's and Keegan's. After a while I found it hard to remember Max and Weng as ever having hair. Our lips split and bled.

It was an oddly gender-free world we lived in. We were all walking skeletons, skin shrunk against our skulls, ribs protruding horribly. The saving grace was that it was happening to all equally. We didn't need mirrors, the differences between us inconsequential. We all stank the same. Without privacy there was no shame. Nudity meant nothing; even shitting into a bucket in the corner did not bother us. Real equality.

A visitor, an outsider, would have found us truly disgusting, but there were pleasures to be found in this solidarity. This was a shared experience; no one person was any better than the other.

Fischer and Mikhail were the lucky ones. They didn't feel the pain.

Max became distant as time passed. The stresses on her pushed us apart, and, never the most articulate man, I had neither the words nor the energy to make things right. As days turned to weeks, to months, I realized it was too late. If there'd ever been easiness in each other's company it was certainly gone now.

Instead it was Weng I became closest to. Only she still refused to interact with Greigor, always unforgiving. Sometimes – in the oddest way – she'd creep over to my bed and silently insinuate herself against me, like a cat nuzzling for warmth. But we never had sex.

No one did. No one had the strength. She and I would just lie together in silence. I never knew what she was thinking. No one asked questions like that anymore.

After the first month the crew ran out of words. We'd been through the arguments and the practicalities enough times, and even our personalities retreated as the cold slowly bit down on us. And as our differences diminished, so did my anger towards Greigor. Without his film-star looks and rugby-player physique, he was just pathetic, and I wasn't human enough to feel anything but numbness for the things I'd lost. Although I knew I'd be haunted forever by the sight of the memcard on the brazier, I just couldn't feel it. Later, if we ever felt warmth again, then I'd cry again.

We survived. We survived, and we lived, and we endured in a twilight world of browns, ambers and grays. Time ceased to exist. There was sleep and there was wakefulness. There were jobs and there was rest. That was all that mattered.

We weren't aware of the bitter chill slowly easing as we passed midwinter. The changes were too small for us to detect. We just knew that the fire was warm and everywhere else was cold. But then one day I went out for more coal, Max by my side, and there was a low yellow arc on the horizon.

We stood, emaciated and exhausted, and stared at it for a long time. Then we went back inside and brought the rest of us out to see it too. The nine of us watched the sky. We thought of the dead and the maimed. We held hands, identical and anonymous in our warmsuits, and stood in silence.

The night shift was drawing to an end.

Finally, a long, long time later, we were rescued.

You know that story better than I do. You came by crawler: you, Dr. Gabriel; Technician Istevez and Operations Executive Baurus. You made the long journey from Tierra to find us. I still wonder what you made of us, whether you could tell us apart, whether you could bear to be near us.

We all knew that there'd be questions, an inquiry, that we'd be drugged and tested. We didn't care. All that mattered was that the night shift was over. The night shift was over and we'd made it through alive.

ACKNOWLEDGMENTS

This novel exists because of the efforts of more people than I can name, but here goes: thank you to all at Flame Tree Press for taking a chance on me, for producing a wonderful cover and for being a pleasure to work with. Thank you to Laura Williams of PFD for her expertise, and to the gallant members of Abingdon Writers', and especially to the AB-FAGgers, for their tender eviscerations of early drafts.

Huge thanks to the lovely people of Twitter for keeping me company through long days of procrastination. But the biggest thanks go, of course, to my family, who have been forced to cope with my feckless, unproductive ways for far too long and really should have complained more than they did.

FLAME TREE PRESS
FICTION WITHOUT FRONTIERS
Award-Winning Authors & Original Voices

Flame Tree Press is the trade fiction imprint of Flame Tree
Publishing, focusing on excellent writing in horror and the
supernatural, crime and mystery, science fiction and fantasy.
Our aim is to explore beyond the boundaries of the everyday,
with tales from both award-winning authors and original voices.

•

Other titles available include:

Thirteen Days by Sunset Beach by Ramsey Campbell
Think Yourself Lucky by Ramsey Campbell
The House by the Cemetery by John Everson
The Toy Thief by D.W. Gillespie
The Siren and the Specter by Jonathan Janz
The Sorrows by Jonathan Janz
Kosmos by Adrian Laing
The Sky Woman by J.D. Moyer
Creature by Hunter Shea
The Bad Neighbor by David Tallerman
Ten Thousand Thunders by Brian Trent
The Mouth of the Dark by Tim Waggoner

•

Join our mailing list for free short stories, new release details,
news about our authors and special promotions:

flametreepress.com